Arianwen

By

Angela Johnson

Black Bee Books Ltd.

First Published in Great Britain in 2020 by
Black Bee Books Ltd
Bryn Heulog
Talley
Llandeilo
Wales SA19 7YH
Copyright © Angela Johnson 2020

Cover Image © Eddie Cloud / Alamy Stock Photo
Cover Design © Huw Francis

ISBN: 978-1-913853-00-6 (Paperback)
ISBN: 978-1-913853-00-6 (eBook)
Printed and bound in Great Britain by Clays Ltd, Elcograf S.p.A

www.blackbeebooks.wales

Acknowledgements

To Seonaid Francis for her support, advice and patience, and to my fellow author Francesca Capaldi Burgess for her support and encouragement.

Dedication

To Angharad and David

PART 1

CHAPTER 1

'I'll be back in half an hour.'

'I'll have the kettle on.' Such is the quotidian nature of daily discourse.

All stories have a beginning and an end. This story begins with its ending, but the story is about the life leading to the ending, a harsh ending, painful, but what came before is the important part of the story. You will soon forget the ending because it is not the important part of a woman's life. Her end was dramatic, but those who knew and loved her, remember her for the life she lived.

I will take you to a spring afternoon, some time ago, not history, a couple of decades at most, when fashions were slightly different, as were political concerns. It is not warm, winter is still digging its heels in, and from the west just a hint of cold in the salt wind, some vague promise of rain before evening.

Arianwen is running late, as she always is, a woman of indeterminate age. She moves so quickly that sometimes you think she is a young woman. She is eager, her life is smoothly content, a warm rounded thing like an egg warmed in the sun.

Somebody is coming to tea. There was a time when she would have made a sponge, all icing powder and smug lick of jam running down its sides. And Welsh cakes, and perfectly sliced bread and butter.

'Don't bother with cakes,' Elwyn says, 'they come to see you, not your cakes.' And he kisses her on the cheek.

When you come to love, gratefully, in late middle age, there are not the irritations of long acquaintance. Love is domestic. Love is ordinary as burps, as the lines on their faces, the grey in their hair and the new creak in the knee.

Friends told her that sometimes they could kill their husbands. So grateful were she and Elwyn for late discoveries that they held hands before sleeping and even staring at each other's ageing faces in morning light; on damp mornings when the distant hills were just gloomy threats they would smile and take each other's hand across the table, looking down towards the road where nobody

1

walked and only a tractor or a jeep passed.

We could surmise whether, if that cake had been baked, or the bread had been fresher and they'd not run out of milk after deciding to have full milk porridge for breakfast, whether this ending would have been different, or whether perverse destiny had decreed that a good woman would be destroyed. Or if the old shop in the village had still been open so that she could walk quite safely to another conclusion. So many imponderables. So does a life find its myriad paths.

So on an early spring afternoon she drove her Mini a couple of miles through the village where she waved to a couple of people and noted the buttery show of daffodils in the minister's garden and cowslips in the hedgerows and decided that she would get some cowslips for the garden, from the nursery as long as they were properly sourced and not dug up from the wild by some amoral shyster.

It was a bright afternoon by the undemanding standards of West Wales afternoons. A bit of sun to the west, too late to do any good, and a cloud getting bigger over the top of the hills. As always, the village was quiet. She glanced at the school. It had an abandoned weekend look about it.

Arianwen was not one to waste time on contemplation of the past. A more sentimental woman could have looked at that playground with nostalgia, after all, a large fraction of her life had been spent there, chivvying children into one of the two classrooms before settling down to a day's teaching.

Happily, she was not aware that this would be the last time that she'd look at that particular sight. At least she was spared that. As she drove the couple of miles to one of those handy little shops which peddle everything, and, most importantly, gossip from an omniscient proprietor, her mind was occupied with mundane domesticity, ironing which no longer could be avoided, and cakes to be made for the school fête. A pragmatic woman, a woman who avoided the darkness in her, the darkness of memory, as she drove her two miles towards an inexorable oblivion.

Unwinding in the peripheries of her vision was the brightness of gorse and even through closed windows the usual accompaniment of new lambs complaining about their world.

***

2

The shop is a bit stuffy. An old fashioned paraffin lamp exudes weak warmth and strong oil fumes

'Heard about Dewi Davies? He died last night. Who'll run the farm now? Steffan's a teacher in London, hardly ever comes home. When he does, pretends he doesn't speak Welsh.'

'I'll call and see Merys with a sponge.' Arianwen is a conscientious woman. In Wales death is attended by cakes. She will call on the widow. There will be no tears. There will be silence, and then she will say her goodbye, turning before she opens the car door to watch the widow's face, calm, not crumpling yet, not till the son comes home to eat cake and tell her what to do.

'I'll be at the concert tonight. Looking forward to you two singing. Should be a good turn out. Ted 's gone to the cash and carry, said he'd be back early to look after the shop while I get us a bit of tea. It'll be quiet late afternoon. He can do the paperwork while waiting for customers.'

Arianwen smiles. Perhaps she has not really listened. To a woman who has seen suffering there is comfort, perhaps, in the mundane, and Mrs. Davies is, most definitely, a mundane woman, not a gossip like the old Mrs. Jones in the long closed shop back in the village, but she must be treated with the utmost courtesy. This is the way of old fashioned villages, even at the tail end of the twentieth century.

She remembers that she'd promised to go into the school on Monday to help with some of the babies' reading. They don't call them babies anymore, now they're infants, or reception, but she always did: other women's babies, briefly her own. There is something strange about visiting her domain, welcome as she always is, and the clever girl with an excellent degree from Cardiff, and the studs in her nose, is charming, and always very grateful.

As she leaves she turns back to the shopkeeper.

'See you this evening. You'll stay for a cup of tea and a chat afterwards won't you?' and she turns away out to the road, looking to a future which does not exist.

Two miles away, in yet another moribund village, a young man swears at his mother who might have refused to lend him some money, or has complained about the drugs found under his mattress with a stash of porn. He is angry, jumps into his car, notes the petrol tank is almost empty. Curses. Thinks of the scene with his boss the day before. He'll have to apologise or he'll be back on the dole. And that bitch from Milford Haven giving him the run round. Fucking frigid bitch. Life is hell. He curses an unsympathetic universe. He drives along silent roads. He is immune to tedious signs of burgeoning spring, or the rather charming bleating of lambs. A scrawny black and white sheepdog barks at his car and chases it without hope, as he chases all vehicles and returns to the curses of his owner. He hits the cross roads at seventy miles an hour. Too fast. He is almost out of petrol. He has no money to buy any more. He is not the kind of young man who thinks ahead. Will he drive till the engine dies on him? He doesn't stop at the give way sign. There is always a hundred percent chance of nobody coming. As there is now. No trundling tractor or spluttering oil tanker to divert the determined trajectory of fate.

Arianwen looks at her watch. Running late. Damn. The Joneses, old friends of Elwyn's, known since his childhood, are always appallingly prompt, driven to constant movement by boredom, and the long silence of their marriage. Prompt at three they'll be there, looking forward to tea and a good helping of anecdote which they will metamorphose into malicious gossip.

She dashes across. If only she had been younger, quicker on her feet.

He doesn't see the small woman crossing the road. His head is full of anger, lifetimes of bitterness churning in his brain. At first he doesn't realise what has happened, there is a spinning universe of noise and screaming and his car slows. For what, he doesn't know. Terrified by the unknown he brakes too late, sees a bundle in the road from which he must escape. He reverses and drives round it.

His is another story, but moralists will be pleased to hear that he didn't get far. He ran out of petrol. Ran for the gorse hills. A farmer checking his sheep found him, a huddle in the dubious comfort of a stone wall.

The woman in the shop went back to her paper, unwrapping with one hand a Mars bar which she will never eat and never will again, the brown and red wrapper, the chocolate caramel smell a sickly menace of Proustian accusation.

There is silence at first. Then the sound of a car approaching very fast. Then a muffled bump. Glass breaking. Inhuman sounds.

She'll never know what they were, but will spend many dark hours in speculation. The car seems to slow down briefly. Then it speeds away again. Something has happened, something momentous, something quite beyond her experience.

On legs encased in concrete, she walks to the door. There is a small bundle in the middle of the road, blood and worse seeping into the tar. There is the smell of burning tyre, the smell of dying. Her mouth opens to scream. She'll never know if the opened mouth, a parody of Munch's painting, ever emitted that scream.

For a long time - seconds or hours - time is uncertain here, as if it has lost confidence in the regularity of minutes and seconds. Then, in the distance, familiar and almost reassuring, comes the trundling sound of a tractor. If only our tractor driver had been earlier, slowing down the killer driver. Then my story would have died happy.

Jim had called for pink diesel at the garage. Life and death spin around such trivialities. The tractor spills the fertile potato growing mud of Pembrokeshire all over the road. That mud will be spread all over Mrs. Davies's lovely clean floor, washed down with too much Flash every morning while her husband sorts out the papers, dropping ash, and spreading the smell of Players all over North Pembrokeshire.

But not today. Jim always calls for his paper after dinner, his perusal of the page 3 girl delayed till later in the day. Today his paper will be unread, the breasts ignored, not that reading is a skill in which Jim has great mastery, particularly in English. He had never needed English much, only for the incomers who, thankfully, don't impinge on his world with their plans for making money and changing his timeless patch of Wales.

For a man in middle age he has excellent sight. He has spent many hours of his life staring into distances: looking up at the hills for signs of weather, looking for errant sheep, whistling his scrawny sheepdogs to heel. Bess, the grand old matriarch, better natured and more reliable than his wife, rides like a stately ship prow at the front of the tractor, the slight breeze of ten miles an hour breathing through her mud encrusted fur.

He sees the bundle in the middle of the road, stops in a different parking place which Bess does not like, and she barks hysterically. Mrs. Davies is standing over the bundle. Bess, who recognises her as a giver of treats and greetings and fuss, runs to her and barks, and Jim watches them, a sheepdog and a white haired woman staring at the bundle in the middle of the road. Mrs. Davies reaches her hand out and strokes the dog's fur, up and down, slowly, deliberately, as if looking for contact with some living thing, something breathing, something warm, as she stares at what lies on the road.

Bess is quiet, her tail wags like an automaton. There is such silence as if the world is ending, the cloud over the hills has deepened and thickened, and there is an apocalyptic gloom over the empty road. Jim has not heard of the pathetic fallacy, but if somebody explained it to him he'd understand.

He climbs down.

'Mrs. Davies, what's happened?'

She turns round as if she's only just realised he's there. She is still stroking the dog's back.

Never has he seen such pallor. And Mrs. Davies always so rosy cheeked. Her ill- advised gash of cerise lipstick, her only concession to vanity and the demands of her public, is a streak of blood in that face, pale as the dead, and the snow on the hills in January before the gorse comes again like sunshine.

He takes off his green and yellow baseball cap, worn back to front, and holds it in his huge chapped hands.

'Who is it?'

'Arianwen.'

'Duw bach. She taught me in school. She was very young then. Taught me to read. Kind. Didn't have any nonsense mind.'

He thinks of her, the last time he saw her, at one of the village fund raising concerts, singing some silly song, Elwyn playing the piano. Laughing, always laughing. Talking to him and his wife over dark cups of tea and a piece of sponge. Her, looking up and teasing him.

'I was always telling you to wash your hands. You and Gwyn Pant Coch, you were right devils both of you,' and then turning, her eyes full of love, to Elwyn. 'You wouldn't think to look at him now, but he was a scrawny little thing.' Laughing, always laughing, that high giggle, as if she was singing. The village loved her. They'd seen her through so much, said goodbye and welcomed her back and now they'd say goodbye again, and somebody would have to tell

Elwyn. O duw bach. The police, that was the next thing. Phone the police.

'Mrs. Davies, come in away. I'm going to move the tractor into the middle of the road, so nobody can get past. Then I'm phoning the police. Get them off their fat arses. See if they can get the bastard who did this. I'd like a go at him.' He clenched his fists at the thought of delicious retribution. He remembered he and Dai Evans giving a good kicking to a school bully in a pub car park in Haverfordwest, and how it felt. The best in the world. All that talk of forgiveness in chapel. Bollocks. Not that he ever went to chapel now that his parents were long dead, ashes carried away in a stream not far from Carn Ingli, part of those crystal waters.

He'd be there for this funeral. What a funeral it would be. The chapel full. And all the old hymns like claws scraping at the heart. He wanted to go on his knees and sob and pray and scream at the universe. One of the hymns came to him as if on the breeze from the sea, the words circling his head.

The tears came. Mrs. Davies looked shocked.

He took her by the arm. She was like a statue. 'Mr. Davies home?'

She was a long time answering as if uncertain whether a Mr. Davies had ever existed.

Then, in a quiet voice, a stranger's voice, 'Gone to the Cash and Carry in Haverfordwest. Back for tea. Got to put the kettle on.'

'That's a good idea, cariad.'

On any other day he wouldn't have dreamt of calling Mrs. Davies *cariad*, far too familiar. And Mr. Davies wouldn't like it. But today was a special day, and it seemed right, that in this enforced intimacy of grief, he should be friendly.

'You put on the kettle and I'll phone the police.'

He heard a car approaching, and then it slowed down. In the countryman's way he checked the Range Rover's reg. Owen Jones, married to an Englishwoman. Thought himself a cut above the ordinary farmers. On mart day went to a different pub after selling stock. Sometimes went on holidays. Expensive wife, they'd heard.

Jones rushed into the shop, face like an overripe swede. Obviously he hadn't seen the bundle in the road.

'Jim, get your fucking old heap of a Fergie out of the road. What the fuck do you think you're doing?'

Jones stopped, looked at Mrs. Davies's face and heard Jim ask for police, his voice heavy and slow.

'What's happened?'

Mrs. Davies pointed to the road.

Jones went out, saw the bundle, vomited in the middle of the road, staining his wax jacket.

He came back into the shop.

'Who is it?'

Mrs Davies told him. He too remembered her: how she'd pushed him into the grammar. Told him he was a fool when he turned down a place at Aberystwyth to read Geography. 'You'll regret it, Owen,' and he did.

Jim's hand is shaking as he puts the phone down.

'A patrol man's coming, and the ambulance. Asks if we've got the number of the car. Daft thing to ask.' And then exhausted he sat down on the chair by the counter where so often he'd sat for a good gossip.

Time passed. They were uncertain how much of it.

Owen Jones forgot his urgent appointment and went to make the cup of tea which Mrs. Davies had found herself unable to do. It was too strong, and he put too much sugar in, and that is how the first policemen found them. Two men and a woman sipping tea together in silence, their faces ghosts of humanity, the bones pushing at the flesh, eyes huge with what they'd seen.

CHAPTER 2

Arianwen was born in a remote valley in West Wales, in a valley of trees and a tough little stream. Her home was the woollen mill passed down through the family, and it shaped the woman she became.

She was a lucky child, much loved, the only one. Her first eleven years were spent in a small world, the mill, then the village school, the long walk holding Mam's hand, up the tree filled lane to the village school. No school run then, children walked, often a long way. Country children took their surroundings for granted, this is no Rousseau idyll. Seasons were only noted by varying degrees of discomfort, and this being Wales the fluctuating volume of rain. Music began early, as if the profusion of song birds and the rhythms of the mill wheel slid easy as butter into the child's thoughts. She sang at school, and singing helped to make the walk home from school, tired and fractious, hungry, desperate for Mam's bread and butter and blackberry jam, a little less painful.

She was a popular girl and the hours between the school days seemed long. Children do not acknowledge loneliness, they note a desire for people of their own age. Adults have their own alien lives to lead. For the only child there is none of the comfort of bickering, of petty jealousies and not even the rare fun of a blackberry fight, coming home in September with faces and hands covered in juice and screaming gripes in the stomach to face an angry mother with face flannel and lifebuoy soap with its reek of overt cleanliness. Her friends were always complaining about brothers and sisters, and her mother was elusive when asked.

'Mam, why haven't I got a brother or a sister?'

'You just haven't, don't ask silly questions.'

'I'd like a brother or a sister.'

'I had plenty and there were times when I wished I didn't have any. You've got Shan.'

And the kitten, a lucky refugee from a nearby farm, wound itself round their legs.

'But Shan's not a person, Mam.'

'Too much to say for yourself, my girl. Now go and shout for your father. Supper's ready, and I don't want it getting cold.'

As she went out to the shed where her father was fiddling with an old wireless which somebody had asked him to repair, she thought of her friend Mair at Ty Mawr. She had three brothers and sisters and the house was full of noise, everybody shouting to make themselves heard above barking dogs and when their father, a dark man, almost like the gypsies who came round trying to sell you things you didn't want, came in, everybody went very quiet and somehow their movements were slower as if they had to be more careful, and when she stayed for tea, they had bread with no butter while Mr. Jones had eggs and fatty ham and the children watched him eating, and Arianwen didn't want to eat the bit of bread. She didn't know why.

Years later, when she talked about her childhood, there was always a light shining in her eyes. At a time and a place where many children were unhappy, and if not starving, underfed, she was, she knew, one of the blessed.

At home she looked at the food on her plate: eggs and plenty of meat and Mam's beautiful cakes, and sometimes felt sad, but she didn't know what she could do about it. And years later when her life was bleak, and the music was gone the only thing she could do to alleviate pain was to help others.

When she was eleven she passed to go the grammar school, and because in those days transport was limited, and the school almost twenty miles away, she would have to board during the week.

Arianwen did not like her landlady. It was hatred at first sight. At eleven years of age she'd not met many people she did not like. Most people she loved or liked in degrees. Mam and Dad, well she loved them, and she liked her cousins who lived up the road, and her friends at the little village school. She didn't like the boys, but then you were not meant to like boys. They were just a different species and her friends who had brothers didn't seem to like them very much either.

None of her friends were going to the grammar school, so they could live at home. Better if she'd failed the scholarship, but Mam and Dad were so proud, and in the first outbreak of joy it hadn't occurred that she'd have to go and live in Cardigan in the week.

'I don't think I'll go to the grammar school after all, Mam. I want to stay here.'

'You'll like it when you get there and there'll be proper music lessons and a choir. There'll be none of that if you stay here.'

'Won't you miss me?'

'Of course I will. Dad as well. He'll miss his little girl. And Shan will miss you. '

The cat rubbed against her legs as if to reinforce this.

She was eleven and must be brave. And there would be music.

And she would still go for piano lessons with Mr. Williams in the village on Saturday mornings, walking through the dark valley and up the steep hill, recovering her breath at the top, before knocking the door of his untidy cottage where he lived with his wife who was strange and sometimes sang very loud to herself totally out of tune. From the valleys, Mam said. Not these gentle Cardiganshire valleys of childhood, the valleys east of Swansea where Dad had come from and swept Mam off her feet. That was the family story, and Mam would blush when Uncle Elfed who liked to tease, told the story in a big dramatic voice.

But imagine waking up in the morning and not listening to the big wheel of the mill turning in the power of the water, not that it had produced any wool for some time. There was a big hairy blanket on the spare bedroom bed which had been made in the mill: full of strange colours, like gorse and grass. Mam said the blankets they made were too tickly and bought hers from a shop in Cardigan, and vans came and delivered things, the drivers cursing the narrow dark hill and having to turn round at the bottom and carrying things across the bridge.

One of Uncle Jim's taxis took her to Cardigan. She'd been there quite a few times before, and back in August to get her school uniform in the poshest draper in the town, and to Carmarthen for special clothes for a wedding, where she'd sung in a pink dress and white shoes. It was good having people listening to her and best of all clapping at the end and then asking her to sing again and she couldn't think what to sing and then she sang *Calon Lan* and everybody joined in, especially the men who'd been drinking beer, who sang loudly, and some in tune, and the women cried.

Years later she would hear it in a chapel in Patagonia, its familiarity enhanced in such an alien place, and her blood ran cold with the beauty and the passion, and she turned to Elwyn. 'I want that sung at my funeral.'

'I'll be gone long before you, cariad. And you'll look lovely in black. And I want you to sing for me.'

And he'd squeezed her hand and afterwards, outside the little chapel they looked at the thrill of the scenery and he'd squeezed her hand and kissed her right there as if they were teenagers, not two stocky little people in their sixties.

She kissed Dad goodbye outside the shed. He was fiddling with something oily and some of the oil had come off on his face, and when he kissed her some of it was left on her cheek and she had to rub it off with her new clean hanky. Mam rolled her eyes, but didn't say anything. Which showed that it was a special day.

'See you Friday, cariad. We'll have a nice long walk and Mam's going to cook something special for supper.'

She was eleven and she knew that a week wasn't a long time. Today was Sunday and she'd had to miss Sunday School, not that she minded that, Mrs. Hughes Hafod was a very silly woman and still told them Bible stories in a breathy kind of voice as if they were three years old. Some of the older boys, especially Gethin the minister's son, who was also going to the grammar school, and said he didn't believe in God, were very naughty, and asked her questions she couldn't answer and then laughed at her and whispered swear words to some of the other boys, just loud enough for everyone to hear. She quite liked Gethin even though he was a boy, and wondered if he was in the same class. He was staying with an aunty in Cardigan. At least he was with somebody he knew, even if he said that his aunt was mad, and had secrets, but then Gethin was always one for a bit of drama.

She'd met Mrs. Daniels her landlady when they went to buy her uniform. They'd arrived outside the house in her uncle's taxi, their legs aching from standing so long in the draper shop while the funny little man with the droopy moustache who spat all the time brought out tunics and blouses for her to try on. Mam complained it should have been a woman.

'Not right a man dealing with girls and blouses and those bloomers for games.'

The lady assistant was looking after a fat woman with a red face and tight ginger curls who was looking at everything the poor woman brought out to her in disgust. In the end she walked out having bought nothing except a box of hankies. As she walked out, the assistant made a rude face behind her back and laughed, and Arianwen laughed, such a relief as the draper was worse than being in chapel when the minister was in one of his gloomy moods and getting into a state about hell and damnation.

They then went to the saddlers and bought her a leather-smelling satchel to carry her books to school every day, and then a shop where her mother bought her boots and a stick for hockey which she didn't fancy at all, as the stick looked as if it could do a lot of damage.

Mrs. Daniels had come to the door. She had a face like a big fat ham. They'd been invited in to the parlour which was full of brass things and a sad looking little man who scuttled out when they entered.

'Cup of tea, Mrs. Evans, and one of my nice Welsh cakes? Just the thing after a day's shopping.'

Her voice was a witch's high pitched whine, and her accent was strange, as if it did not really belong to her.

The room smelled of old lavender. Arianwen tried hard not to sneeze.

Mam put on her important voice.

'That would be very nice, Mrs. Daniels, I'm very partial to a nice Welsh cake. Then perhaps we can see Arianwen's room and discuss terms.'

'Breakfast and high tea will be included and she'll get a piece of bread and cheese and a bottle of cold tea to take for midday dinner. My husband and I have our dinner at midday, and it's too far for the little girl to walk home. I'll make sure she has something hot and nourishing every evening at six o'clock before she goes to her room.'

The school was only round the corner, but Arianwen decided that she would rather stay in school, however bad that might be, and one day a week she was having special singing lessons with one of the teachers who came to the school to teach music. Dad was paying for that.

'My contribution for my little girl.'

Everybody knew that it was Mam who had money and Dad didn't earn very much as a local jobbing gardener and handyman.

A young girl came in with a tray with two cups and two plates and two Welsh cakes on a plate. There were doilies underneath them and there was no butter and they looked dry and old.

Mam took one bite and left hers behind. Arianwen was not offered anything. Mrs. Daniels looked at the clock.

'Well it's 4 o'clock and I'm sure you'll be wanting to get home before dark.'

'There's plenty of time and I haven't seen the room yet.'

'Doris will take you up.' She picked up a bell with *A present from Llandudno* written on it and the little maid rushed in looking breathless. Arianwen looked round the room. No sign of a piano. All she wanted was to be home, and not have to think that soon she would be spending five days a week here, aching for the sanctuary of Fridays.

They followed the maid up the stairs and then up another flight of stairs. Her mother was puffing slightly as they went. The maid took them into a small room with brown wallpaper and brown curtains and a big picture of an unhappy looking deer over the bed. Again there was that smell of lavender. Her mother sniffed and tried the bed.

'Bit hard. You'll make sure the sheets are aired won't you?'

'Oh yes, Mrs. Daniels is very fussy about the sheets.' Unspoken was the suggestion that Mrs. Daniels was very fussy about everything. Arianwen went to the window. She looked down at the garden which looked tired and drained by the long summer. No sound of the stream here, or the reassuring familiarity of the wheel, only the sound of the road: very occasional cars, and the sound of people talking as they walked past.

Doris pointed to a washstand and a chamber pot under the bed and blushed.

'I'm in the room across the hall.' She smiled, and Arianwen realised that she wasn't much older than her, and smiled back.

'I thought I saw a bathroom on the way up.'

'That's for Mr. and Mrs. Daniels.'

'We'll see about that.' And Mam was away down the stairs, her best heels clopping daintily along the bare stairs and shooshing more slowly along the thinly carpeted bottom stairs. Arianwen had seen that look on Mam's face before, when Mr. Williams had caned her for getting her times tables wrong, and when the delivery man brought second rate coal.

Arianwen smiled at Doris.

'My name's Arianwen, perhaps we can be friends?'

Doris smiled. And really she was quite pretty when she smiled and didn't look frightened.

After a few minutes she decided it was safe to go downstairs. She stood outside the parlour. No voices could be heard.

Mam came out, smiling. Mrs. Daniels came out, her face red with defeat.

And now a few weeks later with one of uncle's drivers humming a dance tune in the front, and Mam looking out of the window and not seeing or saying much, they were on the way. All the school stuff and the little suitcase with her nightie and toilet things and the old grey dress for wearing after school were all packed neatly in the back. She felt that here in the back seat of the car she was living her old life, ordinary and familiar, cosy as a winter evening when the curtains are drawn, and, in the boot her new life, frightening, but exciting as well. She thought of her friends staying on at the village school growing away from her, but she'd still see them on Sunday after chapel, running around the gravestones, and jumping out at the little ones and making them cry, even though she knew it was wrong.

She joined in the song, her soprano blending with Ianto's monotone bass and Mam joined in as well, and by the time they got to Llechryd they were all laughing, but she noticed that Mam was wiping away a tear, but she didn't know whether that was laughter or crying.

Mrs. Daniels must have been waiting for them. 6 o'clock, Mam had said and they were there on the dot. By that time they'd all stopped singing, and Ianto was just whistling through his funny black and white moustache which looked as if there was a tiny badger on his face.

'Good evening, Mrs. Evans.' Mrs. Daniels, regal as ever, nodded at Ianto to carry the suitcases. Ianto looked startled. He was not a man used to condescension, but he winked at Arianwen to show that he wasn't intimidated. After all, this was the man who never stood for bullies, and had kicked out a gang of gypsies from the local pub almost single handed, assisted only by the shouts of encouragement from his less courageous mates.

Mam was about a foot shorter than Mrs. Daniels and only reached up to her strangely shaped bosom, but when it came to regality she could outdo anybody.

'Good evening, Mrs. Daniels, how lovely your garden looks even at the tail end of summer like this. Of course our garden is much bigger than this, but even the smallest of gardens takes a lot of work.'

The little man, who had scuttled out of the parlour that first time, was hiding behind a rose bush.

'Herbert, tell the girl to put the kettle on, and to bring tea into the parlour for Mrs. Evans and myself and to give a cup of tea to the driver at the kitchen door.'

Arianwen was shocked. Ianto always came in for a cup of tea when he brought them home from a shopping expedition, and he and Dad would sit on the settle in the kitchen and have a long gossip. Dad, being the favourite village handyman, knew everything about everybody, and after some of his home brew he was very funny, and there'd be a song or two with Mam complaining about the noise.

Herbert was now standing in the hallway, as if waiting for further orders.

Arianwen's luggage was placed all around him and he looked a bit like somebody in one of the boys' comics when the Indians surrounded the wagons, even though he was a very small and lonely wagon.

'Take the big bag up, Doris can carry the rest.'

The little man was dismissed.

Arianwen followed the two women into the parlour and sat in the tall upright chair by the aspidistra. The two women sat each side of the fire, lit, even though it was hot outside. Their chairs were too close together, their faces only inches apart, as if prepared for close scrutiny.

'Has the girl had her tea, Mrs. Evans?'

'Her tea, yes, but not her supper.'

'We don't have supper on a Sunday. We have high tea at five o'clock. We find that after Sunday dinner that is quite enough. Perhaps you'll make sure the girl has her tea before she leaves home on a Sunday.'

'I'll do that, but please make sure that she has a cup of Ovaltine before she goes to bed, full milk mind, none of that watered down stuff, and a biscuit or two.'

The biscuits never appeared, but every Sunday Mam made her a sandwich of roast meat from Sunday dinner with a little cake with icing sugar sprinkled on it, and she ate it in her room at the top of the house with the Ovaltine Doris brought up to her, and as she chewed the sandwich and tasted home, she thought of Mam and Dad in the warm parlour listening to the wireless and the wheel turning, and the water whooshing.

CHAPTER 3

Later on, when she and Doris became friends Arianwen persuaded Mam to pack enough food for two and they would sit up there on Sunday nights laughing and talking, sometimes so loudly that Herbert was sent upstairs to ask them to be quiet, and Mrs. Daniels spoke to Arianwen about the undesirability of befriending servants.

'Arianwen, I am certain that your mother would not want you to be talking to servants, and you a grammar school girl.' And her thin lips were tight as a stretched elastic band, and her eyes cold as she looked down at her.

'Silly cow,' Doris said. 'She was only brought up down in one of those old cottages by the river. Her Grandad was a drover and her Mam was, well, not a respectable woman.' Doris smiled in the certainty of her fifteen year old sophistication. 'And the way she talks, that's not natural, it's just put on. You should hear her when she loses her temper and forgets herself.'

Arianwen loved Doris's stories. And Doris did not need much prompting.

'How did she meet Herbert? He seems a nice man.'

He always smiled at her and said, 'Good day at school? Lot of old homework tonight? I went to that school you know,' but, always, before he said anything interesting, Mrs. Daniels would appear from somewhere with the latest orders.

Arianwen was surprised to hear that Mr. Daniels was a bank manager and highly respected in the town.

'How is it he married that horrible woman then?' She was growing up quickly under Doris's world-weary tutelage and learning the pleasures of malice.

Doris had four brothers and two sisters and seemed to know far more than Arianwen, even though she'd never gone to a grammar school, and only read magazines about lipstick and getting married.

'Had to, didn't they? Got a son, Harry. He's away at university. Never comes home. Hates his Mam, can't say I blame him. The only time he comes home is when his Mam goes, once a year, to visit her sister in Rhyl. It's lovely when he comes. The house is full of laughter and I gets more money to spend on the cooking, and they drink beer and smoke in the parlour. Smells like a pub in the morning. Nice. I like it. We have to open the windows wide before she comes home. I look forward to Harry coming home. And he has a little banjo thing he plays like that George Formby and he sings rude songs and he comes in the kitchen and sings to me and he calls me his darling Dorry.' And her skinny little face pinked up with a blush.

One Sunday evening over beef and piccalilli sandwiches, Doris told her about babies and how they were made. It sounded very different from what they'd been told in biology when the girls were separated from the boys and there was lots of giggling and squirming. As she thought of the strangeness of adult behaviour she quite forgot to be homesick.

CHAPTER 4

The wheel turns. There is the sound of water, controlled, rhythmed water. A blackbird sings. The sounds of childhood. So many sounds in her life: the disciplined sounds of music, of harmony and of love. Later the music clashed with the horror of adulthood. All her life she is sensitive to sound. The creaking of a rope on a rafter heavy with the weight of its burden and the music that mingles with a car driven too fast, a car which will never stop in her lifetime, and the scream which never came because there was no time for it. The last bird she heard singing, a thrush on the lawn singing to the hills and their first gold gorse covering.

She woke every Monday to the realisation that the liquid sounds of the wheel turning were the rhythmic sounds of her own breathing, in her secret life of sleep. In time she learned to throw away the sadness of Mondays. As she got older, time closed in on itself and the weeks were shorter, and Fridays came sooner, and at 4.30 Ianto was always there, with his big smile and his whistling, to take her home. Like most children she learnt the vices of secrecy as she grew away from her parents, and as time passed there were fewer stories to tell Mam and Dad as they ate their Friday supper and listened to the horrors of news from Europe.

In class she becomes dreamy. There is a boy with fair hair who sits in front of her. There is a softness to his neck, and a silky down, which makes her want to stroke it, in the same way as stroking the fur of a kitten. When he looks at her, her verbosity flies away, a silenced sparrow, her mouth drops with longing. This is a long time ago when adolescence was as yet undiscovered, and you were a child until some magic hour when you were grown up, and nothing would happen and the dullness closed around you certain as a mist off the stream in November. Later she would smile back at her innocence, but, without regret, a pragmatic woman, always looking to the future. Her parents grow older and they become fallible. Dad is not as clever, she realises, despite his dexterity with objects, as Mam, who has dreams she cannot articulate.

Arianwen is uncertain of who she will be. There are others who sing better, who will go to music college, who will join great choirs, and those girls who will become mothers and lead unquestioning lives.

And the wheel turns, and one day she is sixteen. And school certificate is behind her, not brilliant, not disgraceful, and her parents say that she can stay for another two years and become a teacher. It would be that or a nurse or a secretary. Nothing else was expected of a woman apart from marriage. And she finally asked if she could find other digs. Doris had left the Daniels to marry her Iwan, and was pregnant and happy in one of the little terraced houses by the river, and Herbert tidied and bullied into his grave. While her mother prevaricated, Mrs. Daniels told her that she was moving to Rhyl to help run a boarding house with her sister, now also widowed.

Arianwen never quite understood why she was allowed to go live with the Morgans, but they had been recommended by the headmaster, and the word of Dafydd Edwards MA Cantab was enough for Mam, and Mr. Morgan was a music teacher so he must be respectable. Mam had spoken to Mrs. Morgan on the phone and had been reassured by her cultured accent, and had not felt it necessary to do the military inspection she had done at the Daniels. And there was so little choice with all the evacuees. Mr. Morgan was one of the visiting music teachers at the school. He taught a variety of instruments, but not piano, which she was learning. She only knew him as the strange, huge man with the beard who crashed along the corridors like an angry stallion. He looked, somebody said, one of the boys who will go to a London art school and come back to live by the sea and paint landscapes and sculpt driftwood, like Augustus John, whoever he might be.

The house was not far from the Daniels' house and was of similar Edwardian design, a house built for a substantial family with an attic for servants. The front door was painted red, slivers of it peeling off, and not the conventional brown or green.

Ianto delivered her to the door, carrying her big suitcase, wheezing in the fading warmth of September.

'Duw, that's bright' Ianto said. 'Nice, mind, I like a bit of colour. Perhaps I'll paint mine red, though perhaps best not till this old war's over.' Ianto was too old to go to war, as was Dad which was lucky. Some of the older boys from the village school were already on troop ships going to places she'd hardly heard of. Mam was at home with a headache, looking tired, and she'd not come on the usual Sunday jaunt, and as for Dad he didn't like cars much and he liked to spend Sunday evenings listening to the wireless and mending something. There was always something for him to mend. Sometimes Arianwen thought that he broke things so that he would have something to repair.

'Garden could do with a tidy.' Ianto looked at the garden, wild and exhausted at the end of another hot summer. It looked as if it was just a collection of unhappy plants and a lawn which was nothing but beaten up earth. 'I could grow some nice veg there. Dig for victory.' He laughed at his weak joke, then looked worried, staring up at the sky, as if waiting for bombers.

A little girl came to the door when Ianto knocked. She was wearing nothing but a rather grubby petticoat and her face was almost completely covered by a great smear of jam. In her hand was a battered teddy bear which she was trailing along the floor.

She stared up at Ianto and then at Arianwen.

'I'm Arianwen, I'm the new lodger.' The little girl continued to stare and was joined by a large, daft looking dog which also came to stare, but at least it was wagging its tail in a kind of welcome.

'Dai,' the girl said as if naming the dog was somehow an imperative part of social interaction and patting it on its tangled head, and the dog accelerated its tail wagging, and licked some of the jam off her face.

For the first time the little girl laughed.

'Is your Mam and Dad in?' It was 6 o'clock on Sunday evening. Perhaps they were in church or chapel, but Mam had said in her letter that she would be arriving at 6 o'clock and five years of Mrs. Daniels had taught her to be punctual.

'Or'r nefoedd fach.' Ianto was getting impatient. Supper was at seven, his favourite meal of the week, Sunday supper, cold meat off the joint and pickles and fried potatoes. And Mrs. Ianto was a bit fussy about being on time. She wouldn't say much but she had her way of showing displeasure and she was such an accommodating woman in so many other ways, especially on Sunday nights as a reaction to too much chapel.

Suddenly, the little girl screamed 'Mam, Mam.' The dog jumped and barked and ran out to the garden where he ran round in circles, the barking growing louder as his speed increased.

A tall thin woman appeared, as if from nowhere, something unreal about her like a beautiful woman from the Mabinogion.

And then she smiled, and Arianwen was lost.

'Arianwen, cariad, I'm so sorry; Blodeuwedd, why didn't you call for me earlier? Silly child.'

Blodeuwedd flung the teddy bear out into the garden and followed it. The dog flung itself on the toy and continued to run his circles with the bear hanging from his jaws and the angry little girl calling 'Dai, bad, Dai bad, Dai bloody bad.'

The mother laughed. Arianwen was shocked. She would never swear like that in front of her mother.

'I'm Mrs. Morgan, but call me Angharad.' She smiled, a smile like sunshine, at Ianto, who took off his cap and breathed heavily through the brindled moustache.

'Would you like a cup of tea, Mr. erm?'

'Call me Ianto' he said. Quite the man of the world. Arianwen looked up at him. Ianto somehow looked taller, and his shoulders were straighter. And his face was quite pink, and he looked young and eager.

The house was full of light. All the walls painted white, no carpets, only the plain wood floors and there were no curtains anywhere. And there didn't seem to be a parlour, only a very big kitchen with two settles and big battered chairs by the old fashioned stove which looked as if nobody ever cleaned it. A boy was sitting at the big deal table which had a vase of wild flowers on it and lots of papers and books. And the window looked over the back garden, wild as the front. There was a huge ginger cat washing itself under the apple tree and a blackbird picking at the fallen fruit on the ground. Mam would have stewed it and put it in preserving jars. Nice with custard or pork.

Then she saw it. A harp. In a dark corner away from the light and the warmth of the stove. In her mind she heard the tinkling notes of the old songs of *cerdd dant* and felt just a little bit homesick. Not for home, but for chapel and the choir and rehearsing for the winter concert and the eisteddfod.

She smiled at the harp. Nobody she knew owned a harp. Nobody could afford it. And you had to have special teachers.

Ianto was now sitting at the table, drinking tea with Angharad, and there were Welsh cakes with lots of butter on them. Just like home.

Ianto was laughing. He was telling Angharad a story about the night the pig he was fattening for Christmas got out of the pig sty and ran into the chapel where Reverend Edwards was full into a hwyl of Hellfire, and did its business right there in front of the deacons with their solemn faces and woke up the rest of the congregation, and entertained the ones who were restless with boredom or fear, and silenced those surreptitiously unwrapping Mintoes.

The serious looking boy was also laughing.

He turned to her.

'Are you going to have some Welsh cakes? They're quite safe, they're from the baker's. You'd better hurry up, otherwise my horrible little sister and that mad dog will come in and scoff the lot.'

On cue the little girl and the dog came in, and Arianwen quickly put two cakes on her plate and sipped her tea. The little girl took four cakes and gave the rest to the dog, which gobbled them up and then went to sleep, his huge haunches against the big stove, snoring loudly.

The smell of the roses and the warmth from the stove and the laughter of the boy and the little girl's prettiness which had now emerged after the mother had taken a dishcloth to it, made her feel quite sleepy as if she was at home, yet a strange fantastical kind of home, as if she'd travelled a very long way. Perhaps tomorrow after school she would go and visit Doris and take some of Mam's cakes which somehow she didn't think she would be needing.

Ianto stopped laughing, looked at his watch, looked alarmed, jumped up.

'Diawl, time I was going. Thank you for the lovely tea and cakes, Mrs. Angharad. I'll see you 5 o'clock Friday, Arianwen.' Somehow she knew that she wouldn't be looking out for him at the window willing the minutes to pass, as she did at the Daniels'.

She went out to the car with Ianto.

'Nice woman,' he said and blushed. He looked quite young and not a bit like Ianto. And he was whistling really loudly.

Mr. Morgan was coming up the path. His long cloak, a greenish tweed which was, even then, rather old fashioned and made him look like an Edwardian relic, billowed behind him, and blew against his violin case and caused the smoke from his pipe to sway like a mesmerised snake.

The dog appeared from the kitchen, followed by Blodeuwedd

who was now smiling at the sight of her father. Mr. Morgan picked her up and kissed her on the forehead.

'How's my beautiful little girl? How's life treating you, my lovely?'

'Dai's been eating Teddy again.' She offered her father the slobber covered bear which he examined with a very serious look on his face.

'We'll give Teddy a bath.'

'Dad, Bedwyr has been very naughty. He called me horrible names and wouldn't play with me.'

'Cariad, Bedwyr is very serious and he's starting at the grammar school and he's far too grown up to play with you, but your Dad isn't. Let's play chase in the garden.' He trotted through the side gate after his daughter and the deranged dog, lifting his hat to Arianwen.

'The talented Miss Evans. Welcome to the Morgan house. You'll never be the same again.'

And somehow she never was. Full of enchantment, she went back to the kitchen stepping over her bags which still lay in the hall, exactly where Ianto had left them.

In the kitchen Bedwyr was still reading, and his mother was sitting at the window sketching the still sleeping cat.

Arianwen stood awkwardly in the middle of the room until somebody noticed her, watching the garden as the dog ran up to the sleeping cat and barked at it. The cat lashed out with a white edged paw, the dog yelped and retreated. Angharad put down her sketch book and turned round.

'That bloody dog.' She looked at Arianwen as if she'd never seen her before. Then smiled.

'Arianwen, such a lovely name. What does it mean? Not that it matters in the least. I like the sound it makes. It's like music, Arianwen, or a stream flowing in the spring when the snows are melted.' She giggled.

'Mam is a bit of a poet, you'll have to excuse her. Dad says there are far too many poets in Wales. He says music is far more important than words, but that's stupid.'

'Cariad, don't call your father stupid. He's a very good musician. You're very lucky to have such a kind father. Now take Arianwen to her room while I get some supper.'

'Can we have something simple, Mam, not one of your messes?

I can't bring anybody home because they never come again because of Mam's peculiar food.'

His mother bent over the table and picked up his books. 'Put these on the dresser.'

Bedwyr picked up the smallest of the bags and left the rest to Arianwen. They climbed bare wooden stairs, every step with something lying on it: books and clothes and bunches of herbs.

'You're in here. Next to Blodeuwedd. Lucky you!'

He put the case on the bed and left.

The room overlooked the wilderness of the garden. Mr. Morgan was sitting on a broken down bench with Blodeuwedd on his lap, and the dog one side and the cat the other. There was something about the father and the little girl in their strange clothes, which made her feel that she was definitely in a dream, a very enjoyable dream, but not real life.

Angharad walked down the garden. She wasn't wearing any shoes, even though it was getting quite late and there was dew on the grass; her long skirt trailed behind her, and her dark hair was red in the dusk. She kissed the little girl and ran her hand through the man's beard, and stroked her hand down his face, then leant over and kissed him and took his hand, and they all followed her up the garden, like a procession of the blessed. Arianwen was in love, not with an individual, but with a family, with the selfish animals, the spoilt little girl and the awkward boy. That night she loved them all and would do so for a long time.

They sat over supper till late, the children as well as the adults. Mr. Morgan called her Arian.

'Such a lovely name, but even lovelier shortened. Arian, meaning silver and you my dear are like quicksilver. My name is Arwyn. Morgan in school, or Morgan the madman, as I'm known by the wags of the lower Sixth, but here, I am Arwyn.' Arianwen knew what the boys really called him, and it was very rude indeed. She tried not to smile.

What she ate she didn't know. All she knew was that it was lovely. Bedwyr complained.

'This is horrible. I want ham and potatoes. That's what I always get at Wil's.'

'Our son is the most conventional creature in the world, Arian. He'll end up a bank manager, like my father. When he goes to stay with my parents in Aberaeron he comes home full of strange ideas about tureens and doilies and table napkins.'

Bedwyr scowled at his father.

'I'm going to bed. It's far past my bed time. Tomorrow is one of the most important days of my life. Is my new uniform ready?'

'On your bed and I've ironed your shirt as it's a special day. I may not do it again. Blodyn, time for bed.'

'My name's Blodeuwedd, I am not a flower.'

'Bed,' her father said. 'I'll come and read you a story.'

As they left, Arianwen rose to help clear the dishes as she'd been ordered by her mother.

'Make sure you help, they're a family with children, and I don't think she'll have a girl to do the work like Mrs. Daniels, that Doris she was always complaining about.'

'Doris worked hard Mam, and Mrs. Daniels was horrible to her, and didn't give her enough to eat.'

Angharad watched her, following her movements with her pale green eyes, a sharpness to them, in contrast to the dreamy swoon of her body.

'Leave those for a minute.' She picked up her sketch pad.

'I'll draw you now, in this light. You've got such an interesting little face, a bit like an intelligent monkey, elfin is the word, I think. I'm not clever with words. Bedwyr is the one for words in this house. I'm hardly literate.'

'But everything you say is so beautiful, and Bedwyr says you're a poet.'

'Don't listen to Bedwyr, he's a little prig, quite a few of them in Arwyn's family. Arwyn's the exception. They must have found him under a tree somewhere.'

Arianwen felt very tired, and the room was warm. She watched as Angharad scratched at the pad.

She tore a sheet off the pad and handed it over.

'There you are, give that to your mother next weekend. She might like to frame it.'

'That's wonderful. You're so clever.'

'Just a skill, but no real talent.'

'You enjoy doing it, isn't that enough?'

'No, it never is.' Angharad's eyes were sad.

'I enjoy singing and playing the piano, but I know, even now, that I'll never be brilliant at it, but it makes me happy.'

'You're a lucky girl, Arianwen, so much makes you happy. My children don't seem to be like that. All this fighting. They seem to be disappointed with their world and with us.'

The sounds of the children had stopped. One door had been slammed loudly, and then silence.

Arwyn came back into the room.

'Why do I have such difficult children? On the rare occasions when we visit other families their children are seen and not heard. Perhaps the Victorians had the right idea after all. And there's us with all our psychology and reading, and modern ideas and we're bringing up a pair of strangers. That dog's more grateful. Aren't you, Dai boy?

The dog thumped his huge tail against the floor.

'C'mon, boy, a walk, I'll clear the table and wash up when I get back. And don't keep this poor girl up too long. The sixth form awaits.'

Angharad laughed at the look on Arianwen's face.

'Does your father not do the washing up?'

She thought of Dad's kind face.

'He'd do it if Mam asked, but she'd never ask and if he did she'd complain it wasn't done properly. Mam likes things done properly.'

'Not like me. I was never meant to do housework. My ghastly mother, who you will meet tomorrow because she's coming to supper to inspect you, brought me up to be a lady. That's why I'm pretty useless at everything.'

'Except drawing.' Arianwen picked up the sketch and looked at herself. There was a truth about it she had never seen in a photograph, where she always looked rather grim and cross, and not really the person she thought she was.

'What time's your mother coming? I want to go and see Doris, who was the maid at the Daniels' after school. I've got some cakes for her Mam made. Is that all right?'

'You don't have to ask me. Mother will be here at seven. Supper won't be till later. I'll do a joint, while you can still get meat. Mother shares her dislike of my messes with Bedwyr. He is her favourite grandchild.'

'Can I help? I enjoy cooking. I'll make a pudding. Treacle if you have suet.'

27

'Heavens, what a blessing you are. I'll get some at the butcher's.' Arianwen tried to hide a yawn.

'Go to bed, an evening of Morgans, and you're already exhausted.'

Arianwen, without thinking, leant over the table and kissed her on her soft warm cheek, then blushed at what she had done.

At first she couldn't sleep. She heard the door slam, and one trumpet loud bark from the dog, and then it was quiet. And then, when she'd become accustomed to the unfamiliar configuration of window and door and the absence of the light hiss of the mill wheel, she slept.

CHAPTER 5

Over the next two years as she laboured towards adulthood, and the war crashed along, Arianwen visited Doris many times, but it was that first visit, when the Morgans were fresh as a revelation, that she would always remember.

It was only a little town then, not so many cars, certainly not the traffic clogged horror that it is today.

She passed the castle and dutifully remembered her history lesson about the first Eisteddfod being held there, and she thought of the National Eisteddfod she had visited before the war with Mam and Dad, staying at a boarding house, and the excitement of being away from home for a reason other than school, and seeing the Druidic circle and wishing she was one of them dressed up in their comic robes.

And readers will be pleased to hear that later, much later, that ambition was achieved.

As she crossed the road to the little lane leading to the river where it meandered on its last few miles to the sea, she noticed somebody waving to her from the other side of the road.

It was a tall young man, rather showily dressed, not eccentric like Mr. Morgan, but his hair was longer than most men at that time, and his clothes smarter, an expensive gloss to them, and he didn't have that air of spiritual greyness most men had in comparison with Mr. Morgan, with whom she was just a little bit in love, in a silly non-committal way which did not cause her any pain. Mr. Morgan was a little old and anyway there was Angharad who you couldn't ignore with all that hair and that smile which made everybody feel that they'd been invited into a special world.

As she crossed she realised it was Harry Daniels, who she had never liked, not as bad as his Mam, but not as nice as his Dad. He was a young man who made her feel uneasy, as if he was laughing at her. Not that she'd met him many times, as Mrs. Daniels' visits to Rhyl had, sadly, become infrequent in the later years.

'Arianwen, the little schoolgirl still, I see.'

She realised he was a little drunk .His face was reddened and his eyes were unfocussed as if he was looking at a world beyond the busy street.

'Haven't you gone to live in Rhyl with your mother?'

'No bloody fear, I keep a good few miles between me and the old battle axe.'

'I was sorry to hear about your father, he was a nice man.'

His eyes softened and he was back in the world again.

'I miss the old boy too.'

'What are you doing here? The house has been sold hasn't it?'

'And she took all the money for it. Not a penny for me. But good old Dad, he left me a good bit. I've just been to see the solicitor to get some things sorted out.'

'Where are you going to live?'

'I've been called up. Be grateful you're not a man or you could have been fighting in a couple of years.' He laughed, but she saw the terror in his face. Others she knew had been called up, and she knew of one farmer's son who had been killed. Mam had been to the memorial service in the village chapel. There had been no body to come back. Arianwen had spent a whole night crying for somebody she hardly knew. And she'd cried for him and herself and a world out of control.

Now standing in the street on a warm September day she shivered to think of it, and even though she didn't like Harry much, she wanted to put her hand on his arm and say, 'It'll be all right.'

A different girl would have fallen in love with Harry, all charm and artifice, his blue eyes glistening with self-love. However, Arianwen did not like dilettantes and Harry was most certainly one. You didn't have to be very old or perspicacious to realise that he was selfish and egotistical. Doris had loved him in a way because he was her mistress's son and he'd made her laugh, a rare enough event in her miserable life.

'Harry, I hope army life is not too difficult for you.' She thought it might do him the world of good.

'Huh, you haven't a clue have you, you girls at home, still in school uniform at your age. Time you grew up,' and he reached out as if to touch her, and she stepped back in the road, where a milkman's horse was pulling a dray.

He laughed at her.

'Fancy yourself do you, there's plenty more girls at your school who'd welcome a kiss from me, and more…'

She stepped away from him. 'I'm going to see Doris, she's

expecting a baby any day. She lives down by the river, in one of those little houses.'

'Who's the father of this baby then?'

'She's married a boy who works at the garage at the top of town.'

'Got some poor bastard to marry her, did she? Poor sod.'

There was no point talking to him. He was full of bitterness and fear. And in his face, thinner than she remembered, she saw the shadow of his mother, coldness to the dried-out core.

'Good bye, Harry.'

She walked away, her head in the air, not looking back, not wanting to see whatever emotion distorted his handsome face.

Arianwen was used to the sound of water. The stream which fed the mill, and kept the wheel turning, had been the background to her whole life, but the river here, wearied on its way to the estuary, was different. Her stream was a kindness, a robust worker. Here, however, she saw the threat in such a huge volume of water. She imagined it in the winter after heavy rain, flooding the houses, bringing with it all the detritus picked up on the way from its source at Strata Florida where the monks had once lived, and the sad lives of all the people who lived on its banks, and all the animals, the otters, the exotic kingfisher. So much was in this river. And when it flooded into the little houses along the banks not only would it bring filth and effluence, but the memories of all those lives, and all their transience, and she felt the most terrible sadness as she stood one early autumn day, in the 1940s, by a river in West Wales, safely away from the fighting, the bombs, and, for a few years, the blights of human existence.

On the last day of the school holidays she and Mam had been to a fund raising concert at the village hall. The choir had sung, not so many tenors or baritones now, a few young ones gone, only the old men singing, their voices croaking and not quite up to the challenge of the music, but fine for the slow Welsh hymns which made the women cry. After the concert they walked home, happy as she always was after any music, yet seeing in the darkness of the lane the beginning of an oppression, as if anywhere other than the valley was the natural place for her to be, as if the weight of family history in the timbers of the mill exhausted her. She was growing away from the valley, as she was growing away from childhood. Before they started the ascent into the valley, to the east she noticed a red glow, like the best sunset of summer, but coming from the wrong direction.

'What's that?' she pointed to the sky.

Her mother turned to look, and then quickly turned away.

'It's Swansea burning. Swansea's getting it tonight.'

And the contented mood of the concert was gone, and she thought she could feel the heat of the glow on her face. She'd only been to Swansea a few times. Long before the war when she was still small, they'd visited a relative of her father's, now dead, a dried up looking little woman who smelt odd, and spoke with Dad's strange accent. They'd been given tea, and old biscuits which tasted of damp and tea leaves, and there were drooping unwatered plants on the window sill, and a bird in a cage, which didn't sing.

But before that there had been big shops and a special place for tea with cakes, and a clock made of flowers by a big building near the sea.

It was all a long time ago. She was now older, and knew what was happening in Swansea and it made her sad, and all those people bustling around the street and the big market with the women shouting at each other. What was happening to them?

'Why Swansea? It's a long way from London.'

'Because of the docks. They want to cripple the docks. Plymouth's another place that's getting it. Wasn't it a lovely concert and you sang so well, cariad.'

Praise from Mam was always good because it didn't come too often, but it wasn't the same when you thought of that great glow of fire fifty miles away.

Arianwen walks along by the river looking for number 5, not aware that she is growing up, that a conscience is being developed and that all experience is turning her into the woman she will become, a woman for whom the mischievous and malicious little gods of spite have many plans.

Number 5 was as narrow and poor as every other house in the terrace, but, by God, it was clean. Arianwen, although not a great connoisseur herself, was enough of her mother's daughter to know it when she saw it. And number 5 shone, from the narrow door step to the little brass knocker in the shape of a fox's head on the door. Doris must have learned all this cleanliness from Mrs. Daniels, so the woman had done some good in the world. Her own mother, she'd told Arianwen, was a right slut.

Doris opened the door, tiny and thin as ever apart from the enormous bump which looked as if it could topple her over at any time.

Her thin little face was rosy with exertion and the green eyes sparkled.

'Come in, come in. Look at me, I'm like the side of a house. Iwan says I'm like a bloody heifer in calf.'

She hugged Arianwen to her and she felt the hardness of the bump against her own stomach and wondered at who was inside, surely desperate to come out by now. She blushed at the thought of how the baby would thrust its way out into the world.

'I've brought you some of Mam's cakes.'

'Lovely, I always liked your Mam's cakes, especially on Sundays when you came back. I was always so pleased to see you. Sundays she seemed worse than ever. All that going to chapel brought out the worst in her. Iwan will enjoy your Mam's cakes after his supper. He's heard so much about them and you. He should be home soon.'

'And what about you? I'm sure you could do with one of Mam's cakes.'

'Don't eat much these days, this little one seems to fill me up.'

Then her face, so resolutely cheerful, saddened, the bright smile wide on the little face was smoothed over in seriousness and her eyes were big with tears.

' Iwan's been called up. Next week, and he was looking forward to the little one so much. What if he doesn't come back? What will I do?'

Arianwen, untouched, as yet, by the world and its sorrows looks at the older girl and knows that there is nothing she can say or do. War is war, and the work of men her mother says. All she knows is that she is glad Dad is too old, and Ianto too. Many of the boys who were in the sixth form when she was a junior are already gone, their lives suspended till it is over and they can start again, if they come back. There was a boy from Llangrannog, a lovely tenor in the choir, who would not be coming back. What if Iwan never came back and what would Doris do without him? The only widows she knew were really old and they sat in chairs by their firesides and were loved or hated by their families.

'I'll put the kettle on and brew up. Iwan will be here soon. After the war he wants to try to set up a little place of his own, car repairs and that, and if it's a boy pass it on to him to carry on.' Doris's face is the face of dreams, so very different from the frightened and bitter girl she first knew five years ago.

Doris turns from the fireplace where the kettle is boiling as if she has heard something. He is enormous, fills the space of the door. He is dressed in oily overalls and he takes off an equally oily cap when he sees Arianwen, neat and tiny in her school uniform, and smiles, not the shy smile which she might have expected, but the smile of a confident man who is quite certain that he has a place in the world.

'This is Arianwen, cariad.'

'I've heard a lot about you. You were a good friend to Doris.' And he shakes her hand with a big oily hand without apology, and then turns and kisses his wife on the lips and taps her bottom.

Arianwen feels uneasy, rather shy, she is not used to such behaviour between couples, not even the unconventional Morgans.

'How is the little one doing?' and he puts his hand on Doris's bump and caresses it.

'Very active today. He'll play football like you.'

'Or she'll be a lovely girl like you.'

'I've just brewed some tea, and Arianwen's brought me some of her Mam's cakes.'

'Lovely. I've heard about those Sunday night picnics. Doris thinks a lot of you. You made life bearable for her with that old bitch. Where are you staying now?'

'Mr. and Mrs. Morgan, same street as the Daniels. He's a music teacher.'

'I know him, he brings his car in for repairs. Right old heap.'

'Doris says you've been called up.'

'Don't want to go before the baby's born. No choice though, have I? I'm telling you, after this, the world will change. It'll be the age of the workers after this war, not your bosses. They've had it their way for too long.'

His face was excited, the words stumbling.

Doris came back with the teapot and a plate of cakes.

'When my child's growing up he won't live in a slum like this.'

'This isn't a slum.'

'I know you do your best, but there's rats come up from the river and there's rats in some of the houses, human ones. When I've got my own business, we'll be out of here.'

'Doris keeps it so neat and clean. It's lovely, Doris.'

He looked at Arianwen, his eyes challenging.

'And you live in a big mill I hear and your uncle owns taxis and buses.'

'My Dad's a handyman'

'Stop it, Iwan.' Doris looked embarrassed by his bravado. 'I'm happy here, and I'll be here waiting for you when you come back.'

And then he was quiet, eating Mam's cakes, and his eyes tired, and Doris sitting on a hard stool by the fire almost asleep.

Years later, Arianwen was to remember so many times this strange meeting, the young man's passion and Doris's contentment. The baby was born, Iwan came back with more energy than ever and became a successful businessman and Doris the mother of three children, and she, deep in the darkness of her first marriage, no sign of children, and living in a damp and uncomfortable farm house, remembered her old friend and the strange exigencies of life. Doris is one of the happy endings in this story. For Arianwen there would be many endings and many beginnings.

CHAPTER 6

Angharad shouted up the stairs, 'Arianwen, somebody to see you.'

Arianwen had been washing her hair in the bathroom, her top half covered by a towel to keep her dry. Blodeuwedd had been sitting on the toilet watching her.

'You're not so flat round the front any more. You're getting a fat chest like Mam.'

Blodeuwedd always spoke her mind, especially at school and to her elders. Angharad had twice been summoned there to explain her errant behaviour.

Over supper she would imitate Mr. Mathias.

'He looks like Hitler with this silly little moustache and bulging eyes, and there's always a bit of spit in the corner of his mouth and I want to tell him to wipe it off in case it comes in my direction. He goes, 'Mrs. Morgan, your daughter is a bad influence on the other children and she asks far too many questions. Miss Jenkins says that she is the most troublesome child that she's ever met. Always asking questions.'

I said to him, 'I encourage my children to ask questions,' he just muttered something about manners. What I should do is take her out of school and teach her myself, but she'd drive me mad.'

'Isn't it against the law?' Arianwen asked.

'No, don't think so,' Arwyn said. 'Anyway, Angharad is a qualified teacher.'

'Are you? I never knew that.'

'I was the world's worst, hated every minute of it, and the head used to summon me to his study to tell me off because I couldn't control the children, and he didn't know how to keep his hands to himself.'

'I've been thinking of becoming a teacher.'

'Are you, cariad? Good heavens, can't you get married or become a kept woman, or go to work in munitions or something?'

Blodeuwedd, who had been playing with her new kitten by the stove, shouted out, 'Can you teach me at home, Mam? That would be lovely,' and looked beguilingly at her father.

'Oh, no. You can forget that right now, you're going to that school and you're going to start behaving yourself, or that kitten's going back to its mother.'

Blodeuwedd glared at her father, stamped her foot and wailed, and Bedwyr threw his books on the floor and walked out shouting, 'This house is impossible. There's no peace and quiet anywhere.'

Arianwen loved the house for its turbulence. It was living in perpetual storm. Her life had always been so quiet with Mam and Dad, and the slow and contented tempo of their lives. On Fridays, when Ianto came and she sat in the front of the car with him, and they sang some uproarious rugby song together and practised harmonies, the weekend was like another world beckoning. She was two people: weekday Arianwen, treated like an adult by Angharad and Arwyn, increasingly so at school where she felt she was coming into her own, a real person for the first time, and then weekend Arianwen, Mam and Dad's little girl again, going to sleep and waking to the steady turning sound of the wheel, and weekdays to the sound of Blodeuwedd's morning tantrum.

It was then she came to know her own capacity for adapting to circumstance, something that she would find very useful in those terrible years hurtling down towards her.

She wrapped her dripping hair in a towel, and came down the stairs with Blodeuwedd and her kitten trailing behind her.

Doris was standing there, her little one year old in her arms: Mair Arianwen. It was the first time Doris had come to see her. She usually went to Doris's most weeks and enjoyed the peace of the simple house, especially since Mair had been born, a sturdy and determined child who threatened to resemble her father in many ways. Iwan was far away somewhere, Doris was vague as to where it was exactly. Mair was already walking a little and when tired of walking moved quickly on all fours

Doris was carrying a box.

'I've brought some cakes. Nothing special with these shortages, but I saw a recipe in a magazine. I made too many, as if Iwan was still home, so I brought some for the children. Hello, cariad,' she smiled at Blodeuwedd, who was showing the kitten to little Mair who was laughing at its antics.

'I'm Blodeuwedd and my brother is Bedwyr and I don't like him, because he says horrible things to me. My mother is Angharad and my father is Arwyn.'

'My name's Doris and this is Mair and her Dad is called Iwan.'

'She pulled Ben's tail and I'm not letting her touch him again,' and she stomped off taking the kitten with her. Little Mair screamed.

Arianwen took the little girl's hand. 'Come on, Mair I'll show you a big dog,' and she picked Mair up and took her into the kitchen and woke up Dai who was in his usual position by the stove. The little girl looked aghast at the huge dog, then laughed when he woke up and wagged his tail and offered a huge paw for her to shake.

'This place is like bedlam most of the time, but I like it here. Put the cake box on the table, not that there's much room, what with Bedwyr's books and all the other stuff.'

Doris, who had been trained in impossible standards of neatness by Mrs. Daniels, and whose little house was immaculate, looked around the untidy kitchen.

'Lived in isn't it? Mair's sitting on top of the dog, he won't bite will he?'

'Dai, who's the only one in this house with a normal name, only uses his bites for eating. The kitten's called Bendigeidfran. Ben, mostly. It's like being in a chapter of *The Mabinogion*. Did you read that at school?'

'All those silly names and the woman made of flowers. Didn't see the point meself.'

The two girls laughed. Doris, who was a wife and mother and always short of money always felt so carefree with Arianwen and loved her for her laughter. Many years later, on that solemn afternoon in the spring, she thought of the laughter of the woman she'd loved and respected for many years and shivered with the waste of it, and took Iwan's hand, and cried as the congregation sang some old hymn she didn't know.

'I'll make a cup of tea to have with the cake. You're thin as ever. Me, I'm getting to be like Mam, a fat little pigeon.'

Doris had suddenly stopped smiling.

'Those cakes, that's not why I'm here.'

'What's wrong? Something to do with Iwan?'

'No, as far as I know he's all right, and I'm expecting another one. Last leave,' a smile of memory on her thin face. 'Things will be tight, but I'm pleased, and Iwan says we will win the war, and he will be home. I know it. And he says the world will change when the war's over. You know him with his ideas, and Mr. Jones is taking him

38

back. No, it's Harry Daniels, he's been killed. Somebody told me in the shop.'

Arianwen felt sick. All her life she had been protected, by today's standards impossibly so. Relatives had died, pets, boys from the village who'd sung in the choir, but, somehow, Harry's death was more shocking than anything she'd known. She'd never liked him very much, and her last memory of him was half drunk in the street, his face swelling with bitterness and fear, and yet she felt an overwhelming sense of loss.

She sat down. Quite cold. The little girl laughed and the dog barked, his tail wagged against the strings of the uncovered harp and played a clumsy arpeggio.

'Sorry, I know it's a shock.'

'I saw him just before he went away. He was horrible. I hated him. I was angry with him. I was on the way to see you. That first time, when you were expecting.'

The little girl, bored with the dog now, came over to her, raised her hand and touched the tears and tasted them in her mouth. She laughed.

'Sh, cariad. Arianwen's upset. I didn't think you'd be like this. You hardly knew him.'

'I know, it's silly isn't it? I was just thinking of those times he came down when his mother was away, it was the only time I saw Mr. Daniels laugh. Do you remember? Harry used to make cheese on toast in the kitchen and he and his Dad would have a glass of beer, and we all laughed. Poor Harry, poor Mr. Daniels.'

'It was the only time I was treated like a friend, not the servant. When she came home, Mrs Daniels used to create about the state of the stove, even though I'd scrubbed and scrubbed. He tried to kiss me once, couldn't kiss like my Iwan.'

'He was nothing special was he, not as a person, not inside, but I feel so sad because there was so much life in him, and it doesn't seem right somehow. I remember losing a kitten once, the foxes got her, and I couldn't believe that something that was so full of life one minute was gone just like that.'

Doris's face crumbled. ' Don't say that, Arianwen, you've not got a husband in the army.'

'I'm sorry, I didn't mean to upset you.' A silence and a distance between them, they sat with their thoughts, and listened to the

39

sound of Angharad's soft footsteps on the wooden floor of the hallway.

She came into the kitchen, saw Arianwen's face. 'What's wrong?'

'Bad news. The Daniels boy killed, Mrs Morgan.'

'So sad.'

'Surely this war can't go on forever?'

'We can't be certain, Arianwen. I don't always believe that Mr. Churchill. All that talk of beginning and ending.' Angharad's face was full of anger. 'Such a waste this war, any war, such a waste of lives.' Her face was bright with emotion, the green eyes' normal languor iridescent with anger. 'I'm just so glad that Bedwyr is the age he is. All those young men lost, and not so long after that other war. If women ran things there would be no wars. Men can be so stupid.'

Arianwen was to think for a long time about Angharad's comments. It appeared to her that Angharad was right, that men did run the world, although at home there was no doubt that it was Mam who was in charge, and she told Dad and all her brothers what they should do, treated them like naughty little children.

If only she was really clever she could have done something important in the world, but she was going to be a teacher of little ones for a while, and then she would marry and have children of her own and help to build this new world that everybody was talking about.

CHAPTER 7

Ianto always looked forward to Fridays, especially when he was picking up Arianwen. Sundays, he was always in a hurry to get back to supper and the wireless, but Friday had a different feeling to it, somehow, Saturday beckoning, only working in the mornings, usually something pleasant like a wedding, and then Sunday, pottering in the garden keeping an eye on the joint while the missus went to chapel, or working on his motor bike which his sons teased him about.

Friday was his night at the pub. Payday, only a couple of pints and then a sing song, light stuff first, sometimes with words the landlady complained about and, *Sospan Fach* and then when everybody was nicely mellowed, the hymns, with the light dim in the blackout, weather beaten faces full of hwyl and furtive tears wiped away.

Picking up Arianwen, he'd only missed once when he was laid up after having a tooth extracted by that butcher of a dentist in Newcastle Emlyn, was a whole part of the lovely smoothness of Friday afternoon, and with luck Friday would end with the wife in a good mood after he'd taken her home a bottle of stout and a good pay packet with all the tips he'd been given in the week. Not that the Cardis were famous for their generosity, but a lot of regulars showed their appreciation for having their bags carried, or a helpful elbow. Ianto was originally a Pembrokeshire man and we will allow him his little bit of chauvinism.

He knocked at the Morgans' door. Often Arianwen was waiting by the door with the little girl and the dog. It was closed, which was unusual for a warm June day. Their door was always open unless it was raining, as if they wanted their rumbustious life to spill out for everybody to see, a kind of circus for everybody's entertainment, not really the thing in this tight arsed part of the world he felt. As he waited he looked at the garden. It looked a bit better. They had a gardener now, because Mr. Morgan had inherited a tidy sum. Angharad had told him one Friday when they were having a cup of tea in the kitchen, another part of the delicious Friday ritual when he would stare at her lovely face with those exotic eyes and feel just a little bit disloyal to Mari and her pretty, but, increasingly pudgy, face.

'We don't really need to have a lodger now, but we'll keep Arianwen till she leaves school. She's so good with the children, particularly Bedwyr. She'll make a lovely teacher, and she's even civilised Blodeuwedd, well a bit. And it's nice to have somebody to sit with the children if we want to go down the pub for a drink.'

Ianto was not entirely sure about women in pubs, the only woman in his pub was the landlady and he was certain she would look askance at any other woman in there, and certainly he wouldn't like to see Mari in one, even though she enjoyed her weekly glass of stout and a port and lemon at a wedding. The Morgans, however, were different. They had rules of their own. Different from most people. That was the way of the world. You had to have all sorts. He congratulated himself on his worldly philosophy.

Today there was nobody to welcome him at the door: no children, Bedwyr looking superior, and Blodeuwedd wild as ever, always on the verge of a tantrum. Mari would have stopped the nonsense with a good smack, but that wasn't Angharad's way.

Ianto was not an imaginative man. Life happened and he let it happen. Days came and went, and he was not one for reflection, but he later convinced himself that the closed door made him uneasy, in the way that the unusual made him wary, a passenger who didn't smile, or driving to a funeral when it was somebody he knew stored away in the coffin.

He knocked on the door. There was a long wait as he looked anxiously at his watch and he saw his lovely Friday evening sliding away into uncertainty, and then Arianwen was there, traces of tears on her round little face and the brown eyes, usually glistening with mischief and humour were red and swollen.

'What's wrong, cariad?'

'It's Blodeuwedd, she's in hospital, they think it's diphtheria, her Mam and Dad are with her. Bedwyr's gone to stay with his auntie in Aberporth. I don't want to go home. I think I should stay here.'

'There's no point in you staying here, there's nothing you can do. They'll be staying at the hospital as long as they need to. They'll probably want to be on their own. They know you care about Blodeuwedd. And your Mam, she wants you home, you can't stay here. And there's the concert tomorrow and they're depending on you for your solo. Go on, girl, go and get your bag, or you'll be late for your supper.'

Looking at her he thought how lucky she was, this protected child who had never faced poverty, or grief, or pain, or cruelty. One of the blessed. At her age his Mam had been in service for three years working all hours, a frail little girl who never recovered from the privations of her lost childhood. Life would get the girl in the end, as it always did. Not for a long time, he hoped. He was fond of the girl.

As he put her bag in the boot of the taxi, a car drew up, a taxi cab. Mr. Morgan got out of the back and went over to the other door and helped Angharad out. They were smiling, but their bodies were eloquent with exhaustion. Arianwen ran to them and he heard laughter, and inside the dog sensing their return, barked.

Arianwen came back to the car.

'She's going to be all right. They did one of those things where they cut a hole in the throat to make you breathe. She'll be a long time in hospital, but she'll be all right, and Arwyn said she'll have to be quiet for a long time. Oh dear, poor Blodeuwedd, she won't like that.' But her face was solemn. As if she'd just realised that even the Morgans, the anointed of the universe, were not immune to suffering, and the butterfly flitting of fate.

On the way home, foolishly, regretting it immediately, he told her about the death of another young man from the village who had been at the village school with her. Looking in the mirror at her face, shocked, but blank yet of suffering, he felt a great tenderness for her. What suffering would she endure in her life by the time she reached his age? As he drove along the familiar road to Llechryd, he was struck by the most terrible sadness. The lovely Friday feeling was all gone, a fleeting fantasy, ephemeral as the smells from the roadside, of tar and flowers and wood smoke, all changing as he drove along those quiet roads more than seventy years ago.

When Arianwen died, Ianto was long dead himself, and didn't know of the last act in her life, but like so many others he watched the early trajectory of her life, the laughing girl, the blessed girl. Strange that such an ordinary girl, a girl whose beginnings were full of light should know such darkness before the light came again.

CHAPTER 8

It was one of those days after Christmas, those empty, rather formless days, when daylight is just a brief illusion. Arianwen was reading by the window of the big sitting room where you could just see the edge of the wheel turning. Through the closed window the wheel's rhythm was hardly more than a murmur now and soon it would stop forever. Its history had come to an end. The woollen mills of West Wales were coming to an end, only a few would remain open and most of them as tourist attractions rather than working mills.

Just two more terms at school now. She was not a child any more, but was still treated as one, as young people were then. Nobody had heard of teenagers, all that rebellion and fashion was in the future.

She was still a dutiful daughter, though there were little periods of insurrection, usually thwarted.

She was going to do teacher training, the expected career for a girl like her, a respectable kind of job till marriage and children came along. There had been arguments when she'd had doubts, arguments always won by her mother.

'It's a good job for a woman, you won't be doing it forever. Then you'll get married and have children. You think how lucky you are, people look up to a teacher, and you'll never have to get your hands dirty. Pity you're going so far. This war's given people funny ideas. Especially women. Perhaps now it's over everything will get back to what it was, and everyone will know their place again.'

'Oh, Mam, the world is changing, and quite rightly too.'

'Those Morgans, they've given you funny ideas. Sometimes I think I should never have let you go there. The Headmaster recommended them. I never thought a music teacher would have such odd notions on how to live.'

'I've been very happy living there, Mam.'

And her mother smiled a rare smile. 'I suppose that's what's important. Being happy. It's not been easy seeing you go on Sunday evenings while you've been at school, but when you go away to college you'll never be our little girl again. I don't know what your father will do.'

'Find more stuff to repair?' And they shared a rare giggle. The war dragged on, yet people were beginning to laugh and hope again. And there was a vision that a brave new world could prevail.

One day in the summer Doris, now the mother of two children, had visited. Iwan was home on leave and had borrowed a car from the boss. Mam had been very gracious and provided a lovely tea, but somehow there was something in the air which said: 'This young woman was a servant. I am being very kind and rather modern having her here in my front room eating cake off my second best china.' Her mother still had old fashioned ideas about class. Arianwen had decided that when she could vote she would vote Labour as the Morgans did. Daring for Cardigan.

After tea Mam had stayed in the house for a rest and they went to see Dad in his shed and Dad and Iwan talked about engines. The two young women sat on the bank, watching Mair paddling in the stream, and Doris fed the baby and the new collie barked and ran, tracing circles around them.

'Doris you look so well and the children, they're lovely.'

'Mair is a little madam, her Dad spoils her when he's home and as for little Harri, difficult to know what he's going to be yet. It's funny, Mair looks like her Dad, big and sturdy, and Harri's like me, even now you can see he's going to be skinny all his life. He's not fat like other babies, even though he's greedy.' The baby burped loudly in acknowledgement of his mother's comments.

'What's it like having babies?'

'Hell, putting them in is nice though.' She blushed, so much prettier now. Marriage and motherhood suited her, and there in the shredded light of the tall beeches she was almost lovely.

'I'd like to have babies, I don't know about getting married.'

'You'll have to get married first. I don't think there's ever going to be a time when you can have children without having a husband first. Have you got a young man, then?'

'No, I'm still at school. I've got to concentrate on my Highers now.'

'Plenty of girls married with children at your age. I like being married and being called Mrs. and having respect and my little house where I can do what I like, no mean old woman nagging me all day long, but I suppose for a girl like you, you've got to go to college. Is there anybody you like? Will there be boys at college?'

'Only old men come back from the war.'

'Perhaps you'll marry one.'

Arianwen was uneasy about all this talk of marriage. Angharad had told her in her calm unembarrassed way about what went on in marriage. It made her feel uncomfortable, but excited, and she felt as if she was blushing from the inside.

Sometimes she still thought of the fair boy who had sat in front of her in the history class, sometimes she breathed his name in the darkness of her bedroom. The back of his neck was smooth, soft like a baby's with none of the spots that other boys had. He didn't like rugby and football and teasing girls, and walked around on his own, his eyes shying away from others. He was very clever, and that did not make him popular with the others. Some girls thought he was handsome, and tried to tease him and flirt with him and were ignored. So they said he was just a snob and a swot, and laughed at him. The boys spread rumours and sniggered and tried to bully him, but grew tired when he walked away seemingly unscathed by blows and insults. She thought about asking her form teacher what had happened to him, but he was not the kind of teacher who answered questions. When she asked one of the kinder boys in the class, he just teased her and made her blush, and told some of the other boys who also teased her until they grew bored.

Later she was to find out that his parents had moved away to the North of England and he was going to start at a new school and it was much later that she realised why he was such a loner, why she had felt he was so different from the rumbustious boys from the farms with their boring loudness and predictable jokes. She often thought of him, and what life would have been like for him in those years after the war, persecuted by the police and subject to homophobic attacks.

And still she saw the thin face with the blue violet blurs beneath the eyes and the hollows beneath the prominent cheek bones and the blond down on his lips and the green eyes full of something deep and mysterious as if he knew all about suffering.

'Arianwen,' her mother called from the kitchen. She dropped the book, one of those romantic books which always made her sad as if there was something she was reaching for, something just beyond her reach, like a friendly hand beckoning her into a new world, a world where she would not feel the myriad little cauldrons of anxieties which worried her these days.

Her mother came in. 'I'm just going out to get the washing in. It hasn't dried one bit in this old murk. I'll put the chickens in while I'm out there. These days are so short, it's dark when you get up, and the daylight goes so quickly. Keep an eye will you? I've got some cakes baking in the oven. About another ten minutes and they'll be ready.'

Arianwen nodded at her mother's voice, not lifting her head.

'Did you hear me? I don't know what's wrong with you these days. You seem to be in another world. Don't forget about the cakes. They're for the whist drive tomorrow. Do you want to come with me? Dad doesn't want to come.'

'I don't know, Mam.'

'You've hardly moved from that chair since Christmas.'

She looked up as her mother went out. The room was so familiar, made crepuscular by the trees, and the reflection of the water shimmering on the ceiling, familiar as her own breathing, and the creaking of the floor boards under her weight. For the first time in her life she felt its restriction, as if in this room the whole tired history of the mill was suffocating her, and the valley, dark, always holding the light away.

The dog barked at her mother, moving ghostlike, insubstantial in the mist of the garden as she shooed the chickens, and there was already in early afternoon an owl calling. She was ready to go back to Cardigan to the rollicking life of the Morgan family and the huge operatic drama of every day. It was disloyal to Mam and Dad, but there were times now when she felt the oppression of the valley and its busy history like the aftermath of a bad dream.

At school, reverberating with laughter and discipline and daily extolled to virtue and industry, and the loyalties and feuds of adolescence, she didn't have time to think of her life and the thoughts of dying which assailed her. Not her own death, she was still at the age of certain immortality, but the death of others. She had been a late child of a late marriage. Mam and Dad were getting old, and sometimes she felt that she was a stranger to them. There was a duality to her life: two existences which had always led their parallel courses quite amicably but, now, they seemed to clash like badly played music, a jarring disharmony.

Too late she smelt the cakes burning in the kitchen, the reeking smoke mingling with the wood smoke from the fireplace. She opened the oven, took out two blackened sponge cake halves, burning her fingers because she didn't use the oven cloth correctly. Her mother found her at the kitchen table scraping away at the burnt cakes, tears falling down her round little face and bits of burnt sponge all over the kitchen table.

She put down the washing basket and put the peg bag on the dresser.

'You silly girl, did you let them burn? For heaven's sake, there's no need to cry. You're not a child. I'm going to put a bit of butter icing on them, well margarine and a bit of sugar I've kept by, a bit of colouring and it'll be fine.'

Arianwen was still crying, sobbing into her hanky. Her father put his head round the door ready for his afternoon cup of tea and a piece of cake, saw Arianwen crying, and a grim look on his wife's face, and closed the door again and went to sit on the outside step with the dog and a cigarette, till this latest storm died down, and somebody called him in, rescuing him from the damp murk of late afternoon.

Back in the kitchen her mother sat down at the table and looked at her daughter.

'What's wrong? You've been miserable since you came home for Christmas. Your Dad's bewildered, you're not his little girl any more, and I feel you're a complete stranger. It's as if you don't want to be here at all.'

'You treat me like a child. I'm not a child. Doris had children before she was my age, and I'm still in my school uniform, and when I leave school I'm just going to another kind of school and all that studying and then when I finish it'll be back to another school and that'll be my whole life.'

'Now you're just being silly. Everybody gets a bit low after Christmas. It's these short dark days when the night seems to go on for ever. Come on, wipe your eyes. You've got all your life to look forward to. You'll make a lovely schoolteacher and you can carry on with choirs and singing and playing the piano. It's those Morgans. They've given you funny ideas. I should have found a more ordinary family. The headmaster recommended them so highly.'

'I don't know whether I want to be a schoolteacher, I think I'd prefer to be a nurse and work in a hospital and do some real good.

And I love living with the Morgans. It's so quiet here.'

'Don't be silly. You're going to training college in September, and don't you think teaching children is doing good? I'd have loved to be a teacher.'

Her mother went to the cupboard and took out a bowl and then margarine from the larder and a little twist of sugar from the food cupboard and started the business of beating the buttercream mixture. As far as she was concerned the conversation was finished.

'Go and tell your father there'll be a cup of tea and a piece of cake in five minutes. I'll make some nice sandwiches from the ham, and we'll have some Christmas cake We'll sit round the fire and listen to the music. That'll be nice.'

Arianwen went outside where her father was sitting on the bottom step smoking one of his Woodbines and stroking the head of the collie. It was completely still, not a hint of a breeze in the trees, tall and somehow just a little sinister in the gloom. There was complete silence, apart from the dog's occasional little yelps at nothing,

'Cup of tea in five minutes, Dad, by the fire Mam said as it's such a miserable day. We'll listen to a concert.'

'That'll be nice. I like a cup of tea by the fire. Bit of a treat. Just let me finish this cigarette.' They sat in silence and watched the smoke waft upwards, quite straight in the stillness. He took her hand and squeezed it. A tawny owl called at the top of the woods and somewhere down in the valley another answered it; their calls skimming the sluggish stream, muddy and brown after heavy winter rain, tired and melancholy, as if aware that its years of production had ended and it was now redundant.

Many years later she would often think of that dreary afternoon and her futile little attempt at rebellion, her mother's unyielding will and her own weakness. She considered different narratives for her life's arc. How could her life have been different? That great jagged pattern of her existence. She always pleased others, wanted to be liked. Had she been too passive? Her questions were unanswerable, and later, when she was happy, there was no time for reflection. Questions were as futile as night time anxieties.

The dog followed them in and went to sit by his bowl in the kitchen, his eyes bright with hope. She gave him some biscuits and the frenzied tail wagging lifted her spirits.

Her mother was loading the tray. 'Take this in and put it on the table.'

The room was warm, her book still lying by the window where she'd dropped it. She picked it up and lay it face down on the chair, drew the curtains to shut out the endless burdened motion of the wheel, and the dark and damp of the afternoon. Looking round the room, at the big fire, the Christmas tree, the stuffed badger in its case, her father sitting content by the fire and her mother coming in with the big brown teapot in its cosy, she felt the burden of familiarity and safety fall about her like the mist creeping around the mill.

'Put the radio on, Arianwen, the concert should be on soon.'

And sipping her tea to the sound of a harp playing an old song, she tried to forget her worries and exiled them to the stream and the mist and the darkness lying waiting for her outside.

CHAPTER 9

Bedwyr was in a bad mood.

'Where's Arianwen? She said that she'd be back tonight to help me with my history.'

'You don't listen to anything she says when she helps you. You just want to impress her by showing off how much you know.'

Arwyn Morgan tried not to laugh at his son's angry face and the blush which gave away the ongoing crush on Arianwen, which Bedwyr fiercely denied when the family teased him.

Bedwyr, at thirteen, was growing too fast, and was at the most unattractive stage of that growth. His face was covered in spots and his voice was a battle between soprano and bass, and the unlovely blushing merely accentuated his blemishes.

Arwyn was convinced that he'd managed the transition between childhood and adulthood quite without all this attendant drama, and showed no sympathy towards his son.

'Boy's a complete fool, all this drama and fuss. Takes after your family, Angharad.'

Angharad came in carrying a bundle of badly folded washing, took one look at her son's angry face and walked out again singing *Ar hyd y nos,* and shouted up the stairs, 'Blodeuwedd, can you come down here for a minute, I want you to take some clothes up for me.' There was a loud protesting wail from above, then a heavy clomping on the bare stairs.

Blodeuwedd came down dressed in one of her mother's long dresses, its sequinned hem threatening to trip her up. Dai followed her, barking and biting at the dress. Blodeuwedd had decided, after a visit to the cinema, that she was going to be an actress. The preparatory process involved moving around the house in her mother's dresses, her mouth slashed precariously with Angharad's bright lipstick.

'Go and get changed. That's the dress I was going to wear for the dance tomorrow night. Look at it, Dai's bitten it and trodden on it.'

Blodeuwedd looked down on her mother from the middle stair. There was the familiar cold contempt in her eyes and she turned to the dog, 'Bad dog, Dai,' and patted it lightly on its rump, setting off a manic cycle of barking and tail wagging.

Then she continued her stately progress down the stairs, passing her mother in the hallway without a glance and sauntered, head held high, into the kitchen, the dog following her like a faithful, if rather lunatic page. As Blodeuwedd passed, Angharad noticed that the little girl smelt strongly of her best perfume and that the dog was carrying a piece of the sequinned hem of her dress in its mouth. Never had she wanted to hit her child so much. She bit her mouth in shame, and clenched her fists tight against her thin hips.

In the kitchen, Bedwyr was glowering at his homework as Blodeuwedd twirled in the middle of the room. Arwyn was stirring something in a saucepan on the hob, bits of ash from his cigarette falling into whatever was being stirred.

She thought almost longingly of the long despised order and tranquillity of her childhood home, and picked up her sketch pad which Bedwyr had swept on to the floor with the imperious disregard he showed for anybody else's possessions.

Always she'd had a rather silly affection for her kitchen and was proud that it was full of vitality, the centre of her family's life. Now everything was changing: Bedwyr growing up a hostile stranger, and Blodeuwedd's behaviour more disturbing each day, and Arwyn seemed to have become quite estranged, never touching her. Her once ardent lover turned his back to her every night.

In the warm kitchen she felt a sudden coldness coming to her as if her life was changed and something enormous had been taken away from her.

Blodeuwedd stopped her twirling and rather unsteadily sat on the stool by her father's harp; she plucked harshly at the strings, releasing an arpeggio of discord into the room.

'Stop that at once.' Another clumsy tug at the strings. 'Did you hear me? How dare you treat that harp like that. It was left to me by my grandmother Morgan, and it wasn't meant to be ill-treated by a spoilt inconsiderate little girl like you. Now go and get changed and go to your room and when you come down I expect to see your face washed.'

Blodeuwedd was her father's darling. Her pretty little cat like face crumpled into tears and she ran out of the room. By the time she'd got to the top of the stairs she was screaming hysterically.

Angharad looked at her husband's angry face, and noted Bedwyr's pleased snigger, and felt a weight of despair envelop her.

Arwyn looked across at her as if noticing her presence for the first time.

'Haven't you any control over the children at all? I've been teaching all day, no supper ready and Blodeuwedd screaming like a banshee, and ruining my harp, and Bedwyr sulking because Arianwen's not here. And you, what do you do? Sit there doodling as if you've got nothing else to do.' He scooped up the cat and nuzzled his nose in the soft fur. He was crying, her strong husband, her tolerant husband, crying.

He looked up at her, his face wet with tears.

'What's wrong, cariad?'

He shook his head, nuzzled his face deeper into the struggling cat's fur.

'We chose to live our lives in this way, Arwyn, to give our children the freedom we didn't have. Are you saying that we've been wrong, that our whole philosophy was misguided?'

He looked up. His eyes were dead. He spoke slowly as if to a stranger.

'Perhaps it's to do with being middle aged and a failure. Neither of us is what we set out to be, and the children make me feel old and hopeless. Sometimes I think that Arianwen is the only pocket of sanity in this house. I don't know what we'll do when she leaves in July. We're all going to miss her. I'm going out. I'll have a pint with Edwin. With any luck he'll ask me home for a bite of supper. His wife's a good cook, very well organised. Don't wait up.'

She heard him in the hall, greeting Arianwen who had just come in. He said something in a deep voice and she heard the welcome sound of Arianwen's musical giggle. Bedwyr blushed and started to shuffle his books, and she heard the padding sound of Blodeuwedd's bare feet on the stairs.

They came in together, the little girl, and Arianwen, her hair glistening with rain, her face radiant with youth and music, and Blodeuwedd, face washed, shabby in a cotton dress, a parody of normality. She was clinging to the older girl and dragging her in. Bedwyr stared intensely at one of his books.

Angharad looked up from the almost bare page of her sketchbook.

'Arian, cariad, how was your rehearsal? Supper will be ready soon.' She looked in despair round the kitchen and at the abandoned saucepan.

'Shall I do us scrambled eggs on toast? And then we'll have some of Mam's cakes.' Mam always gave her eggs and cakes to bring back on Sundays, fearing for the nutrition of the children in such a disordered house.

'Lovely, lovely, lovely,' screamed Blodeuwedd, dancing round the kitchen.

'Blodeuwedd, you tidy up the kitchen and Bedwyr you clear the table and then lay it nicely with the knives and forks and shall we have a candle because it's still not very far from Christmas and after we've washed up and cleared together, perhaps, I'll have a little play at the harp and we'll have a bit of a sing song shall we?'

Blodeuwedd cleared everything and put a whole pile of stuff in the corner. Immediately the cat went to lie on it and kneaded a pair of mismatched gloves with loud purrs.

Bedwyr pushed his chair back hard, glowering to hide the blush which always threatened when Arianwen was in the room. He carefully avoided looking directly at her, fortunately unaware that she was really quite oblivious to him as anything other than the bright, rather serious son of the house who she quite liked, but would probably not have liked as a brother. He was certainly not the paragon who she had created in rare moments of only child self-pity: good looking, perfect tenor and a sympathetic listener to all complaints.

Bedwyr piled his books in another corner and went to the dresser to fetch the cutlery. Angharad stood up at last and went to draw the curtains. The garden was full of shadows and she touched the glass, wet with condensation, and sketched a smiling face in it with long hair. She touched her face with the cool moisture. She felt tired. All she wanted was to go bed and sleep and really forget her troubled family. Tonight she would quite easily have walked down into the town, past the castle, through the dark riverside terraces with their sounds of scurrying rats in the shadows and the shouts from ill-lit houses, and walked into the cold river and allow herself to be swept out, a piece of flotsam, down to the estuary, out to the sea.

She was forty years old, and she felt the weariness of an old woman.

Arianwen was standing by the stove stirring eggs while she super-vised Blodeuwedd buttering the toast, and all the time humming something cheerful from some musical comedy, her tiny feet tapping as if she would dance at any minute, her face alive with the harmony of the music. She turned to Angharad and smiled; a strangely maternal kind of smile.

'Angharad, sit down, you look so tired. Are you sickening for something?' Angharad shook her head.

'No, I'm fine. Depressing weather this. I'll feel better when the days lengthen again.'

'Supper's ready, Blodeuwedd come and sit by me.'

Bedwyr ate his food too quickly and mumbled something about homework and picked up his pile of books.

'Aren't you singing, Bedwyr?'

'No,' he growled, and left the room, in some strange way easing the tension in the absence of his unhappy male presence.

Arianwen looked at Angharad.

'I think I'll just listen to you two. Half an hour and then bed. I'll come and read you a story, Blodeuwedd, and make sure you have a good wash before you get into bed.'

Blodeuwedd looked as if she was going to protest; her lower lip, always indicative of trouble to come, jutted out showing the pink moistness of her mouth, and remnants of scrambled egg. Arianwen gave her a song sheet which she always kept in the kitchen, and played on the harp with the gentle reverence Arwyn so much admired and appreciated, an old song which made Angharad want to cry, and pacified Blodeuwedd who sang in her thin sweet voice, her face composed and cleansed of its anger, and Arwyn coming home to apologise, having found the company at the pub loud and unfriendly, came in unseen to the kitchen and watched them as if they were on a stage far away from him, strangers from another place, his beautiful wife in the chair by the stove, the cat on her lap, and the dog's muzzle in her hand, smiling sleepily, and Arianwen singing, holding the hand of a smiling Blodeuwedd, now singing slightly out of tune, and he joined in in his fine tenor in a verse of *Calon Lan* and Bedwyr, cold and miserable in his little room at the top of the house, came quietly down the stairs and stood in the kitchen doorway feeling somehow reassured by the sight of a harmonious family and the smile on his mother's face sensing that, somehow, equilibrium had been restored and the light was come again on that dark and dank January evening.

'I'm trying to work up there. What's all this row about?' but despite his better efforts he was smiling, and when they laughed at him he wasn't angry, and while everybody was laughing it was a good opportunity to have a really good look at Arianwen who was looking very pretty in the white blouse she wore for choir, and her face shining with warmth and music and her dark eyes full of happiness as she looked to her future which he knew, even then, would not include him at all.

CHAPTER 10

And soon, as if childhood was a bright day fading, she went to college.

And the mill wheel turned, its turning increasingly listless, and watched as the family changed: Arianwen now a woman, her parents grown older, and the dreary post-war world began to change. The little river carried its secrets, and the birds sang along its banks and in the surrounding trees, and the village was changing and the farmers were prospering.

She still came home at weekends, but not always, on the little train to Newcastle Emlyn, and was met by Ianto, growing brindlier, proud of his new National Health teeth, all pink gums, the colour of tinned salmon, or one of the younger men who tried to flirt, although it was not advisable because she was the boss's niece.

Her life grew beyond the confines of West Wales. One weekend she went to Rhyl to the home of a college friend. On Saturday, they had a giggly afternoon on the prom. Chins deep in ice cream, artificial tasting, and leaving the tongue numb, they sat and stared at the sea.

'What's wrong?' Siwan was laughing, which only made her look even more beautiful. A couple of young men walking past nudged each other. 'You look as if you've seen a ghost, and you've slurped ice cream all down your chin and neck.'

'Over there, that's my first landlady I was telling you about. She was really horrible.'

Mrs. Daniels tall and thin, apart from her improbable bosom, and a woman who was probably her sister, she could not possibly have friends, a squat and square woman, were coming towards them on the prom.

'Like Laurel and Hardy,' Siwan said, and like schoolgirls, they ran behind a shelter, watching the two women, giggling at their own wit, and drunk on youth and freedom.

Siwan had an older brother who was studying medicine at Cardiff. He was home for the weekend to play for his rugby team. What a catch her mother would consider him to be, a doctor, she'd never need to work, a practice in Cardigan, a fine house on the Gwbert Road, and a lot of babies to keep her happy. Mam was ambitious for her, but only within the parameters of convention.

Peter was a serious young man, a bit like an older Bedwyr, but less disturbing. There was no sense of anger seething underneath the outer dignity.

On Sunday he asked her if she'd like a stroll along the prom while his mother and sister prepared Sunday lunch, and his father, who was a teacher at a local grammar school, marked exercise books. The family had not mentioned chapel or church and had looked surprised when she'd asked where the local Baptist chapel was. Siwan, being a polite kind of girl and determined to be a good hostess, took her to the local chapel and sat through a morning service taken by a minister who was very young, rather vapid and himself seemed to be grappling with the complexities of faith. Siwan watched it all with the rather sceptical air of one who is studying the rituals of a primitive race. She didn't sing at all even though she was one of the finest sopranos in the college choir. The singing was good and Arianwen joined with her usual enthusiasm. Sometimes she thought that one of her main reasons for going to chapel, even though she knew that compared to the easy purity of Siwan's voice hers was just a passable working instrument. As for faith, her life was too busy for too much contemplation, but she considered herself a believer.

'You didn't sing, Siwan.'

'No, we're not a religious family. Peter's an atheist, and so is my father, I think, not that he speaks to me very much.'

She was shocked, but, perhaps, not surprised. Siwan's was an educated family, unlike her own. Was atheism a consequence of education? On the way home they talked of other things. Arianwen was having far too good a weekend for such seriousness.

As she and Peter walked along the prom it began to drizzle. He turned to her and pointed to one of the shelters.

'Let's sit down here and stare at the sea like those old folks over there.'

An ancient couple sat in the adjoining shelter eating sandwiches out of a tin box. The old man was holding a thermos flask and pouring tea into a tin cup with shaking hands, most of the tea spilling on the pavement.

'What's the point of living till you're old like that? I'll make sure that I've got something to put an end to things when I get to that stage.'

'You shouldn't talk like that. We go when our time has come.'

'When God's ready to take you for a sunbeam? You don't believe in all that fairy tale stuff do you?'

'Of course. I go to chapel and I pray and I believe that there is someone looking after me.'

'Easy for you. You've not been tested. Who looked after all the Jews? Who looked after all the men taken prisoner by the Japs? One of our neighbours came back from Changi. He was hardly alive, I doubt whether he'll ever be alive again. He's dead in his mind. God knows what he suffered. Don't talk to me about a God. Have you ever seen a dead body?'

'No.'

'When we do dissections, there's a body there and you know there's nothing there, just a dead body, just meat.'

'Yes, because the spirit's gone.'

'Don't talk to me about spirits. Ever read Darwin?'

'No, I've heard of him though.'

'Read him. Everybody should read him.'

'Siwan came to chapel with me.'

'She's a polite kind of girl, we're a polite kind of family, we're brought up on what you might call Christian principles even though my parents are not believers; consideration for others is their credo. Perhaps it's one of the reasons why I'm training to be a doctor, and it's well paid, and I want to travel a bit before I settle down. I was called up a couple of months before the end of the war. I only saw Catterick. I was one of the lucky ones. Some boys from school, a bit older than me, they never came back. I'm going to live my life, every bloody minute of it. Training to be a doctor's hard, but it'll be worth it.'

'I wanted to be a nurse, I thought it would be more useful.'

'And you want to do some good in the world. Won't you be doing that as a teacher?'

'Yes, I suppose so.'

'Why didn't you become a nurse then?'

'My mother, she wanted me to be a teacher.'

'And you did what your mother wanted. And you'll let your mother choose a husband for you like they do in India.'

'It's easier for a boy to get his way than for a girl.'

'Perhaps you're right. Siwan wanted to go to art school you

know, she got a scholarship to the Slade. Apparently she's very good. I don't understand anything about art, I'm just a simple scientist.'

'Why didn't she go then? I can't imagine anybody stopping Siwan from doing what she wants to do.'

'That's what I thought. Something happened, I was in Cardiff, didn't come home much that summer term because I was busy with exams. I think there was a boy and there were lots of tears and a lot of drama from what I could pick up in Ma's letters. 'Siwan is being a bit difficult,' was the code for trouble. She's never said anything to you about it?'

'Nothing.'

'I think there was a boy and staying out all night and all a bit racy for boring old Rhyl and Dad put his foot down, and said she can do art as a hobby and that she'll only end up getting married and having children and what will be the point of gadding about in London with a lot of people with loose morals. Something to that effect. Then the next thing is, Siwan is going to train to be a teacher. She's never forgiven him. In some ways the old man is quite liberal, but there's a lot of the old Victorian paterfamilias about him. Are you going to get married and have babies, little Arianwen?'

She blushed. She wasn't used to young men who were quite so direct, and she had after all met some of the strange people who came to the Morgan household, once a thin and strange woman who had modelled for Augustus John and was rumoured to have been one of his mistresses, a gnarled waif who sat on the sofa all evening until she fell asleep with a cigarette in her hand which burnt a big hole in her flimsy dress.

'I haven't really got any plans for anything. Just go ahead with living and see what happens.'

'Perhaps you're right. Siwan and I rush at life as if it's some great battle.'

He took her hand, and they sat and watched the sea, turbulent in the south west wind, and the couples fighting against it before returning to their hotels for Sunday lunch, and the long snooze of Sunday afternoon.

They watched the old couple in the neighbouring shelter walk arm in arm, their frail bodies bullied by the wind, but they were both smiling as if they were young and all life in front of them.

'Right, better go or Mam will be cross. Great believer in punctuality my mother, and my father will be wielding the carving knife like the best surgeon in the world.'

He kept her hand in his till they turned into his street then they walked a little apart as if they'd done something wrong.

After lunch which was noisy and cheerful and not as good as Mam's, he left to go back to Cardiff, and the next time she saw him he was a surgeon, home from the States for Siwan's first exhibition at a prestigious London Gallery, a lifetime away from Rhyl on a grey post-war morning.

CHAPTER 11

The summer at the end of her first year was dry and hot, and she spent a lot of time reading by the stream with her feet dangling in its cool but shallow flow, and walking through the woods, and sometimes up to the village shop to get a few bits and pieces for her mother. The holidays were long and they threatened to become dull and formless. One day, shocked by her listlessness and inability to enjoy such a lovely summer she went to her uncle's taxi firm and asked if somebody could teach her to drive.

Mam was not pleased.

'Why do you want to learn to drive? We've got a taxi company we can use any time.'

'I want to be independent.'

Her mother glared at her. 'Independence. What do you want independence for?' Then took a tin of polish and a duster from a cupboard and walked out into the hallway. Soon there was the sound and smell of polishing. No more was said.

Ianto took her out in one of her uncle's old cars every morning for an hour between washing the coaches.

'Duw, you're a natural, girl. You'll be driving a coach soon. Why do you want to be a teacher when you could drive coaches for your uncle? You'd be the smallest driver in Wales. I can see you driving a coach load of supporters up to the Arms Park for an international. You'd keep them under control, you with your teacher's voice and that glare in your eye when you're cross. Watch that bloody pheasant, they're too stupid to live, those bloody things.'

When Siwan came to stay a couple of weeks before they went back to college for a second year, the weather was still warm, and one sunlit day they had a taxi to take them to Cardigan where they were to visit the Morgans. They were invited to tea which seemed rather formal for the Morgans. She knew that Siwan was the kind of girl who would appreciate their informality.

The girls dressed in their prettiest dresses: Arianwen in pale blue with a white cardigan to show off her dark hair, and Siwan in red, her blonde hair loose against tanned shoulders, rather exotic for Cardigan, and the most beautiful gold sandals. Siwan looked like a Hollywood star.

Ianto was at his most gallant. By the gate to the garden where he always parked the well-buffed Morris he took off his cap, and opened the back door for them.

'Good afternoon, ladies. I hope the wife doesn't see me with two beautiful girls in the back of the car. It'll be round the village in no time. Ianto off to Cardigan with two lovely girls. Oh what a lucky man I am.'

Out of respect to Siwan he didn't start a sing song, but kept a respectable silence as far as Llechryd where he started whistling *Sospan Fach*, and the two girls joined him and Siwan impressed him with her knowledge of alternative lyrics.

'Duw bach. Where did a lovely girl like you learn those?'

Siwan giggled, and Ianto blushed a manly blush.

After shopping for some essential stationery for the much dreaded teaching practice in October they walked up the main street towards the Morgans' house.

'Angharad, Mrs. Morgan, is a very good artist. Perhaps she'll show you some of her work, she does lovely sketches of the family.'

Siwan had never said anything about her desire to go to art college and she was studying history as her main subject, but everybody had seen the brilliant visual aids she prepared for teaching practice, quite the envy of all in their group, sitting till late at night struggling with pieces of card and glue and bits of tissue paper.

Siwan looked bored. Her visit was not going well. Arianwen had so enjoyed the visit to Rhyl and the walks by the sea and the prom, and the interesting Peter who, though rather intimidating in many ways, had talked to her as nobody had ever spoken before, as if she were a real adult, somebody in her own right with thoughts and opinions. The beauty of the mill and its surroundings did not seem to move Siwan, which was surprising for an artist, because many had come to the valley and praised its beauty and the subtle changes of the light on water.

When she arrived and they walked along the stream to the house, she'd looked surprised, her body undulating in a little shiver, and stopped, a strange look on her face, as if she'd suddenly remembered something.

'That's really quaint, it's like something out of a children's story book; you expect a witch or a goblin or something to come out of the woods.' She shuddered, and jumped, as the excited collie came out and barked her welcome.

'Do you like living here? It's so out of the way from anywhere. I can see why you had to stay away for school. It must have been very strange coming back here after a week in a town.'

'I was always glad to come home.' Not strictly true perhaps in the last year or so when everything had been so colourful in the Morgan household, and when she felt they needed her more than her parents, set in their cosy undemanding routine, but always so glad to see her. It was her home and she was not happy to hear her home being dismissed in this way. Other people who had come home with her had all been charmed and envied her living somewhere so different, *so romantic,* somebody had said.

But Arianwen was a tolerant girl, and she was very fond of Siwan, or so she had thought.

As they walked up the slope towards the Morgans' house, Siwan was puffing slightly, and her face was pale even though the sun was warm.

'Are you all right? You're looking very pale.'

'I'm fine, I didn't sleep very well last night. I can't get used to the sound of that wheel turning. It's just a bit spooky that's all. And the owls calling. My Nain always said that the call of an owl meant somebody was going to die. Silly old wives' tale.' Then she turned and smiled and Arianwen remembered why they were still friends.

'I'm really looking forward to meeting your second family. They really sound interesting.'

And, briefly, harmony was restored. Many years later, when Arianwen got married, Siwan gave her a huge picture of a barn owl as a wedding present. It was flying over the mill, something caught in its claws, the bird a rapture of gold and white, a great round-faced slash of light across a strange, disturbing sky. It was the essence of owl, not the wise creature of lore, but an efficient killer, and somehow it looked bigger than the mill, which was lying by the stream, a waiting victim with nowhere to escape to.

The picture was on the wall of the parlour for many years and often when she went in there to dust, or play the piano, the owl made her think of death and the day came when she had to take it down because she couldn't bear to look at it any more. It went into the auction. Somebody got quite a bargain, and sometimes she wondered if it was still sitting on a farmhouse wall, the owner quite unaware that it was the work of a famous artist.

The Morgan garden, although now far more respectable thanks to the attention of the elderly gardener, still stood out from its neighbours, gardens where nature was tamed rather than nurtured, and neurotically tidy as if any aberration would give away family secrets hidden behind well painted doors and scrubbed doorsteps.

The Morgan garden no longer displayed a collection of rusting toys long abandoned. Now there were pieces of driftwood lying on the lawn, all bleached and rather beautiful in the bright sun as if they were alive, not long dead. Right in the middle of the lawn there was an enigmatic item which might have been an abandoned collection of disparate pieces of metal, or a piece of modern sculpture. Angharad had let it be known that she was widening her artistic repertoire.

Siwan rubbed her hand along a piece of driftwood pale as bone from the bleaching of sun and salt wind.

'That is beautiful. I'd like to draw it. I've never seen anything like that on the beach at Rhyl.'

As was usual, the front door was open, and inside they could hear a puppy barking.

Blodeuwedd came through the door carrying a dark puppy .

'This is Dai two. Dai one died last week, so we've got a new one this week'.

The two young women tried not to smile at this pragmatic, if callous, view of death.

Blodeuwedd seemed to have grown since the last time she'd seen her at Easter when she'd called round with a basket of eggs for the family and Angharad and Blodeuwedd had been on their own, Blodeuwedd dancing in the garden while her mother sketched from the kitchen table. She'd refused to come into the house to speak to Arianwen even when she'd been called into tea and had continued with her manic dancing until she collapsed on the grass and went to sleep.

'I can't do anything with her, Arwyn is the only one who can make her do anything. She's quite wild. The school writes letters complaining about her. We can't afford for her to go away to school. She never looks me in the eye, always looks over my shoulder, and she and Bedwyr ignore each other. I've taken her to the doctor. He just says that there's nothing wrong with her physically. You used to be so good with her. I think she misses you.'

'Why doesn't she come and speak to me then?'

'She knows you're only staying a short time so there's no point. She'll sleep now, and, later, she'll be wandering back and fore up and down the stairs till she tires herself out all over again. Arwyn is trying to get somebody from the education department to see her. Do you have any idea what might be wrong with her?'

Arianwen shook her head. 'We've done a bit of educational psychology but it's more about how children learn, it's nothing very sophisticated. Have you tried music lessons? Surely Arwyn knows somebody?'

'Oh, Arianwen, music the answer to everything. Of course we've given her piano lessons, Arwyn says she's got quite a musical ear, but he lost patience with her and she went to Mrs. Jones up the road. It lasted a few weeks till Mrs. Jones sent a very stiff little letter saying she didn't want to teach her any more. We haven't done anything about it since.'

Arianwen felt the familiar sense of exasperation she felt with the Morgan family. Angharad sat there surrounded by the debris of breakfast with page after page of torn sheets of abandoned drawings scattered amongst it. She was thinner than ever and her cheeks were hollow. Her lovely face was ageing and the bright hair was fading. A good haircut and some sensible clothes would have improved her. She couldn't go round looking like a pre-Raphaelite muse for the rest of her life.

'It might be an idea to try and introduce her to another instrument.' She looked over at the harp in the corner, a constant, a calm icon in this turbulent household. How she'd always loved it, the cool medieval charm of its sound, and Arwyn's lessons in the evenings had been one of the joys of her schooldays.

'Arwyn won't teach her the harp. He hates her even touching it. She's so rough, and pulls at the strings. There's so much violence in all her movements.'

'Could you teach her to draw? She's probably frustrated at school. Some of these primary schools can be very old fashioned. When I start teaching I hope I'll be able to do something more than just teaching them to read and write and do sums. There's lots of new ideas coming through now.'

'Play me something on the harp, something melancholy and

beautiful. Arwyn hardly plays now.'

She played *Dafydd y Garreg Wen*, its sadness almost unbearable. When Blodeuwedd, eventually, came in to the kitchen she saw the two women: one playing, the other listening with that dreaming look she hated on her face, and the tears on both their faces. She ignored both, and got herself a biscuit from a jumbled tin on the dresser. When Arianwen said, 'Hello, Blodeuwedd,' the girl stared at her, cold and unrelenting, and went out to the garden where she sat underneath the apple tree and stared hard at the sky.

Today when she answered the door she looked calmer, and had grown taller and thinner, her face less babyish and you could see the striking woman she would become.

She looked at Siwan, ignoring Arianwen's smile and greeting.

'Who are you?'

'I'm Siwan, Arianwen's best friend at college. We're both learning to be teachers.'

'Yes, I know that. I've known Arianwen for a very long time. She used to live here, but she doesn't any more. Would you like to come and see my room?'

'We've only just arrived, Blodeuwedd, Perhaps later.'

Leaving them on the doorstep she ran up the stairs throwing down some shoes and books which had been left on the stairs,

Angharad came to the door. She ignored Blodeuwedd's tantrum. Immediately Arianwen could tell that she looked much better, not so old, not so strained, as if some of her tension had been squeezed out. She was languid and lovely again.

'I think we've upset her.'

'Blodeuwedd is always upset. I'm learning to ignore her tantrums. She loves attention.'

'Is she still going to be an actress?'

'Yes, I'm afraid, and I suspect she's going to very beautiful.'

'It's a pity that there's not an amateur drama group with a junior section she could join.'

'There's nothing for any one as young as her. They don't do anything at that useless school of hers.'

'When she goes to the grammar school there'll be plenty of activities for her.'

'I doubt she'll get to the grammar school. The secondary modern for her, I'm afraid, learning how to cook and sew and to become a good little wife and mother, unlike her mother.'

'You've been a wonderful mother to the children.'

'I like your garden. So original.' Siwan walked to the window and stared out, her artist's eye enjoying its anarchy.

At this point Bedwyr came into the room. He was in the fifth form now, and he'd lost his spots and gained a new equilibrium to his voice. He smiled at Arianwen, looking down at her, and then, quite confidently, kissing her on the cheek.

'Nice to see you, Arian. I no longer need you to help me with history. I'll be doing English, Latin and geography for my Highers. I'd like to do a Master's and then a doctorate and become a Fellow.'

'He's got his life mapped out, very different from me at that age. I was like a butterfly flitting from one idea to the next.'

'I don't intend being like you and Dad.' There was no malice in his tone as he answered his mother, more a bored condescension. Angharad just ignored him.

'You've changed so much, I didn't see you at Easter.'

'I was out with some friends. We cycled to Aberaeron for the day.'

How he'd changed. Where was the gauche young man who'd trailed her with his longing eyes? He was gone, almost into adulthood. It was good to see, but she felt an irrational regret.

'Blodeuwedd's mad as ever, you know.' He addressed Arianwen, but he was looking at Siwan, taking in the cornucopia of femininity: the fair curls, the blue eyes, the red clad bosom and her tanned legs beneath the dress. She tried not to feel jealous of her friend's starry beauty, and her talent for making all accomplishments look so easy.

'Don't be daft, Bed, she's not mad, just a bit eccentric.'

'You mean just like the rest of the family. At school, they call Dad Mad Morgan when they're being polite, and I'm Mad Morgan minor, but I'm not mad at all. I'm the one who tidies up, and remembers to pay the milkman, and all sorts of things my parents forget.' He spoke of his parents as if they were rather hopeless children.

Siwan looked as if she was about to laugh. Arianwen hoped not. Laughing at Bedwyr was something that no one dared do. It was too cruel, like kicking a loyal family dog.

He put his hand out and touched Arianwen's arm. 'I'm not

exaggerating, I think there's something seriously wrong with her. Mam and Dad just think she's very naughty, and pretend to each other that it'll all turn out all right, but she's definitely getting worse.' He looked at his mother.

Angharad said nothing, and picked up her sketchbook and slashed angrily at it with a piece of charcoal.

Blodeuwedd came into the room wearing one of Angharad's dresses. Her hair was the strange dark copper her mother's had been and even though the dress was huge on her, she looked less like a pantomime act. There was a strange and rather frightening dignity about her. The puppy lay like a baby in her arms.

Angharad let the sketchbook slide off her lap.

'Time for tea, Arwyn will be home soon.' The table was strangely bare. Somebody, probably Bedwyr, had been tidying up. All the usual clutter was in neat piles on the floor, half hidden by an old shawl of Angharad's. Precisely at the centre of the table there was a bunch of flowers in a jug, roughly arranged, but pretty, and the jug was primitively glazed earthenware, setting off the flowers' tangled colours. There was a tray with cups and saucers and plates laid on the dresser, and the whole scene had a charm which recalled her first sight of the Morgans, and the initial enchantment she'd felt then.

Siwan seemed similarly charmed, sitting on the big settee by the window, smiling and looking round, stroking the old cat, looking as if she was quite at home, which she never did in the old mill, always looking askance at its cosy darkness.

The puppy jumped from Blodeuwedd's arms, barking hysterically in the style of his predecessor, and Arwyn, bringing with him the discordant notes of the outside world, came in. He was larger than ever, and something about him, perhaps his blatant masculinity, changed the atmosphere of the room.

Blodeuwedd went up to him to be kissed. Angharad looked up and smiled and Bedwyr gave his father a little wave of acknowledgement. All on the surface, harmonious, but Arianwen felt the duplicity of it, and heard with an inner ear the disharmony which hummed in the afternoon heat.

'Hello, everyone. Hope you didn't wait tea for me. Got talking to someone. What a magnificent cake. I presume we can thank your mother, Arian, cariad.'

'No, it's one of mine.'

'What a clever girl you are. You'll make someone a perfect wife one of these days, my darling. Lucky man.'

And then he saw Siwan, who had stood up, her beauty framed in the window, and her hair blazing silver in the sun. And suddenly the song of the room changed again, a clashing of brass notes, loud and foreboding and the known world of the family changed too. His children, his wife, and his pupil and friend, Arianwen, they were on the peripheries of the world.

Siwan gulped, almost gasped, as if somebody had kicked her. Her face was almost as red as her dress.

'This is my college friend, Siwan. She's staying with me for the week.'

He smiled that smile which had charmed so many women.

Now as she looked at him holding Siwan's hand a little longer than was necessary, and her friend's blush, Arianwen felt a coldness fall about the warmth of the room.

'Come and sit at the table, let's have tea,' and he led her, still holding her hand, to the table and pulled out a chair.

'Is that kettle boiled yet? Blodeuwedd, come and sit down, and wash your hands. They're filthy.' Blodeuwedd looked shocked; occasionally Bedwyr or Arianwen, or even Angharad might issue such an order, but never her great henchman, her father. Without protest she washed her hands at the sink, turning the tap on full so that the water splashed everywhere. She was scowling, and her face was a threatening puce like a warning of thunder. She turned while she dried her hands and glared at Siwan.

'Angharad, make the tea, Bedwyr, lay the table.'

Arwyn was enjoying himself in full paterfamilias mode. Usually everybody laughed at him. Not today.

Bedwyr put the cake in the middle of the table, and a plate of roughly cut bread and butter and a pot of jam, and two more plates of cakes which looked as if they'd come from the baker's. Angharad came to the table, the big pot shaking in her hand. Arianwen felt the turbulence of the unknown in the room, a dark threat to equilibrium.

Blodeuwedd threw back her glorious hair in the gesture which suggested she was centre stage.

'Dad, I've learnt some poetry to recite for you.'

Her father ignored her. He was pouring tea for Siwan, smiling at her. She smiled back at him now, unembarrassed by his attention.

Angharad turned to Blodeuwedd.

'Perhaps you can recite that to us later after tea, perhaps if you're good enough you can enter the eisteddfod later in the year.'

'Did you hear that, Dad? Can you take me to the eisteddfod?'

Her father ignored her.

Angharad stood up to refill the teapot.

'That would be a good idea wouldn't it, Arwyn?

'Dad, would you go over some *Hamlet* with me later? I've got to do an essay on the soliloquies.' Bedwyr looked angry with his father, and looked at Arianwen as if pleading with her to help him out of the unknown.

'Do you like music, Siwan?' Arwyn's voice was soft and intimate.

'I sing a bit in the college choir.' She hadn't touched the tea or any of the food.

'And my mother is an artist,' Bedwyr said, looking at his mother and smiling, that rare smile which suggested the charming man he would become.

Angharad looked pleased by her son's intervention.

'My mother is a very good artist,' Bedwyr continued.

'Would you like to see some of Angharad's sketches? I'm sure you would.' Arianwen tried to hide the desperation in her voice, but she was aware of some momentous upheaval as if the world was suddenly spinning too fast or in the wrong direction.

Angharad stood up as if to pick up her sketchbook, then stopped as Siwan turned to smile vaguely at Arianwen as if she'd barely heard her, and turned back to Arwyn, gesturing at the harp.

'I'd love to hear you play the harp, Arwyn.' Arianwen heard the throatiness of her voice, the low timbre which men loved, and felt that she was in new, unknown lands.

'Of course, and perhaps you'll sing.'

Arianwen thought of the evenings when after her lesson he'd played while she sang *cerdd dant*, or folk songs, and felt ridiculously jealous of her friend and the beautiful voice which would soar, far too big even for this room, and pass through the open window down towards the coast like the very essence of beauty. Tears threatened, ridiculous tears. Looking round the table with the smiling Siwan and Arwyn and the two children and Angharad looking bewildered and angry, she regretted bringing Siwan here, inviting her to stay, befriending her, going to college, abandoning the Morgans. The whole beautiful day had turned against her, and some deep turbulence, a huge displacement, was happening which she did not even understand.

Blodeuwedd stood up, knocking over her full tea cup, and suddenly she was dancing round the room and singing in a high pitched voice, more keening than singing, and the puppy barked round her heels and snapped ineffectually at the dusty hem of the dress.

'Dad, Dad, look at me, I've learned a new dance, I made it up for you, Dad. Watch, watch.' She twirled towards her father, turning his face round with both hands, 'Look at me, look at my dance.'

She was screaming now and the wild glitter in her eyes was terrifying.

Angharad stood up and shouted, 'Calm down, calm down.'

This only made things worse. Blodeuwedd threw herself on the floor and banged her head on it and kicked her legs.

Arianwen stood staring at her, and still Arwyn and Siwan were in an insulated world beyond the room, two spirits floating in another world. Arianwen picked Blodeuwedd off the floor, shook her and slapped her face. It was not the way she behaved, she did not believe in hitting children, but something had to be done to stop the dreadful keening.

Blodeuwedd looked at her in shock. Then sat on the floor, calm and quiet, and the puppy went up to her and licked her. Arwyn came back from whichever world he had been inhabiting, and standing up looked across at Angharad.

'I'm taking Siwan out to look at the garden. It's not the tidiest of gardens but if you stand on a little bank at the bottom you can deceive yourself that you can see the sea.'

Siwan followed him out of the room, an enchanted smile on her face, a child's face full of wonder.

Blodeuwedd had gone to sleep on the floor.

The kitchen felt desolate and cold.

Arianwen started to clear up the table; very little had been eaten, the magnificent cake was untouched, the refilled teapot accusatory, accusing her of some moral infelicity. After all it was she who had brought this girl into the house, causing havoc to an already volatile family.

'Bedwyr, put the cake in a cake tin, and if you cover the little cakes and the bread and butter with tea-cloths they'll do for supper. Angharad, you wash up, and I'll dry.' The three of them worked in silence stepping round the sleeping child.

Arianwen, all her life hating silence, as she did disharmony, as only children do, began to sing a cleaner version of Ianto's favourite: *Sospan fach*. For her there would always be a Martha role, solving the problems of others, but when it came to her own she was alone.

Bedwyr joined in in his respectable tenor, and Angharad in her weakish soprano, but it didn't quite do the trick, and when, eventually, Arwyn and Siwan came back in, looking like strangers from another world it was to the recumbent girl and three silent people standing round the room like amateur actors waiting for direction.

Arwyn was hearty and smiling, the genial father enveloping all in his sense of well-being, not sensing the coldness descending like the first autumn frost on his family.

'Right, time for some music. Let the concert begin.' He placed himself at the harp as if embracing an old friend. The actors stood and watched, not moving, not speaking,

He touched the strings and played a neat little arpeggio to tune up.

'Something cheerful. What about *Ar lan y mor* as it's such a beautiful day?' His bonhomie was a reminder of a past fiction of family happiness.

'Siwan, do you know that?' He ignored his family and ex-pupil and played a twinkling introduction and waited for Siwan. Already they were in harmony.

She sang her pure notes, transfixing her audience, as she always did, standing quite still, expressionless, hands straight at her side like a shy schoolgirl, initially an unworldly look on her face, but now she was looking at Arwyn, and every now and then he looked up from the strings and they smiled enclosed smiles.

The voice carried outside to the silent, tired summer twilight, silking over the sky to the sea, beautifully attuned with the cool notes of the harp and then Arwyn sang an old Welsh lullaby in his fine tenor and together their voices united, they were more beautiful than the blackbird's song. The young woman, and the man well across the far borders of middle age, created their own exclusive world where ordinary beings were not welcome.

Blodeuwedd woke up. 'Can I sing now?' Her face was dark, the known precursor to a tantrum. Outside the sound of a car stopping broke into the momentum of the music. Ianto. It was 6 o'clock. Wonderful Ianto, on the dot as usual. Three rhythmic bangs on the door.

'Right time to go, Ianto's here, Siwan.' Arianwen picked up her bag. She noticed, as if she was staring at herself from some faraway place that her hands were shaking and her mouth was dry, drier than it ever was after a long choir practice.

Angharad went out to let him in. He came in smiling as always, a man sure of his welcome in this strange house, but he noticed as she opened the door that the strained look he'd noticed a few times when he came to pick up Arianwen was back like an unwanted lover.

In the kitchen Arianwen was looking serious.

Arwyn who had seldom met Ianto, greeted him as if he was one of the family.

'Ianto, a quick chorus of *Sospan fach*, clean version,' and he and Siwan sang, laughing, but Ianto didn't join in; somehow he didn't feel like it.

'Time to go, Siwan.'

Siwan looked cross, and looked at Arwyn as if expecting him to keep her there, an adoring acolyte, singing forever.

Then she saw the look on Arianwen's face and went around the room to thank the family, a parody of a prim child remembering her manners. She shook hands with Bedwyr, kissed Angharad lightly, and coldly, on the cheek, and turned to kiss Blodeuwedd who turned away and then she went back to the harp where Arwyn was still sitting plucking rather sulkily at the strings and reached for his hand to shake, then she kissed him just to the left of his lips. It was not the most contained of kisses and Ianto looked away in embarrassment, Angharad picked up her sketch pad, Bedwyr picked up his copy of *Hamlet* and turned the pages furiously, and Blodeuwedd stroked the dog, singing to him in a high keening voice.

'Ready,' Siwan said, her face pale now, all passion spent. Bedwyr stood up and turned to the window where his violin lay and picked it up and without tuning it played something furious and loud and off key and they could still hear it as they got into the car, Arianwen sitting in the front with Ianto.

***

And the music of Arianwen's life lives on till the very last clashing note.

This was a long time ago, long before mobile phones and easy communication, long before many homes even had phones. The Morgans had one, and, somehow, it transpired, Siwan and Arwyn found a way to continue that relationship farther than the end of a song.

Arianwen always looked to see if there was a letter for her in the hostel pigeon hole, not that she got much, her mother still saw her most weekends except when she stayed at college to work, or went home with a friend, though she was never asked to Rhyl again and had been surprised to get a virtually indecipherable letter from Peter in Cardiff.

> *Dear Arianwen,*
>
> *How are you? Life in Cardiff remains a relentless cycle of long days and long nights and the unmemorable faces of the sick. There are days when I think I should have been a bank manager growing a paunch in an office in Colwyn Bay, and visiting the parents on Sundays with a smug little wife.*
>
> *When I'm qualified I will go the States for a while, despite Mam's protestations. Soon you'll be qualified as well and what a wonderful little teacher you'll make, all bustle and kindness. Siwan still continues to worry Mam, and no sign of a respectable suitor. Tears on all sides when she goes home at weekends, I hear, and all very fraught. What on earth is going on in your dreary college?*
>
> *One day will you come and visit me in the States when I'm sporting a strange accent and a cigar and we shall sit in diners and eat large steaks and I'll find you a lovely little Baptist chapel where you can show them how real singing is done.*
>
> *My very best wishes,*
> *Peter.*
> *PS Look after that silly sister of mine.*

Too late she'd thought. Since the holiday a coolness had grown between Siwan and herself. The uncomfortable stay came to an end, to everybody's relief. Siwan spoke of Arwyn all the time and asked questions about him incessantly. When Ianto came to drive Siwan to the station she said that she preferred to be on her own. No need for Arianwen to see her off at the station like that scene from *Brief Encounter* which they'd recently seen, and cried over happily.

'We'll soon see each other again. I'm sure you have plenty to do, Arianwen.' Arianwen watched as the car turned the bend, Ianto revving it for the challenge of the hill. Siwan didn't turn to wave.

A little note of thanks came for her mother, polite but lacking warmth, nothing for Arianwen. She was not surprised. Friendships ended, especially when you were young; there would be later ones which would endure, and later, when Siwan declined an invitation to her wedding she was not surprised and not unduly saddened, yet when the present, the magnificent owl painting arrived, she felt again some of that warmth towards her that she felt gone forever on that day in August

Back at college they both relied on other friendships, as if there was unspoken between them an understanding that nothing would ever be the same again

One Monday morning, there was a letter for her in the pigeonhole. She recognised the handwriting: it was the large stylised calligraphy of an artist: Angharad. She knew nobody else who wrote that like that. She shivered, felt the cold invasion of unease. Perhaps it was something about the children, asking for advice about Blodeuwedd, but in her heart she knew it was something she had evaded since the summer. Peter's letter had been a warning. She took the letter to read outside in the still mild October air. Another student, a quiet girl who sang in the choir, waved to her and beckoned to her to come and talk to her, but she shook her head and smiled.

'Busy, see you later, I'll see you at choir tonight.' She sat on a bench under a willow tree and opened the letter. It was typical of Angharad, informal in lay out.

Arianwen cariad,
   How are you? The children are well. Bedwyr is doing very well at school and Cambridge has been mentioned.

*We are very pleased. Blodeuwedd is quieter and has
started having dancing classes in the town with a rather
strange woman who claims that she once danced for the
Royal Ballet. We all have our doubts. Blodeuwedd,
however, adores her and talks about her constantly!*

*Arwyn continues to work hard at school and is now
helping to produce Carousel for the end of Christmas
term. This is quite avant garde for Cardiganshire. Letters
of complaint are expected from the more reactionary of the
governors. We all look forward to it. The children send
their love, and the puppy, a squeaky little bark...*

and then the writing became blurred as if she was exhausted by
her cheerful little note.

*'I would like to ask a favour of you, dearest Arianwen.
Can you keep an eye on Siwan for me? I'm certain that
she's having an affair with Arwyn. He's been going away
at weekends. Could you speak to her, explain the folly of
what she's doing? He is a silly, vain man, but he is the
father of my children. They know nothing. I am so very
unhappy. I don't know what to do.*
Angharad.

Arianwen looked at the letter again. Nothing had changed, yet
everything had changed, the thing which she had tried to ignore
ever since the end of the summer was now a huge storm, gathering
force out to sea, and she was marooned waiting, and, somehow,
implicated. What could she do, not yet twenty and faced with this
- and what was she expected to do? Spy on Siwan, follow her like a
detective in a novel, wearing a hat pulled low over her face and a
long mac and her collar turned up? Was Angharad expecting
weekly bulletins about what she saw? It was all ridiculous, the
fulminations of a neurotic woman implicitly blaming her for
introducing this catalyst into her home.

However, she guessed that it was true. Siwan was strong minded,
an intelligent and educated woman who had been thwarted once
by her father, and hid behind her beauty a bitterness which made
her tough and intractable. She wasn't going to listen to a woman

who was no longer even a friend, and an innocent in the ways of men and women.

Angharad was asking too much of her. She was, however, her mother's daughter and that deep Non-Conformist sense of duty was strong in her. In the evening, after lectures, during the couple of hours before supper, she went along to Siwan's lodgings. They had looked for lodgings together, and couldn't find one who could take them both and almost at the last minute Arianwen had been asked to be a senior student which meant she could have a hostel room again as long as she was willing to help the warden with certain tasks. As an only child, she'd enjoyed the life in hostel and the late night chats over cups of tea and toast, and when the rift came she was more than glad that she didn't have to share with Siwan.

The landlady answered the door.

'Is Miss Hughes in?'

'Yes, come in. She's back now, she was late coming back after the weekend. She had to go home because her father was ill.'

Siwan was sitting at her desk, but her desk was bare. She looked up when Arianwen was shown in. She looked bored, as if her visitor was of no interest to her.

Arianwen had seen Siwan at some of the big lectures, but as they were being trained for different age groups and studying different main subjects, they never seemed to meet up close any more. It wasn't the same as the first year when they shared a room, and laughed the terms away, and their friendship seemed inviolable.

'What do you want? I'm ever so busy. Late with an essay as usual.' No smile.

Her face was thinner, her eyes bigger, and she'd grown her hair much longer: she was dauntingly beautiful. The huge eyes looked beyond Arianwen as if she was waiting for somebody else to come through the door. Then she looked at her as if remembering something, then judging her to be of no account, studied her nails, painted bright red and predatory long, quite unsuitable for teaching practice in a week's time.

'Isn't this term hell? So much to do. I've dropped choir. I'm concentrating on getting a Distinction, and I've switched to secondary training. I don't think I could possibly cope with all those horrible snotty little ones.' She laughed. She was a stranger.

'I've had a letter from Angharad.'

Siwan flushed and, briefly, looked again like the girl who had been her friend.

'Yes.' She looked at her watch, and turned back to her empty desk and took a notebook from the bookshelf above it.

'She says you're having an affair with Arwyn. She's very unhappy.'

'She's talking nonsense, she's just one of those neurotic clinging wives, no wonder that little girl is so peculiar.' She laughed. 'Honestly, cariad, you can't believe what she says. She's probably just got rather a lively imagination, and she's bitter because she's middle aged and knows her looks are going.'

She looked towards a mirror on the wall, patted her blonde waves with a smug little smile on her face.

'I'm ever so busy. I've been given a reprieve till tomorrow with this, so I've got to get on.' And she picked up her pen and looked down at her notebook.

'Will you promise me that you'll stop seeing him? There's plenty of men who adore you. You don't want another woman's husband. What would your parents say if they knew?'

'Are you threatening to tell them? I'll never forgive you.'

'So you don't deny it then. What if you get pregnant?'

Siwan smiled a knowing smile.

'Don't you have any conscience at all?'

'Don't spout me all that Baptist stuff.'

'It's not about religion. It's about common human decency.'

Siwan stood up.

She smiled her cold infuriating smile.

'You'll never prove anything, and keep your nose out of others' business. You don't know anything about being a woman. I think it's time you left now. Don't interfere in my life again.'

Arianwen walked back to the hostel confused and unhappy. Nothing had been achieved. What did Angharad expect? Siwan was a cool and clever adversary, and there was no point in appealing to any sense of morality. It had always been Siwan's lack of social constraint which had appealed to her, that glamorous lack of concern for others' views. Now she saw it for what it was, a myopic self-regarding weakness, made worse by her infatuation with silly, selfish Arwyn.

It was choir evening, somewhat of a relief. She didn't want to sit in her room brooding over Siwan and the Morgan family. There was quite enough to think about with teaching practice coming up, a prospect she dreaded. Should she have insisted on being a nurse, but could she have coped with all that suffering?

She was late, as were others, and the choirmaster, a round little fusspot of a man was talking to the pianist who looked bored, checking her already deeply scarlet lips in her compact mirror.

'Arianwen, another soprano, thank heavens. What's the point of choir practice if nobody turns up?'

Behind his back one of the men was flapping his hands in imitation of the choirmaster, and making ferocious faces. Trying not to laugh she bit her lip and tried to give the little man her full concentration.

'It's second year teaching practice next week and there's some essay deadlines as well.'

'Will these people never learn to organise themselves? To think they'll be let loose in classrooms next year. Where's Siwan these days? The sopranos are a bit weak without her. I was going to ask her to do a solo in the Christmas concert, but quite honestly, if she misses more I'll have to assume that she's left us. Great loss, such natural talent. What about you, Arianwen, would you like to have a try at it?'

'I'm not sure. I don't have a voice like Siwan's, you need a stronger voice than mine, perhaps you'd better find something for one of the tenors.'

'Well, have a think about it.'

'I don't think that I'll have much time for thinking for the next few weeks, it's teaching practice for a month and I'm out at Llanelli and the bus back takes about an hour each evening, but I'll make sure I get to choir practice once a week.'

'You're a good girl. I wish more were as conscientious as you. I saw Siwan last week in a café in Swansea. She was with a man, must have been her father,' and he walked away towards the tenors.

Edward, an ex-RAF man, came up to her.

'You don't look very happy, not your usual self at all. Not had bad news, I hope.'

'No, not really.'

CHAPTER 12

Later as the choir master packed his case and some of the men planned an evening in the pub, which of course was not an option for the women as they had to be back in hostel for 10 o'clock, this being a time when young women had little freedom and had their virtue protected at all times, Edward came up to her and asked her to come to tea with him the following Sunday. As a mature student doing the emergency training course he had lived outside college since he arrived.

He was staying in the house of a widow who welcomed the money, and the company of well-spoken and respectable young men.

'Come and meet Mrs. Pugh on Sunday. She is impeccably refined, and she welcomes lady friends as long as they stay in the sitting room. Tea will be rather good, I can assure you. She thinks I'm too thin. I've been too thin all my life. Quite useful for scrambling in and out of planes. Better than hostel tea I'm sure, stale bread and bad jam and dry cake I hear.'

'Well it's not as bad as that, but not really much better.'

She wasn't certain that Mam and Dad would approve of her taking Sunday tea with an older man from Shropshire, who like the other mature students, had an air of having lived his life twice over and more, with tired eyes which seemed to have seen everything.

She was rather looking forward to tea with Edward, and she managed to forget Siwan for a couple of days, knowing that there was little she could do, although her conscience told her that life was not that simple, and that she was being a moral coward.

'Keep out of other people's business,' her mother always said. 'There'll be enough pain in our own lives to worry about.'

By the end of Sunday Siwan and all the turbulence of that life was quite forgotten as she briefly thought that she was in love, but that silliness didn't last as Arianwen, being a pragmatic young woman, realised that a nice tea and a chat with a pleasant man on a Sunday afternoon did not constitute true love.

He picked her up outside the hostel at 2.30. He had a racy little car. She was gratified to see some girls hanging out of the window and watching her as he came round to the car door for her.

'Shall we have a little spin out to Laugharne and back? Mrs Pugh

81

says tea at 4.30. Are you hungry? I hope you are. There was talk of boiling a ham and a table for two has been set up in the dining room. Being charming to Mrs. Pugh has its rewards. I don't ask her where the things come from. We do seem to eat very well in these straitened times. Perhaps she has a brother who's a black marketeer.'

They drove along to the estuary and he pointed out Dylan Thomas's house to her sideways on to the shore as if half turning away.

'I had started at Oxford you know, when I was called up, reading English. I was going to go back, then, somehow, after the war it seemed rather pointless: three years in academe. I thought I'd do some good as a teacher, some cosy little village school somewhere where I'll find time to write.'

'Poetry?'

He laughed. 'No. I know every other person in Wales is a poet, but I want to be a novelist, although I like poetry. Houseman was born near where I live. I've got no great ambition. I want to write good stories people will enjoy, perhaps something about the air force and teaching. My parents aren't happy, of course, but I'm too old to listen to them too much. I wonder if we'll be the last generation to listen to our parents. The world's changing and I welcome it. Do you?'

'I don't know, I haven't really thought about it. You remind me of somebody when you talk like that, he was full of plans for the future as well.'

He turned to her, his face solemn.

'Did he come back?'

'Yes he did, and he and his family are doing well. I knew quite a few who didn't, boys from the village.'

'And what do you want, Arianwen? What plans have you for your life?'

'Just to live, be happy. Do some good in the world. I think it's going to be a better world now.'

'Not one of those Welsh Nationalists are you?'

'I sometimes think that I might be. I believe in the language and I don't want it to die out, it's an old and beautiful language. Where I come from we speak it all the time. When I look for a teaching post I shall look for a place in a Welsh-speaking village somewhere,

I don't like big towns. That's not for me.'

He laughed and took her hand.

'That's what I like about you. You're so different from the other girls I've known, you're quite solemn most of the time and then when you laugh you light up the world. I like to listen to you singing. When you're singing you're so intense, as if you're going into another world. A world that's full of light and glorious sound.'

She tried not to blush, looking away from him to hide her face.

'You're just being silly. I'm a very ordinary singer, I just get by, but I do enjoy it. I can't understand people who don't like singing and music. It is important in my life. My mother's family are very musical. Dad is tone deaf. I can't sing like Siwan. Her voice is glorious.'

'Oh, the Marilyn Monroe girl. Good voice, but doesn't she know it.'

'She's a very good artist too, got a place at the Slade. Her parents wouldn't let her go there. She never talks about it, but I think she's rather bitter about it.'

'It does seem a shame.'

'If she'd been a boy, they might have let her.'

'Are you a feminist? Quite a hint of battle in your eye when you said that.'

'If being a feminist means wanting the same as men, then I probably am, but I'm not the kind who will go out and fight for it. It's not my way. So many women did men's jobs during the war and did it well, but now they're just expected to go back home and be housewives again, and women teachers don't get the same pay as men for doing the same job. That's not fair is it?'

'You're right, of course. I'm not one of these men who want to keep women down, but' – he looked at his watch – 'time for tea or Mrs. Pugh will be most displeased and Mrs. Pugh has ways of showing her displeasure in subtle little ways. Toast will be burnt and breakfast a little meagre and shirts will not be collected for laundry and other little discomforts.'

He took away his hand. Her hand felt cold. She felt a little sad. There was something rather comforting about having her hand held by this nice man who made her feel that she was not quite so ordinary at all.

She looked at the estuary. How calm it was. And the birds flying

83

and feeding, how purposeful they looked, how busy, and Edward, looking at some sparrows in a bush thought that she was like a little sparrow, not particularly exotic to look at like the curvy friend, but somehow cheering and dependable.

'Why does your friend not come to choir anymore? I thought she rather liked the adulation and the admiration. She's a natural prima donna. She knows quite a few of the older men have a bit of a thing about her. Not me though. She's a dangerous woman.'

Later in the week, when she saw Siwan at a psychology lecture looking sulky and tired, she thought about what Edward had said and wished she'd told him about Siwan's misguided and doomed affair, but that was not what friends did and she supposed that Siwan was still a friend of a kind.

As they drove to Mrs. Pugh's it started raining and the little car which had seemed so dashing, started leaking, and drips of rain fell on their heads, but they both thought that this was quite hilarious and by the time they got to Mrs. Pugh's, absolutely on time, they were singing *Singing in the Rain* and laughing hysterically and when Mrs. Pugh opened the door she looked suspiciously at their flushed faces and their sparkling eyes.

Inside it was very warm, and Mrs. Pugh was very gracious. She smiled at Edward as if he was her long lost son and shook hands with Arianwen in a very regal way while scrutinising her up and down as if judging her as a prospective daughter-in-law or servant.

She showed them into an even warmer dining-room where there seemed to be a lot of red: carpet, walls and curtains.

Edward whispered, 'Mrs. Pugh's bordello, I don't think she's realised what it looks like!'

Arianwen tried not to laugh.

'It's all laid up. I'll just bring the teapot in and then leave you in peace.'

Late in life Arianwen would be known as a woman who could do a good spread, could produce a table full of food with a magic efficiency and this is what Mrs. Pugh in those post-war days had done.

The table was laid in the big bay window looking out towards the big conifer which dominated the front garden. The garden was desolate in its bleak November bareness, but Arianwen felt one of those rare boosts of joy which so rarely come in life to those of anaemic religious feeling. It was not just the stimulating and strangely comfortable presence of Edward, but the feeling that she was on one of the straight paths of her life and that after all she had chosen her direction well, and it wasn't till Edward dropped her off at the hostel rather later than planned, and had left, after kissing her decorously on the cheek with rather dry lips, that the warmth of well-being disappeared and she felt cold again, remembering an essay, a very dull and uninspiring one on child development, had to be written, and that Siwan and all the trouble she'd caused, was still there, a nasty little disturbance on the peripheries of conscience.

And it had been such a lovely afternoon.

Despite Mrs. Pugh having promised to leave them in peace she appeared at intervals of five minutes to check on them.

'Have you got enough tea?'

'Do you want more hot water?'

'Is there enough milk?'

'Do you want more bread and butter?'

'Shall I put another log on the fire?'

Once, she came in just as Edward was taking Arianwen's hand, and looked suspicious as the hand then hovered over a slice of Dundee cake.

'Dear Mrs. Pugh, she has concerns for your virtue. I have told her that you're a good chapel-going girl and that you had assured me that you'd been and made your peace with your deity this morning, but she regards all young men as rapacious and not to be trusted, even though she thinks of me as a very well brought up young man of impeccable parentage. Mention of Oxford works wonders.'

Mrs. Pugh finally ran out of reasons to come into the dining room like a demented automaton and they were left on their own. They talked of music, and their courses, then he turned away from looking at the dusk falling, and took her hand.

'Tell me about where you live.'

'I'm not clever with words like you. Words are just a tool to me, not like you. For you they're something to be loved, and my English isn't good. We speak Welsh at home; although my Dad's from the industrial part of South Wales, he learned to speak it when he was courting my mother, and all my friends speak Welsh and at school we spoke Welsh all the time except in lessons.'

'And where you live?'

'It's a little valley. A bit dark I suppose, especially in winter, but cool in summer and there's a little stream and there are mills in the valley where they made things out of wool, big warm blankets mainly. In Welsh we call them a *carthen*. We live in an old mill and the top part was converted into living quarters, and it creaks a lot. There's a lot of wood, and the old wheel is still there. Still turning slowly, just outside my bedroom. I miss the sound of it. Turning. Turning. When I was child I thought something dreadful would happen if it stopped turning, like the end of the world. How silly I was. So that's it.'

'How romantic it sounds. I'd love to see it. Perhaps I could even write poetry there. Yeats talks about *peace comes dropping slow* in *The Lake Isle of Innisfree*. It sounds just like that.'

'How about you, Edward? Now it's your turn to describe where you come from.'

'Too dull really, a between-the-wars house on a street on the outskirts of Shrewsbury. All the houses look the same, only variations of paint and gardening taste to assert individuality. All in good middle class taste. Mainly men like my father who work in banks and offices and woman who take the bus into Shrewsbury to shop, and bring up obedient children like themselves, peace and dullness and routine. I suppose it was what that generation wanted after all the horror and turbulence of the first war. They just wanted to settle to a quiet life. Before the war I was full of wild ideas about changing the world, now I'm so relieved to have survived, that I'm settling for something similar: a village schoolteacher.'

'But you're going to be a writer.'

'Oh yes. I'm quite serious about that, quite determined. I want peace, that's why your secret valley sounds so seductive.' Then he looked serious.

'There were times when I didn't think I'd come back, each raid looked like my last, and the law of averages spelt out my doom, and sometimes I was so frightened when we were joking and joshing in the mess while we waited to scramble that I just wanted to run away into those dark nights and hide away so that they'd never find me again. A little valley like yours, sanctuary. I was at a place called Biggin Hill in Kent.'

'Were you one of The Few?'

He looked away into the now dark garden and shuddered, and she saw the look of pain on his face as if he was a stranger turned in on himself.

Then he smiled. It was a smile like the sun coming out, and she was glad. There was something rather frightening in all this talk of war, though it was interesting, but she had just been a schoolgirl in the war, doing nothing, missing sweets, not even aware of making do.

'Enough of the war, that's all in the past,' and then he took her hand again and she felt its warmth and the feeling of absolute sanctuary that she had never felt before.

Mrs. Pugh came in to clear the table.

Arianwen stood up.

'Shall I help you?'

'Isn't it time you were getting back to your college?' and she looked at the ornate grandfather clock standing by the door. Nine o'clock.

Her face indicated that her spring of welcome was run dry. Duty was done.

'Yes, I really must be going. I've got an essay to do, and we start teaching practice next week and I've got a lot of preparation to do.'

Mrs. Pugh went out with a laden tray.

'Mrs. Pugh has ways of reminding one about the proprieties. There are no written rules, but it seems that young ladies are not to be entertained after nine o'clock, nine o'clock must be the time for immorality.'

Arianwen tried not to blush at such talk. Some of the girls talked like this, some of the ones who'd worked in munitions during the war, unmarried women coming late to teacher training. Hearing them talk as they smoked and drank gin out of their tooth mugs had rather shocked her. She didn't envy them, but really she felt she was such a dull little village girl. As she sat in Edward's car waiting for him to drive off, she looked at his pleasant face, ordinary, miraculously unscarred by war. She would like to fall in love with him, but to do the things the women talked about and at which Doris hinted with a pleased little smile on her face, terrified her, but she would discover that secret world one day, and she felt that she was starting on some unknown journey and she felt frightened and rather thrilled.

CHAPTER 13

Edward never asked her to tea again. He was friendly and waved to her in college corridors and spoke to her at choir nights in the same friendly way that he spoke to everyone.

That Sunday evening when he dropped her off she had felt so thrilled and excited, full of food and anticipation, but, somehow, as soon as she opened her note book to make notes on child development, and thoughts of Siwan came back, and the room was chilly and she felt rather bloated after so many cakes and sandwiches, and she couldn't, even after so short a time, picture his face in front of her, her practical down to earth side asserted itself and she was herself again, not some silly romantic creature, but an ordinary woman in an uncomfortable room with the wind whistling through the window and somebody singing out of tune in the next room, and the glorious few hours with Edward had seemed to happen to someone else, someone rather more glamorous, more sophisticated, someone like Siwan, one of the blessed of the world. So it was a blessedly ephemeral kind of love.

***

'This is Miss Evans she will be teaching you for the next three weeks. I hope you are going to be good for her and do everything she tells you and work very hard. Say good morning to Miss Evans.'

They sat at their little desks in neat rows, seven year old veterans, varied in degrees of cleanliness, and most had lost the round baby features by now, although there were some who looked so tiny that you wondered whether they should still be at home with their mothers.

They chanted in their squeaky sing song, 'Good morning, Missus Evans.'

All female teachers were awarded marital status by young children, as if they were a species on their own, generic creatures with no individuality.

And there were so many of them. At her previous school practice, in a little village in North Carmarthenshire, so remote she had to lodge at the headmaster's house with his resentful and unfriendly wife treating her as a nuisance, there had only been a dozen children, all rather sweet and well behaved under the rule of an ancient spinster whose fate she began to rather fear for herself. Since Edward, who was now escorting a rather flashy looking girl from the secondary course, there had been no young men desirous of her company.

Now looking at the class of thirty-five looking at her, but somehow not with the same awe and fear as the village children, she felt that she had completely lost confidence and would gladly marry the first man to ask her, to escape the cruel fate of teaching for forty years.

The class teacher, a fleshy kind of woman with cold, unyielding eyes, looked her up and down.

'I'll leave you for a little while with them and see how you get on. They're quite good, but you've got to be quite firm. Any sign of weakness and they'll take advantage of you. You don't come into teaching to be liked. That's the mistake some of you young girls make. Don't be taken in by their innocent little faces, all children are little savages.'

Then she whispered, 'I'm getting married at Christmas, there's a little one on the way. We were going to be married at some point anyway, but he was biding his time, so I moved things along a bit, you might say. Don't look so shocked, dear, that's the way of the world. Dewi Jenkins, stop pulling Mari's pigtails or it'll be the ruler for you my boy. Two strokes.'

Arianwen had sworn that she would never hit a child. Nobody had touched her since that long time ago in the infants and she was quite certain that you could rule children through love rather than cruelty. Arianwen looked at the older woman's face. She looked tough, as if life was something she took on like an unruly dog to be tamed. Somehow she didn't think she could take any problems to her. At the cosy little village school there never had been any, and the four weeks had been easy and enjoyable with biddable little children and all very pleasant apart from the headmaster's wife who always viewed her with suspicion, especially when Mr. Hughes made her laugh with his little anecdotes about when he had taught in the East End of London before the war. As Miss Davies left the room the children sat less straight in their chairs, little backs slumped and there was a visible relaxation. One little boy in the back laughed, and then another joined him and soon a couple of little girls joined in, with tinkly little laughs which were somehow louder than the boys'.

The little boy pointed, and there was a man at the window scrubbing away with a cloth and making funny faces at the children. She glared at the children and then turned to glare at the man who raised his cap to her and continued to grin.

She went to the window which was too high for her to open and had probably never been opened in the last century since the school had been built and waved him away. He waved back and then disappeared. She clapped her hands, 'Right, get out your reading books.' She pointed to a rather self-satisfied looking little girl sitting in the front row.

'What is your name?'

'Tabitha, miss.'

'You start reading from the top of page 24. Mrs. Davies said that you have read this far. After we've read I shall be asking you to write a story about a little dog and you will be doing a nice drawing as well.'

The little girl began to read laboriously, following the text with her index finger. There was a brief moment of peace and then she realised that once again the children were becoming restive, and looking towards the window on the other side of the classroom.

The window cleaner was still waving and gesturing, but this time she decided to ignore him rather than feel foolish once again.

The window cleaner eventually disappeared, but left the children fidgety and restless as if they were waiting for further stimulation, far removed from the tedium of the ordinary. She knew that at 10 o'clock it was time for the times tables before mental arithmetic, and then geography which entailed little actual information and much careful colouring in. As far as she could see the children were learning very little from this tedious exercise.

She had watched Miss Davies for two days of observation at the start of the week, and had quickly realised how bored the children looked. Certain that she had never been bored in this way at her little village school, she had prepared lessons which she considered to be stimulating and informative as dictated by the formidable Edwina Lloyd, Senior Lecturer in Educational Practice, a woman considered to be one of the leading exponents of progressive education.

When she had shown her lesson plans to the blessed Edwina, as she was known to all, she had been full of praise.

'Excellent m'dear. I think you've fulfilled all the criteria here, I love the way you've incorporated so much music into your teaching scheme. I shall try to come and observe you. This looks really promising. Although you must always expect resistance to our enlightened methods. Older teachers are reluctant to change their ways.'

Miss Davies had looked at her plans, and then looked at her and then passed them back to her, her lips curled into a cynical smile.

'Well, we all know that you prepare all this nonsense to keep your lecturers happy and to get your distinctions, but, honestly, you can't do this in the classroom. The children get over excited and silly and they don't learn anything. And as for all this music and dancing, well I don't like them moving around. The children come to school to learn, not to play. That's what the parents expect. I want you to follow the scheme I've given you: reading, writing, times tables, sums and religion, and a bit of history and geography. It's quite easy. I've been teaching for ten years now and I know it works. It's only since the war ended that you young things are coming in with all this new nonsense about how children learn. So leave the piano alone, dear.'

She smiled her insincere self-satisfied smile.

'You know I'll be writing your report at the end of your month here and they'll be looking at it when you apply for a job. The reading books are over there. Make sure that you collect them in. The ruler's here, you can give up to three strokes. Some of the boys have a rebellious streak.'

'I don't think I could hit a child.'

Miss Davies rolled her eyes, but didn't say anything.

'Can I do some songs with them, just for the last quarter hour of school?'

'You can try if you like, but I'm sure none of the mothers will thank you if they're overexcited and silly when they meet them after school.'

And every day she sang a different song with them, and they were silly and excited and one fiercely Methodist mother complained. Miss Davies wore her 'I told you so' look, and then the blessed Edwina came to observe her, and it was Monday morning in dull early November and they were doing the ritual chanting of the five times tables and Edwina, kind Edwina, sat at a desk with a malodorous little boy, and rolled her eyes and, afterwards, before Miss Davies came back in said: 'Oh dear, that was quite diabolical but you were doing your best and you will be a splendid teacher when you have a classroom of your own. Don't look so worried. It's not your fault that the class teacher is such a dreary old dinosaur.'

Then she turned to the children who were fascinated by her colourful clothes and heavy make-up, and the patrician accent; a goddess from another sphere.

'Shall we sing? And Miss Evans will play the piano. *Sospan fach*, Miss Evans, such fun I always think,' and in her tuneless voice she sang, and being English, quite unaware of the utter silliness of the lines.

The children loved it and were quite riotous when Miss Davies came in, rage burning in her eyes, and saw the lecturer standing there, singing in her outlandish clothes and the little student teacher smiling broadly as she thumped away at the badly tuned piano, and the children in a state of uproarious enjoyment.

When the report came in from the school a few weeks later, Arianwen's tutor called her in. He was a serious man, but he was smiling as he read Miss Davies's report.

'This has come in from the school in Llanelli. The headmaster is, on the whole, rather flattering, he says you were punctual, smartly attired, and always polite to the rest of the staff. However, the class teacher was less fulsome. There are suggestions of revolutionary ideas in the classroom and over-stimulation of the children, and that you were less than complimentary about her schemes of work and seemed determined to pursue your own ideas. Personally, I don't think you can over-stimulate children and a certain independence of mind is a valuable property in a teacher, and your first report was exemplary.

'My colleague Miss Lloyd says, in her observation report, that she was most impressed by your teaching and thoroughly enjoyed her visit and that the children were suitably taught. I have never seen you teach, Miss Evans, but I know that your academic record is good and the college will be giving you a favourable reference when you apply for a post. Just a piece of advice, you are a young woman who has modern ideas about the teaching of children. I think it would be best to keep these to yourself when you attend for interview. Some of the governors of schools are people of conventional views and have little knowledge of modern educational ideas, people informed by their own memories of school. You and I know that things are changing. I believe that schools in the future will be much happier places, and young women such as yourself will be an important part of that change.' And then he laughed. 'And plenty of music, Miss Evans, let the children sing.'

And over the years, the happy years, and even in the sad dark years, the children sang.

CHAPTER 14

Looking back at that time, after she had been teaching for a year or two, she came to regard it as the happiest time of her life. Once teaching practice was over, Christmas came, and went, and at home she no longer felt the sense of displacement that she had done over the past few years. The village was prospering, and some of the Italian prisoners of war who had been imprisoned in a local camp had come back to set up smallholdings. English families looking for a life in this far pocket of West Wales were moving in. The village was changing; Welsh was not the only language you heard in the village shop. There was resentment from some, but Arianwen rather liked it, and felt that she was not so far removed from modern life hurtling along.

One day, with Ianto as technical adviser, she went to Cardigan to buy herself a little car. Mam had been saving for a long time for Arianwen's wedding, but being a sensible woman she realised that at this time her daughter was in greater need of a car than a husband and a wedding.

'You'll be a teacher soon, then, Arianwen fach, pity there's no position at the village school, that would be champion, that would be, you teaching the local children and you so strong in the choir.'

'Oh I don't know, Ianto, I've been living away from home for two years, and it would be difficult to move back with Mam and Dad now, and difficult for them too.'

'No chance that those two great lummocks of mine will ever leave, eating us out of house and home. Time they found decent girls both of them. Mari makes it far too comfortable for them at home, with their slippers waiting and a hot meal and they get the best bits of the meat that stingy old butcher has. Where are you thinking of going then? Not Cardiff or Swansea?'

She laughed at the look of horror on his face, Cardiff and Swansea being synonymous with danger and sin for Ianto, although he was used to driving rugby supporters to Cardiff for the Arms Park.

'No, Cardiganshire, Carmarthenshire and Pembrokeshire.'

'Not Tenby way, they only speak English there.'

' No. North Pembrokeshire.'

'Look in the local paper, that's the place for jobs.'

'No, what you do is apply to the education office for each county and wait to see what they've got.'

'Nice job in Newcastle Emlyn would be good, could drive there every day from home.'

'No, Ianto. I'd be happier paying for lodgings and having my little bit of independence. Don't boss me around. I'm not a little girl now,' and laughed at his fatherly concerns.

'What happened to your friend? That girl who came down in the summer. From North Wales wasn't she?' He thought of the girl who looked like a film star, exotic in her red dress and the way her brown legs swung into the car and the little bit of soft breast showing above the neckline. He couldn't help but think she was a dangerous sort of girl, that one.

'She left college, decided she didn't want to be a teacher any more. I think she might have gone to Art School. She's a very good artist.'

Ianto nodded.

'Good looking girl. Friendly enough, but she was very quiet when we were going back that day in August after you visited the Morgans.' He remembered the silence as they drove back, Arianwen sitting by his side, and Siwan in the back looking out of the window, and so much silence in the car, like another body, and there had been no singing, no singing at all. When they got back to the mill, the girl got out of the car and walked away without saying goodbye or thank you, and Arianwen had said goodbye and thank you quietly without a smile, her little face quite glum and rather puzzled as if something strange had happened.

'You've not been to see the Morgans this holiday then?'

'Haven't really had time. You know what it's like with Christmas and everything. Perhaps I'll try to see them when I've got my little car.'

'Those children must be growing up now, I'll take you up after we've chosen the car if you like. There might be a bit of time.' He liked sitting in the Morgans' chaotic warm kitchen with Angharad, elbows on the table, holding a cup of tea in both hands, smiling, her wild hair untidy over her shoulders and those oh so glorious eyes, that made a man feel quite young, as if the spring was coming again.

'No, not today, Ianto. I want to take my time choosing my car.

It'll be the biggest thing I've bought in my life.'

How could she tell him the truth? Siwan having a baby, angry parents coming down to Carmarthen, her mother's disappointed face and her father's grey with anger, Siwan coming to see her to say goodbye, some of the wonderful fight taken out of her, her face thin and hollow with sadness.

'He never made me any promises you know, but I thought he loved me. I thought I was more worldly than that. I loved him and wanted him so much. Didn't listen to you, I should have, cariad. You'll always be the wise one, helping people with their lives. The baby'll be adopted, I'm going to one of those homes in Liverpool. It'll be me and a lot of poor Irish girls. And then I'm going to the Slade. The offer's still there. They won't stop me now. The worse has happened. I'll be tougher now. I'll break hearts but nobody'll break mine again,' and in the setting of the chin in a belligerent thrust there was a little echo of Siwan as she had been in the first year, a lovely friend.

'Write to me, Siwan. Let's still be friends.'

Siwan hugged her.

'Of course. You'll never make a fool of yourself like me. You're far too sensible for that, little Arianwen.'

'I want to hear of you as a great artist, a picture in the Royal Academy, and I'll come up to see you and we'll have tea together in a nice hotel.'

And in due course a wan little letter came, saying that a little boy had been born and had been taken for adoption. Arianwen could not even send a card, or a present for a little boy with no name who was out there somewhere, never knowing that he was the child of Arwyn Morgan and her friend Siwan: two of the chosen of the world, two people who made the world spin faster, something vertigo inducing about them. What heroic creature would come out of their blended genes? What a dull little thing she felt, knowing those two.

Ianto was very important that day at the end of December. He took her to the dealer that the family used, and a second hand Morris Minor was chosen, and a date was set for Arianwen to pick it up.

They took it up the Aberystwyth road to test it out, and on the way they passed Angharad and Arwyn walking up the hill towards the grammar school together. They were walking well apart.

Ianto waved, looking pleased.

'Shall we stop and say hello? Pull in.'

Arianwen put her foot down, and they sped up the hill. He looked at her angry profile, puzzled.

***

On the day Ianto dropped her off to pick up her car, she went to see Doris, who was suitably impressed by the Morris Minor.

'Oh Arianwen, you're quite the independent girl now. Come in and have a cup of tea. I made some Welsh cakes. Do you remember that old cow Daniels' Welsh cakes? She kept them for too long and never put butter on them. Not even margarine, mean old cow.'

Doris now lived in a good sized house on the Gwbert road. Quite the middle class matron. Iwan had got a loan from the bank and had a tidy little business down by the river. Doris had put on weight with the two children and looked as if she'd already settled down to middle age.

'Where are the children?'

'Gone to stay with Iwan's parents. They live at Aberporth now. The children always go there for a couple of days after Christmas before school begins again, gives me a chance for a good old tidy up.'

The house was immaculate and there were few signs of the existence of children. There was a lovely Christmas tree in the corner of the living room which had a window looking out over the garden which looked rather lost in the desolation of winter.

Arianwen felt a little shudder of dread in her blood as if the cold had intruded on its circulation. Occasionally, even at happy times, these shudders came. She didn't know why.

'Are you cold? I'll put another log on the fire.'

'No, somebody walked over my grave.'

They laughed.

Doris poured more tea.

'Have you been to see the Morgans this holiday?'

'No, I don't know whether I'll have time. The holiday goes so quickly and I've got a lot of work to do. Essays to write and then my finals in June, and then out in the world, and I've got to start looking round for a post.'

'Imagine you being a teacher, you'll be grand. I wish you could teach my two one day when they're older. Did you hear about Arwyn Morgan?' Arianwen tried to compose her face. Doris liked her gossip, and if she disclosed anything, Doris with her skilled interrogation techniques soon get more out of her than she wanted to divulge.

'Angharad threw him out. He's back now. Middle of the night it was and him out there in his pyjamas banging on the door and swearing. Mrs. Edwards next door told me. She's friendly with their next door neighbour, and she told her everything. He'd been drinking, they reckoned. Never any trouble before, even with them being a bit artistic. He's back now though, and they're all luvvy duvvy again. They had a party for the neighbours and smiling at each other and hugging as if they were just married again. He was away for a couple of weeks she reckoned. Then she must have taken pity on him. Well, it's only right isn't it, once you're married you're married aren't you? For better for worse, that's the promise we make.'

'I suppose so. Poor Angharad.' They hadn't looked particularly luvvy duvvy that day they'd passed them on the Aberystwyth road.

'She likes the men they say.'

'No, it's just that the men like her. That's different.'

'The children are still odd, they say. The boy's very clever, they say. Going to some college in Oxford and that girl who looks so like her mother, is a bit of a handful. Always dancing in the garden like a madwoman. All long dresses and that red hair, all uncombed.'

'Well I don't know, Doris, your neighbour shouldn't be looking out of the window so much and spreading gossip, and really you shouldn't encourage her. They were very kind to me and I was always happy with them.'

'They think there might have been another woman. Usually is, if a woman throws her husband out, isn't there?'

She saw the expression on Arianwen's face.

'Oh come on, cariad, don't go all chapel on me.'

Arianwen looked at her watch, and the dusk falling on the rimed grass of the lawn.

'I'd better be going. I don't want to be driving home in complete darkness in my new car.'

Doris looked disappointed

'Sure you won't have another cup of tea? Iwan won't be home for a long time yet, and I don't start the supper till six o clock.'

97

'No, I'd better go,' and she stood up and kissed Doris's round face.

'I'll write to you and I'll try to call in at Easter. Perhaps we can take the children out for a spin in the car.'

'That'll be nice,' but there was a coolness in her voice, and when she came to the door to see her off she didn't wait for long in the rectangular light of the door, and didn't wave.

As she drove home Arianwen thought of the mess of the Morgans and Siwan's predicament. How did people lead such untidy lives? How free she felt, and her life was there in front of her, waiting to be unfurled.

CHAPTER 15

One morning in February, when the rain was pouring down and an evil wind coming up the river, and you felt, rather than saw, the college buildings across the quad, Arianwen found an official looking letter in the pigeon holes. Her mother had forwarded it from home, because it had been sent there. It was postmarked Haverfordwest, so Pembrokeshire had come back first to her. It was a thick letter, which looked promising.

She was invited to attend an interview at a school in a tiny village in North Pembrokeshire. They wanted a teacher to teach children of infant junior age, the range for which she was training. It was possible she had been to the village before on the way to Haverfordwest, but she didn't know it that well. It was a village where you could see the Carn hills in the distance, part of Pembrokeshire which was still distinctly Welsh. She had in mind a bigger village with plenty going on, but she decided that she'd go and have a look and then decide. After all, she might not get the job. There would be others attending interview, perhaps all new young teachers like herself, keen to embark on their careers. It would be wrong to take things for granted, but she was determined that she would not go to work in a big town, or in London or Birmingham as some of the more adventurous girls were contemplating. A future in Wales was what she wanted, preferably in Welsh speaking West Wales.

Two weeks later on a sharp as a knife edge Thursday morning, the sun bright behind her, she drove into the little village. The sun made everything bright and clean and bleached even though it was too early in the year to see much sign of new life emerging. She imagined it when the gorse was bright, and the heather's first late summer budding, a dream in yellow and purple. It was very different from the dark enclosure of the valley: wide vistas of moorland and streams, and always the Carn hills dominating the whole scene. There was one small cloud over Carn Fawr which spoke of rain before evening. A few lambs were bleating in the open moors, no tidy fields here, and few trees.

The village was tiny, a Baptist chapel she noted, the manse, a shop, but no pub, a little village hall with a lot of ragged notices on the notice board outside it, and then on the left, on a little rise, almost a mound: the school, a grey stone building with large high windows.

As she opened the car door she heard the voices of the children playing, playtime, and somewhere far above a buzzard mewing its cat-like call, and a curlew calling its musical song across the moor.

She parked her car in a tiny space, and walked across the playground weaving between the children and their complicated games. The boys were shouting, some quiet girls talking in a corner and looking at her curiously, scrutinising her neat dark green costume and the court shoes which had cost far too much in the best shoe shop in Carmarthen.

There was a small lobby, just like in all the other schools she'd visited over the last two years. A woman came out of a tiny office on the right holding a sheet of paper.

'Are you Miss Evans? You're the first interview this morning, please take a seat here,' and she pointed to one of three seats placed along the wall.

'I'll tell Mr. Jones you're here.' Then she whispered, 'If you want to go to the ladies it's at the side of the headmaster's house, across the playground, over there.'

Outside, she heard the ringing of a hand bell, and the children were silent, and then the sound of reluctant footsteps on the stone floor.

She crossed the playground and used the toilet and checked her hair in the tarnished mirror hanging on a nail on the wall. Her face looked tired and anxious and far too young. She applied more of the lipstick she'd bought in the chemist. It was called *Pink Sunset*, but it was more scarlet than pink but if she rubbed over it, it turned into a pleasant pale strawberry colour which she felt made her look more sophisticated, but somehow still very young. Some of the girls had bought hats for interviews, but being so short, hats didn't really suit her and her hair was one of her best attributes after all, almost black, shiny with a bit of a wave, and she had started to grow it a bit longer, and the green suit made her skin look creamier, so, on the whole, she felt quite pleased with her appearance, but that wouldn't help her answer difficult questions.

It might be better to regard this interview as a practice for all the interviews which might come after. Surely she would get better?

As she walked back to the lobby she could hear the children singing, something old fashioned, and somebody was banging away on a rather jangly piano. It was cheerful and the children sounded as if they were enjoying themselves. It seemed then, on that cold February morning, that here in this little village school there was a brief chimeric vision of how schools could be very different from the school in Llanelli where the children had looked bored and sullen, any enthusiasm bullied out of them. These children would be no richer, the children of farm workers and labourers and smallholders, yet if they could sing with such gusto there was something happening which they could remember for the rest of their lives, and be enriched by it. *'Let the children sing,'* she reminded herself.

There were two other people sitting in the lobby now, a woman who looked as if she might have been teaching a long time, her plump face well lined and rather self-satisfied, and a young woman with long hair and a confident and worldly look to her. She was wearing a black costume, surely you only wore those for funerals, not for job interviews? The black costume suggested a higher degree of sophistication than you might expect in a little village school in the Carn hills with the sheep bleating and nothing much ever happening.

Arianwen had told her tutor about her interview at her weekly tutorial.

'I don't know anything about the present head, but the school is famous because a previous head was:…' and he named a famous poet who had written one of the best loved poems in the Welsh language. It gave her a little thrill to even think of going for an interview at the school where such a famous man had taught. Looking up at the sky through the lobby skylight and listening to the children singing, she thought of poetry and song, such a grand foundation for a school.

A tall man came out of the door leading to a classroom.

'Miss Evans?' and she put her hand up diffidently, feeling rather silly.

'I'm Hugh Jones, the headmaster. You're first, come this way. This is a two teacher school and as I'm interviewing, Miss Davies is taking the whole school today. I said some singing practice would be a good idea so you may find that your interview will take place against a background of song. They sing with gusto. They have healthy lungs most of them. It must be the fresh air here. Quite pure,' then he looked serious, 'although I'm afraid there have been some cases of TB in the area, but you're a relatively local girl so you'll know all about that.'

She followed him through the door, and as she had expected there was a panel of governors. Not a single woman. They mainly looked like farmers, stocky with the ruddy skin of the man who spends his life outdoors, and one pale man with a self-important air who was probably a justice of the peace and would ask all the questions.

The JP looked her up and down in a way which she didn't really like. 'I'm Hefin Morris, the chairman of the governors.'

He looked at the sheet of paper in front of him as if searching for something, and in that little gap, Hugh Jones sidled in with questions about education and philosophy which Mr Morris obviously found irrelevant, and the farmers looked as if they would have preferred to be out mending fences on their land or were thinking about their midday dinners, and of a little nap afterwards before milking.

While Hugh Jones was asking her about her methods of teaching very young children, one of the children's songs came to an end, and there was a brief silence so that her answer about Piaget, conscientiously revised, sounded unnecessarily loud, and the JP was rolling his eyes at such foreign nonsense. Then a voice began to sing, a boy's voice, pure and sweet, out to the fields and the moors, and it was so lovely that despite the solemnity of the situation she had to smile and the Head smiled too and the farmers nodded and the JP looked less supercilious, and as the song moved around them, she felt that she could stay in this place forever.

The headmaster came to the door with her. 'Thank you very much Miss Evans, you'll be hearing from us very soon.'

The woman came out of the office.

'Would you like a cup of tea before you start your journey back?'

'No thank you. Are you the secretary?'

'Nothing so grand. I just come in to help on occasions like this.' They both stood at the door and looked out to the hills.

'Wonderful, isn't it? I've just moved here from Cardiff. I feel I've come home, even though I was born in Tredegar. I'll stay here forever. I hope we meet again, Miss Evans.'

Before she got back into the car, she looked around, the cloud over Carn Fawr was getting bigger and it was bitterly cold in the wind blowing from the west, but as she looked she knew she was smiling, and really she would like to come here very much indeed. Next week she had an interview near Aberystwyth, which she'd always liked, but she knew the place that really beckoned.

CHAPTER 16

The letter came a week later, straight to college. The interview for the Aberystwyth post was the next day. She'd have to go whatever happened, even though it was a long drive. She was staying with a friend of her mother's, who had a small house in Llanbadarn, and if she got the job she would probably lodge with her.

The school was a bigger one than the one in Pembrokeshire, would have more teachers which would perhaps be nice and livelier, but she knew where she wanted to be.

It was what she had hoped it was, a rather formal letter from the Pembrokeshire Education Office offering her the post of assistant teacher. Her hands shaking with excitement, she looked round hoping to see somebody with whom she could share her news.

Eating her breakfast on her own, she kept looking at the letter to check that she hadn't read it wrong. It was not till two days later when she received a letter from Hugh Jones that she really believed it was true.

Dear Miss Evans,

How delighted I am to welcome you to our school in September. I was very impressed by your interview and your obvious affection for children. We pride ourselves on being a musical school in the grand tradition of the area. Perhaps you would like to visit the school after you finish your final examinations and meet the class teacher, Miss Davies, who has built up a reputation for the school's music and we hope that you will continue it for many years.

As you know, ours is a tiny village, and I am sure you would not want to drive from your home every day, the weather conditions in this area can be very difficult in winter. Accommodation is limited and as I have two growing children there is no space for a lodger in the schoolhouse. I have, therefore made enquiries around the village. The Rev and Mrs. Richards have excellent accommodation for a paying guest and have helped us out before with student teachers. Mrs. Richards is known to be an excellent cook and you would be well looked after. I

know you are a chapel goer and I'm sure they would
welcome you in their home. If you are happy with this I
shall mention you to them and Mrs. Richards will write to
you. And perhaps you could meet them when it is
convenient for you.

Welcome to our school, Miss Evans. I hope you will be
very happy.
Hugh Jones.

***

In that last summer of freedom before life began its demands on her, Arianwen and her friend Edna spent a week in Paris. They were intoxicated by their own sophistication. Paris was recovering from the war, and a joy in life was asserting itself again. Beautiful women, and interesting men who looked as if they didn't wash quite enough, sat outside cafes smoking those smelly cigarettes and looking clever. They might have seen Sartre and de Beauvoir, and one day they thought they had, or a couple who looked similar.

They allowed themselves one glass of wine and the nasty tasting coffees at Left Bank cafes. Mornings passed, and the afternoons found their own lazy momentum, so much freedom, and one conscientious visit to the Louvre and the disappointment of the Mona Lisa, small, not exciting and they stared at the rose window in Notre Dame. But the best times were those mornings and evenings, in little cafes, eking out the coffees, not admitting that they'd prefer a cup of tea, and eating meagre little dinners, but so different from anything they'd tasted before. One night was so warm they sat out till late delaying the return to the pension with its smelly drains, and unsmiling concierge, and the hard beds and the nasty little poodle which snapped at their heels.

They were sitting at a little round table. Edna put her head up and looked at the sky.

'It's the same sky as at home in Llanelli, but not the same at all. Imagine sitting out in our little garden at midnight sipping wine. The neighbours would be talking for days.'

'May I join, lovely ladies?'

A man with dark eyes and hair which needed cutting, the collar of his shabby jacket turned up, and his hands yellow with nicotine had come to sit, quite uninvited, at their table. He had dark eyes like a Welshman, but everything else about him was gloriously exotic, the yellowed tan, the stubbly jaw, his confidence, and a complete lack of self-consciousness. Arianwen thought he might be one of those dangerous men her mother had warned her against.

'Be careful with men, cariad, some of them can't be trusted.'

Most of the men she'd met at college and at the eisteddfod had been pretty quick with their hands, but not dangerous as such.

'You are English ladies on holiday?'

'Welsh,' Arianwen said sharply.

He looked at her, and smiled. Then turned his eyes to Edna.

'Welsh, yes you are more like us than the cold English. My name is Jacques, and yours?'

'Edna.'

'A beautiful name for a beautiful woman.' Edna blushed. Arianwen looked at her. Edna was very susceptible to male charm, usually the wrong kind, and although she had a curvaceous figure, and a face whose heavy lidded eyes suggested a sensuous nature, she was really quite innocent. The promise of face and body was deceptive; Edna was rather a dull girl with antediluvian views on sexual relations. A prim and avaricious mother had prevailed upon her the importance of keeping herself till marriage.

Arianwen, who read widely, was not so certain that virginity should be some kind of bargaining weapon, and despite her Non-Conformist upbringing, questioned its value. Although, as yet, her deliberations were theoretical.

Jacques turned to her.

'And you, the little dark one, what is your name?'

'Arianwen.'

She smiled at him as he struggled with her name, his tongue and teeth entangling with vowels and consonants. His teeth weren't perfect, but then whose were? She remembered Edward, his lovely middle class teeth, the teeth of a child whose parents took him regularly to the dentist, not just when he had toothache.

Somewhere, in the distance, church bells rang and a clock struck. Arianwen shivered.

'Cigarette?' He offered the battered packet. Edna took one, and her hand was shaking. Her face was pale in the wan light of a street lamp.

Arianwen shook her head.

'I think it's time we headed back, Edna. It's getting cold and I'm tired, and we're up early for the trip to Versailles tomorrow.'

'Where are you staying?'

She named the hotel, proud of her pronunciation, then realised that it was probably a foolish thing to do.

'I know it well. If you want to go back, I will escort your friend back later.' He clicked his hand and an elderly waiter hobbled over to the table. Jacques spoke to him so quickly that she couldn't interpret a single word

He turned back to Arianwen. There was a challenge in his eyes, a darkness which spoke of alien histories and a knowledge denied her. How had he spent the war? It was perhaps best not to dwell on that.

As he looked at her, laughter and contempt in his eyes, he lit the cigarette which Edna was holding in her mouth looking rather silly with her thick red lips pursed in kissing fashion around it. She took one puff, then held the cigarette away from her, film star style and let the ash drop on the pavement, and Jacques smiled at her then took her unoccupied hand and stroked it lightly, rubbing her palm with his thumb.

Edna was staring at him, mesmerised, her large eyes vacuous, licking the lipstick off her lips. All the time, Jacques stared over at Arianwen, triumphant, challenging.

She stood up,

'Edna, we'll have to go now, or that monster of a concierge will lock us out, and I don't think my French is good enough to plead or reason with her. Now let's go.'

Edna heard the voice of authority and looked at Jacques. She dropped the cigarette on the cobbles and wrapped her cardigan defensively around her.

'I'm coming, don't make such a fuss.'

As they walked away the sound of their shoes on the cobbles disturbingly reminiscent of marching soldiers, Edna looked back at Jacques, but he was already talking to the waiter. There seemed to be some kind of altercation, and the sound of angry voices followed them along the street. When they got back to their room they were both so tired they hardly spoke as they prepared for bed.

At some point in the night Arianwen woke up and as she always did when she couldn't get back to sleep, went to the window and stared out at the quiet street: nothing but a cat and an old tramp bending down to pick up cigarette stubs. There was a dim light from a street lamp and as she climbed back into bed looking over at Edna who was fast asleep and snoring slightly she saw that her face was wet with tears.

Next day everything seemed as normal. Versailles was overwhelming, and their eyes ached with staring at so much splendour. The week was coming to an end, and she looked forward to a couple of weeks at home before the term started, and, there, in the dingy room redolent of something animal, something dark which she preferred not to contemplate, home was desirable, and she thought of the cool murmuring of the stream and the comforting motion of the wheel. The encounter at the café and Edna's easy capitulation had disturbed her, but she didn't know why.

For the rest of the week whenever they sat in a café, Arianwen noticed that Edna looked round at every table as if she was looking for someone she'd lost, or a fragment of her existence which had eluded her.

They didn't quite lose touch, and Arianwen went to Edna's big wedding in a dull little chapel in Llanelli. Her husband was a mousy haired solicitor already doing well in the family firm. Arianwen thought him extremely dull. Edna's mother's pride in her daughter's acquisition was swelling out of her beige and black outfit, bought from the very best outfitters in what was left of Swansea. When she thought of Edna and Paris she wondered whether she had saved her, or condemned her to servitude.

CHAPTER 17

Her first thought when he stood in the village hall, cup of tea in hand, was that his eyes were just like Edna's Frenchman, dark and restless. Whereas the Frenchman's eyes were full of confidence Tom's eyes were always looking round as if he was looking for hidden assassins. A typical farm boy. She'd dismissed him as of no importance. There was another young man in the choir full of laughter, stocky, rugby player type, popular, lovely tenor voice who sometimes did the solos, but he never looked at her. Somebody told her that he belonged to a popular men's group of singers who went round singing at concerts all over West Wales, singing, sketches and telling little jokes, mainly clean, some satire at the expense of pompous ministers and vicars.

Arianwen was a soprano and because she was tiny, always sang at the front. If she turned round Tom was always looking at her. Not her type at all: healthy farmer's scrubbed face, clean corduroys and an old respectable tweed jacket, but old fashioned with a hairstyle that looked as if his mother had attacked him with basin and scissors.

The other young man, the desirable one, was growing his hair a bit longer and wearing a black polo necked sweater: A touch of the bohemian about him, more like some of the older men at college.

'There's a drama on in Narberth Village Hall on Saturday night, Saunders Lewis. I've got two tickets. Would you like to come with me?'

She looked round. The desirable tenor was talking to a pretty red haired girl. She was laughing so much that her cup was quaking in its saucer, and her tea splashing on to the floor.

'Elwyn,' someone shouted, 'leave the women alone, especially that one, she's my brother's girl, and he's got a punch like a charging bullock, and we don't want to lose our best tenor.' Everybody laughed and the red head threw her long hair back, enjoying the attention.

Elwyn, so that was his name. Not a very glamorous name for such a glamorous man.

'What do you think, Arianwen? We can have supper at The Pentre Arms after.'

Tom's eyes were pleading and she was a kind girl. It was difficult to refuse those pleading dark eyes. And this was the third time he'd

108

asked, after staring at her obsessively ever since she joined the choir.

'That'll be nice. Just to see the play. I always have supper early with the Richards on Saturday evening. It's the night he finishes his sermon. He tries it out on me over supper.'

It meant she wouldn't be going home at the weekend, but she'd been the previous weekend, had felt restless as if she no longer belonged there and the mill was no longer her home and the wheel loud at night was a hindrance to sleep rather than a comfort. The stream had been overflowing after heavy autumn rains and the valley, dark, enclosed, was so different from the open moors and sheep pastures and the distant view of the Carns. Her mother had asked too many questions. She'd spent a long time talking in the shed to her father who never asked her questions, as if he knew everything there was to know about her and his questions were already answered.

She complained to her father.

'Mam's questions! On and on.'

'She's missing you. It's her way. If she knows every last thing you're doing then you're closer.'

'It's less than thirty miles.'

'To your mother it's the other side of the world.'

'The Richards are so kind, they treat me like their daughter. I feel really at home.'

'That's what she's worried about. This is your home and we're your parents, girl.'

'Oh, Dad, of course you are.' And she kissed his chubby red face.

When she phoned the garage which housed the taxis to get a message to the mill, Ianto answered the phone.

He sounded uneasy. It was not often he answered the phone, but Miss Harries the clerk was on her lunch half hour, eating her sandwich in the corner of the office and resolutely not answering the phone.

'Ianto, it's Arianwen, can you take a message to the mill? Tell Mam I won't be home this weekend. Something's cropped up.'

'Your Mam won't like that. She's been up the shop buying a lot of flour for baking. You got a boyfriend?'

'Mind your own business, Ianto. How's the family?'

'Myrddin's getting married at last. Farmer's daughter from Cilgerran. Tidy farm. Boy's done well for himself there. Wife's excited and keeps on going down to Newcastle Emlyn to try hats on, and she says I've got to get a new suit. Perhaps you'll have a wedding soon then, I'll drive you to chapel.'

'Don't you go marrying me off, Ianto. You're as bad as my mother. I've got my career to think of.'

'Duw bach, girl, you're made for marriage and two little children, singing all the day.'

'You're an incurable old romantic, Ianto. Give my regards to the family.'

When she told the Richards she was going to see a play, they looked at each other.

'Tom's taking you, that'll be nice.' Mrs. Richards smiled, a knowing smile.

'Fine writer Saunders Lewis, although you could say his politics are a bit extreme,' Rev. Richards said looking down at his paper.'I'm a patriot, but there is a limit to how far one should go in pursuit of one's ideals.'

'Would you like to ask Tom to have tea with us before you go? He's been so lonely since his parents died. He's got a housekeeper, a slovenly type, I've met her in the shop a few times, buying cigarettes, and I know Tom doesn't smoke. '

Mrs. Richards plain little face was animated with conspiracy.

'Good sized farm he's got there, good catch for some young woman.' Now even the ascetic Reverend Richards was match making. Village life! It was probably the same on inlets of the Nile and the African plains and the South American pampas. Really, she might have been better off teaching in Swansea with a nice private little bedsit to come home to, and nobody knowing her. No, she'd be miserable. She smiled at the Richards, they were so very kind and their food was excellent, despite the deprivations of rationing. She was putting on weight. Time for some long walks across the moors.

On Monday morning she was laying out some mushrooms she'd collected on Sunday afternoon for the nature table. Mr. Jones walked in.

He picked one up.

'Beautiful smell, lethal of course, if the children touch them make them go and wash their hands, not too good on washing hands some of these children, most of them don't have bathrooms, just outside privies and a sink in the scullery. They look healthier than town children though their diet is probably not much better. Where's the brave new world, Arianwen, our glorious Welfare

State? It's coming but taking its time. Sorry, you don't want to be treated to my rapacious brand of socialism on a Monday morning.' He gestured to the window. 'The sun is shining, no wet playtime. How was the play on Saturday? Great playwright. The Welsh Ibsen.'

He smiled at her surprised face, 'You know, village life.'

It had not been a very exciting evening. The play had been too intellectual for the amateur group, there was one really talented actor, the others had been intent on remembering their lines, and lacked the confidence to examine the characters they were playing

'It's a fine play. I studied it at college. Not a good choice for an amateur group. They'd have been better off with something traditional. The audience were desperate for a bit of a laugh, and kept on laughing in bits when there was nothing funny at all. Still they tried hard, and I'm all for people doing their bit for the Arts. I must admit I prefer a good concert.'

'I'm glad you're enjoying the choir, they asked me to join, they seem to think because I'm the headmaster I should have an innate musical talent. My children laugh when I sing. I love music but I've got no talent at all, that's why I'm so glad that I've got a musical assistant. Old Miss Davies did sterling work, but she banged away at the piano as if it was an enemy, or the bloke who probably jilted her about a century ago. Don't leave me to get married, will you?' He looked at his watch, '9 o'clock. Time for the bell.'

And so another week began and she didn't think about Tom again. Mondays were always hard work, there was always a crying little one who had not expected to have to come back again after the weekend, and the anxious mother who was convinced her large obnoxious offspring was being bullied, and would not accept that it was the other way round and that he was the perpetrator of atrocities behind the boys' toilets. There were the usual accidents amongst the little ones and spare knickers and pants had to be found. At the end of the day she was exhausted, and looked forward to tea in the Richards' parlour with too much home-made cake, and then prepare for the next day, before a big supper in the kitchen with Rev. Richards quiet and Mrs. Richards, her eyes huge with news, telling her all she'd learned from her daily excursion to the shop.

The nights were drawing in and she'd still not been on the long walks on the moors that she'd intended and it always seemed to be raining: a different kind of rain from the valley where the rain fell softly and the trees dripped for hours after. Here in the village you saw the rain blow towards you from the sea, a determined creature which could not be diverted, but when the sun shone and the sky was clear of clouds you saw for miles and you could believe in the infinite breadth of the world. Sometimes in the valley she felt as she did as a child, that the edge of the valley was where the world ended and that nothing beyond was real.

Wednesday was choir night, and she looked forward to it, but this week she would have to see Tom again and she wasn't certain she was looking forward to that, but she would see the glamorous tenor. When she got in on Tuesday, Mrs. Richards was in the hallway looking excited.

'Tom telephoned a few minutes ago, I said you weren't back from school yet. He's ringing back soon before milking. He had the phone put in when his father died. Everybody was surprised, they've always been careful with their money that family. I'll make you a cup of tea and you can sit in the study and wait for it. Rev's gone to a meeting in Carmarthen. He won't be back till suppertime. Scones today, blackcurrant or strawberry jam?'

'Just a cup of tea will do.'

Mrs. Richards looked shocked. 'You'll be starving by supper.'

'School dinner was pie and mashed potatoes. I don't think I've digested that yet.'

'You'll waste away.'

'I doubt it. '

She took her tea up to the study where Rev. Richards liked the phone to be located so that he could answer it before his wife, though Mrs. Richards complained. She sipped her tea and looked at a sheet of paper where he had made an early start on Sunday's sermon. There were lots of crossings out. Poor man. All that work. She didn't always listen to them, sometimes she planned her lessons for the week, some people just rustled sweet papers and one or two of the farmers up since dawn for the milking went to sleep. His sermons were rather too erudite for villagers who just wanted time to pass as quickly as possible so that they could go home to dinner with cleansed consciences for another week.

The phone rang.

'Arianwen?' He sounded nervous.

'Hello, Tom.'

'Are you going to choir Wednesday evening?'

'Yes. I hope so.'

'I'm looking forward to seeing you again.' There was a long silence. The phone made strange noises as if pursuing its own conversation. 'It was a nice evening last Saturday, wasn't it? Good play.'

'Yes.'

She was finding it difficult to think of anything much to say to him, she, Arianwen, who chattered with everyone. Let him think she was shy.

'I'm going to a ploughing match on Saturday. Would you like to come with me?' he blurted out as if in shame.

Ploughing matches: mud and beer tents, and bored women, and the wind attacking you from all directions. Her wellingtons were at home and she hadn't worn them since she had tried to catch trout in the stream a few years back. They still fitted her tiny feet, and she thought of the lovely leather courts that she'd bought out of her first month's salary. Not to be wasted on ploughing matches, not the way to spend a precious Saturday afternoon.

'I'm going home this weekend. My mother's invited some cousins to tea.' Half true.

A lazy weekend at home suddenly seemed appealing, a good book, and her favourite seat overlooking the wheel with its stories of her childhood, and a brisk walk up to the village to hear the gossip in the shop, call in at the garage for a cup of tea. Yes. Home did have its attractions.

'Well we can talk tomorrow at choir, perhaps,' and there was a long pause and a bit of preliminary coughing. ' I can walk you home, or if it's raining I'll take you home in the car.'

He sounded eager and she felt sorry for him.

'That's very kind of you, but it's not very far. We'll see what the weather's like.' She hoped it didn't sound too much like a yes.

'I'll see you tomorrow.'

'Yes.' She put the phone down. Mrs. Richards was on the landing looking eager.

'I'm just going to have an hour or so preparing my lessons for tomorrow. I've really got to do something about the little ones' reading. Some of them are so slow.' She smiled at Mrs Richards as she closed the bedroom door.

As she sat at the desk looking at some of her college notes about reading schemes and methods which did not really apply if you were teaching children to read in Welsh which was much easier, she thought of Tom. He was a nice man. That's all she could say. A gent yes, but rather dull, after the college boys with their wandering hands and the banter and colourful language. Brought up a chapel girl, life with the Morgans and then college had liberated her and enlightened her. Her views were very different from her mother's. However, chapel teachings were far reaching.

Wednesday was a day of rain sweeping like an enemy across the Irish Sea, stopping for reinforcement over the Carns, and then ditching its load over the village. As she walked across from the manse, her umbrella fighting against the wind, the hills were drowning in rain and the gorse was faded to a dull bleached yellow. There were times like this when she thought that it might have been a good idea to get a teaching job far away, somewhere hot where the rain was a desired stranger not an everyday familiar. When she'd studied the Times Ed, there'd been seductive posts in the West Indies and countries in Africa with strange names, and there was a little thrill in finding them in the atlas. And they were tempting, but Mam would have been so upset if she went, and Dad worse, with his smile of encouragement masking pain, and, after all, she was just a girl of the valley, and now the moors, and she didn't know whether she would have the courage to sign away two years of her life.

The school building was a brave little infantryman against the on-slaught of the weather, its grey squat shape seeming to grow out of the surrounding green. Some of the boys, quite unconcerned by the rain, were playing football in the playground, but most were inside, huddling near the coke stove which was blowing smoke into the classroom.

A couple of the girls were coughing dramatically.

'Open the window.'

The room was stuffy with steaming bodies and the smell of smoke would linger all through a day which would be very long and the children would be silly and fractious without a decent break outside after dinner.

Mr. Jones came to the door. The little ones scrambled to their feet. He came in and whispered.

'It's going to be one of those days. I can feel it in my bones. I sat up late. I'm struggling with that poem for the Eisteddfod. I'm not a natural like my glorious predecessor.' Mr. Jones saw it as a personal challenge to carry on the tradition of poetic headmasters.

'I shall look forward to seeing you being chaired at the Eisteddfod.'

She looked up at his pale, dark-eyed face. He was only five years older than her and sometimes she thought she was a little in love with him, in a way which was quite unthreatening because he was married to Sal, who was tall and beautiful and clever. Anyway, he couldn't sing, not like Elwyn who also intruded on her dreams, but in a more disturbing way. Really she had quite enough to be thinking about, without Tom being so obviously infatuated with her. It was all rather glorious. As he left to shout rather louder than usual at his class, she turned round to look at hers, who relaxed after he'd left, already looking as if, collectively, they'd decided to be rather a trial today. Miss looked as if she wasn't really concentrating and it was sums and then reading, and it was a long time before story time.

Lucy Davies was crying. She knew what that meant and the children who sat close to her were histrionically moving away and holding their noses, and Ann Hughes, a smug and officious little girl, a future head girl and pillar of some unsuspecting institution, was putting her hand up.

'Lucy Davies has wet herself, Miss.' The boys laughed. Louder than was necessary.

'Get your books out and turn to page four. Ten sums in half an hour.'

This was not what she'd learned at training college and was not the usual pattern of things in her classroom, but there were times when the old despised ways had their compensations.

'Lucy, come with me. And if there's any noise there'll be no singing today and no story.' Her head was already throbbing as she turned to the cupboard for spare knickers.

It was still raining at four o'clock when she left school, but after a day of incarceration in a damp and smelly classroom, the outside world was a giddy freedom. The rain was soft and slow now, a last ditch drizzle, the air was fresh, and the wind had dropped and there was a sliver of blue over the hills, tiny like a fragment of old cloth, and she knew it would be a lovely evening, with everything fresh and the Irish wind warm with its memory of salt about it. She called in the shop for a packet of aspirin.

'Headache, cariad?' Mrs. Jones was an archetypal Welsh woman:

short, big bosomed, reddish face. So would one of her ancestors have looked in hat and shawl and long flannel skirt. She spoke little English, only words like Cadbury's and ginger nuts, Lifebuoy soap and Persil. When the commercial travellers came round with their practised charm, her husband, who ran the post office with a pompous awareness of his own importance was called to exercise his English, fine honed at the grammar school.

'What rain we've had today. Not good for the children being cooped up all day. Poor little things.'

'Not very good for me either, Mrs. Jones. They miss their playtimes outside.'

'Yes, indeed.' She smiled her gentle smile to which so many succumbed their secrets, and learned to regret their folly.

'Choir tonight, I hear you've got a lovely voice, and play the piano really nice. There's some nice young men sing in the choir. Do you know Tom Davies? Lovely farm his parents left him. Forty acres! That's a good size for round here. He needs a wife. Fine singing voice he's got. I remember at last year's Christmas concert.'

'I'll just pay, Mrs. Jones, got to be going.'

Mrs. Jones, however, had not finished with her. It had been a quiet day in the shop.

'Any sweets? You've not been using up your rations.'

'No thank you. I'm cutting down on the sweets and cakes. Mrs. Richards feeds me too well.'

No, she shouldn't have said that. Customers would now be treated to stories about the young teacher starving herself and complaining about Mrs. Richards' cooking. The benign peasant face hid a mind which was not so much malicious as imaginative with a tendency for exaggeration and distortion. Mrs. Jones should write stories, preferably for the more lurid magazines. Pity she couldn't write in English.

'Look, it's stopped raining.'

Mrs. Jones looked disappointed. Perhaps people stayed longer and divulged more when it was raining.

***

When she walked over to choir practice, it was a beautiful evening and a bright sunset lit the tin roof of the village hall to a Mediterranean ochre, but there were signs of accelerating autumn, the few trees in the village were almost bare, and soon the clocks would go back, but

116

back then she was too young for the rhythms of melancholy and all her life she had created light in dark places. The nights were drawing in and despite the showy dusk it would soon be dark.

Later on in her life when she had discovered the true nature of darkness, she would look back at such innocence, that child blithely walking in sunlight lit by love and the benisons of chance, shivering in sympathy as she watched that former self.

Arianwen was a practical young woman and despite her intelligence she was not one for philosophy. As yet she accepted the simple creed of a chapel childhood. Not for her the intellectual rebellions of her generation, the lapse from certainty into uncertainty. Life was generous. She would be a good teacher, perhaps, one day, have her own little school, such as this little village one. Marriage was a possibility and motherhood the inevitable consequence.

The choir master, nurturing his creative talents, allowed himself the occasional bout of ill temper, a bank manager by day, staid in suit and dark tie, tactful with the wealthy, diplomatic with the recalcitrant. Choir night was the high point of his week and he was indulged in this by the choir, who appreciated his musical skills.

He'd had a puncture just outside Haverfordwest and had got oil on his casual trousers bought from the best draper in Carmarthen, and had been nursing a fit of pique. The choir, like children released from school, excited by sun after rain, were restless, and the tenors, apart from Elwyn, whose voice soared perfectly through the open window to an audience of startled sheep, were lifeless.

'That's enough.' He shouted so loud that the sheep ran away, bleating, to higher ground.

'That was bloody terrible.' He blushed. 'Sorry, ladies, but this isn't good enough. We'll have our tea early and then I'm hoping for much better. Tenors, you are not concentrating at all, not at all. We'll have early tea, and let's hope that we all try a little harder after refreshment.'

Emboldened by his own expletive, he swaggered to the men's toilets. Two obedient women scuttled to the kitchen and turned up the urn and opened packets of ginger nuts which the men always demolished before the women got near them.

Tom came up to her as she stared out of the window at the darkness. There was even a star in the distance above Carn Fach, a rare clear night. There might be a frost, and in the morning a sprinkle of rime on heather and gorse, and the sheep would come down to huddle against stone walls and the little moorland streams would sparkle in turgid movement.

His cup and saucer were shaking in his hands and some dark brown tea had spilled in the saucer. He looked down at her with the dark eyes which she was certain some women would find attractive, but not her. Swivelling her eyes to the left she saw that Elwyn was watching her. Her with the red hair wasn't there. Rumour was that she was expecting, and spending most of the time being sick. She smiled a welcoming smile at Tom.

'Lovely evening, Tom.' She shook the dark waves of her hair and she watched him trace their ripple across her neck. 'So nice after all that rain. Price is in a bad mood, isn't he?' She giggled, certain that Elwyn was staring harder.

'He shouldn't have sworn like that, not in front of the ladies, it's not right.'

'I've heard worse when the boys are playing football during playtime, and you'd be surprised at the vocabulary of some of the children in Llanelli.'

He didn't smile, a man with little humour she thought, not like Elwyn who was laughing loudly and she wanted to look round, but stopped herself.

'I'm sorry you're going home this weekend, you'd have enjoyed the ploughing match.'

She aborted a little shudder with a wide smile.

'When Aunt Ada and her daughters come on a visit the whole family obeys.' Aunt Ada was actually paying a stately visit to her son who had escaped to Bristol, but it was half true.

He looked out of the window. 'I'll walk you home after choir.'

'It's only a few hundred yards.' She smiled a smile which was not completely dismissive, and which viewed by an interested observer would suggest promise, but when she turned round Elwyn was still laughing, but deep in conversation with a huge young man who looked like a farmer but was actually the local vet and every farmer's wife wanted her daughter to marry him, a vet, almost as good a catch as a doctor, and better paid than a minister or a doctor judging by what he charged for attending a difficult calf birth.

The choir master was in a better mood after tea and four ginger nuts, and a sympathetic conversation with the buxom English-woman from one of the rundown cottages at the moor end of the village, and some useless advice on how to remove the oil, and the choir, briefly, very briefly, caught the full joyous mood of the Messiah, and their voices soared, despite the young vet's baritone being rather slower than anybody else's, finishing a few beats behind. They were rather pleased with themselves. She looked round for Elwyn, but he'd gone in a great scrum of men heading for their cars and probably the pub in the next village, or home brew in one of the farms. Tom was there waiting, his cap low on his head, the dark eyes anxious under its peak and putting on an ancient tweed coat.

'I'll walk you home,' and there was nothing she could do about it. When she came out of the cloak room with her coat, everybody had gone, except the two women washing up and she suffered the scrutiny of their eager eyes and imagined their knowing looks as Tom proudly opened the door for her, a look of knightly mission and purpose on his ruddy face.

It was a beautiful night. Such a romantic night. At school she'd read *The Merchant of Venice* and she remembered the poetry of Jessica and Lorenzo at the end of the play: *On such a night as this...* and how she'd loved the words and allowed herself wild dreams of Venice and a young man. How silly she'd been then. She was not a dreamer now. Certainly not with this young man. And there was a huge moon between her and the hills, dazzling low, beckoning as if speaking to her some tale of the future. She turned to look at him, desperately thinking of a way of walking home alone.

'Would you like to come to supper with me, at the farm house, one day, after school?'

No, she thought. I wouldn't. I prefer to go back to the manse, allow Mrs. Richards to fuss over me and stuff me with cake and fatten me up, and feed me with the day's gossip from the shop. Tomorrow I'll be the gossip, and sweet Mrs. Richards will pour me another cup of tea and sit with me, that expectant look on her little face, and her eyes bright with curiosity like a little dormouse come out for the spring.

He didn't wait for an answer, as if there was so much to ask and he'd been rehearsing a long time and was desperate not to forget his lines.

'Would you like to come to a concert one night in Haver-fordwest? It's a bit of everything. It's the weekend after next.'

It was difficult to invent more visiting relatives, and her mother would be entertaining a visiting preacher from Carmarthen, a particularly pompous character, a prodigious and messy eater who always spoke as if he was addressing a congregation.

She always enjoyed weekends when she didn't do her duty and go home, and had planned a self- indulgent couple of days: a visit to St. Davids, perhaps Tenby, and a bit of shopping. Another month's salary to spend, meagre as it might be, but she could certainly allow herself a nice dress for going out, and another pair of shoes.

'That would be nice, Tom. I don't think I'm doing anything next weekend.'

She tried not to see the delight in his eyes. Somehow it hurt her, as if she had committed an unplanned sin.

He walked slowly and she had to curb her natural tendency to gallop along as if on some important mission. Like Mam, she was restless, full of movement, as if life was too short for stillness.

At the gate she turned to say goodnight. He held out his hand. It was a strange gesture, and she didn't know how to respond, and she held out her hand as if she was being introduced to a stranger. His hand was warm and he touched her very lightly, as if frightened of her. A great pity for him and his loneliness overcame her and she smiled up at him. His face was dark, silhouetted against the huge brightness of that enormous moon, then he dropped his hand, and turned away from her.

'I'll pick you up on Saturday at 4 o'clock.' And he was gone.

As she turned the key in the lock, she could hear Mrs. Richards scurrying from the kitchen. Cocoa would be offered and she would have to sit at the kitchen table and avoid the expectation in the poor woman's eyes. She was very tired.

'Cup of cocoa, cariad fach, and a nice slice of cake, before you turn in. '

'That's very kind of you, but I won't. It's been a tiring kind of day. I'll go straight to bed.'

'Breakfast at eight. I've got some lovely fresh eggs and a nice bit of bacon.'

'Goodnight, Mrs Richards.'

***

He picked her up at four o'clock as they'd planned. His old car was polished and the inside was clean, almost as clean as Ianto's taxi. In fact she felt that she should be sitting in the back like a customer. Tom was very formal in what looked like a suit for a funeral and he smelled of some strange old fashioned cologne. He opened the door for her, and looked at her as if he was proud of her.

'You look lovely, Arianwen.'

She'd brought her favourite dress from home, bright red, which showed up her dark hair and her pale Celtic skin. She was proud of how she looked, although it was tighter round the hips than she remembered. Her black patent court shoes showed off her slim ankles and she had her best coat on, bought on a shopping trip to Carmarthen.

It was a cold afternoon, and the old car offered little comfort, and she was glad when they got to the town.

They walked to a popular little café near the town centre. The waitress greeted them, and then looked Arianwen up and down with envy.

'Can we have a table by the window, please?'

They looked out at the street rather than each other.

'Is it warm enough for you here? I always like sitting by the window. I like to watch the people walking back and fore. All busy. A farmer doesn't see many people. Only on mart day. That's full of noise right enough. I always come home early after I've bought and sold stock. I never was one for pubs. Rough places some of them. Once or twice I've been in, for a bit of company like, but I don't stay long.' And then he was quiet, as if surprised by his unaccustomed eloquence.

Again that treacherous surge of pity. She could imagine the long evenings at the farm. She knew what these farmhouses could be like, especially with no woman to make them comfortable: damp, cold, always the smell of the farmyard, dark corners, a radio in the corner, and an old range perhaps, blowing out smoke when the wind was in the wrong direction, and the slatternly housekeeper who didn't really earn her money, and his lonely suppers, and voices from the radio offering false friendship.

But it was none of her business.

She smiled at him.

'I'm looking forward to the concert. I like a bit of variety.'

'You should be singing in it. I love to hear you sing. It seems to make you so happy.'

His eyes were full of pleading. Arianwen turned away.

The waitress came to the table.

'Have you decided what you want?'

'Just a cup of tea and a Welsh cake for me, please.'

Tom looked disappointed.

'Is that enough?'

'Mrs. Richards cooked a big dinner today. I can hardly move.'

'Do you mind if I have something more substantial? I only had a bit of bread and cheese for my dinner. I'll have egg and ham and chips please, and tea and bread and butter.'

The café was filling up with tired looking shoppers. A couple of women sitting in the corner were staring openly at her. One looked familiar, a large woman with hair which looked dyed, and great beefy hands like a butcher. Then she remembered, she'd seen the woman in the playground, the mother of that boy in Mr. Jones's class who he had to punish for bullying a timid little new boy. Mr. Jones didn't believe in caning, but had made the boy stay in during play time, and the mother had come to the school to complain, very loudly.

It wouldn't take long to be round the village then. Mrs. Richards would be pleased. How long would it take to travel the twenty or so miles to her parents? West Wales spread gossip like fertiliser. Ianto did a fair amount of travelling during the week and he knew everybody and everything, and enjoyed talking!

When the food came Tom ate without speaking and she was left to drink her tea in silence and nibble at the dry Welsh cake with its mean little smear of margarine. As bad as Mrs. Daniels' offerings so many years ago. And always when she thought of the Daniels, then came thoughts of the Morgans, certain as thunder after lightning, and that sadness that comes with such happy memories. One day she must visit them again. The last couple of years were like centuries. She felt that several histories had been enacted in that great surge of youth. And would she want to see Arwyn again, knowing about Siwan's suffering, and that unknown little boy, Bedwyr and Blodeuwedd's stepbrother?

Tom ate everything on his plate, every flaccid looking chip and fatty slice of ham. Arianwen stared out of the window. There was something intimate about watching him eat, something which made her feel uncomfortable. How strange to live with a man, to see him washing, all the routines of everyday life. It was how it was for her parents, but she couldn't imagine the same thing for herself; anyway she was too young, marriage could wait. If it had been Elwyn sitting at the other side of the table she might have felt differently. She was like a woman in one of those romantic novels, the wrong man was interested in her.

After his egg and ham and chips he ordered another pot of tea and a selection of pastries. She looked at the cake stand with its selection of synthetic looking cakes and refused to take one. Not a patch on what she could have made herself.

By the time they'd finished, and the sullen waitress had brought their bill, it was time to go to the concert. It was obviously a popular event. The hall was full, and from the kitchen at the back, she could hear the sound of steam hissing from the urns and a clatter of plates. Not more tea and cakes. The whole of Wales lived by tea and cakes.

He bought her a programme, and the only act that interested her was the Lads of the Mountains. Elwyn sang with them. The evening which she had dreaded and had, hitherto, only added to her mood of ennui, suddenly seemed brighter.

The first part of the concert was the usual mixture of children struggling on violins and recorders, and sopranos identifiable only by the varying degrees of size and exposure of bosoms. The last act before the interval was a fine tenor: squat, bald, face ruddied by wind and rain. His homely appearance was contradicted by the histrionic romanticism when he sang a passionate Italian aria.

At the height of emotion his three chins waggled. Arianwen had to take her handkerchief out, to blow her nose to suppress her giggles. The informal policing of Welsh community life was quite familiar to her. There was always a ready-to-be-offended relative or friend on surveillance. The KGB had nothing on Welsh country life.

'Miss Evans, isn't this a lovely concert? Though, to be honest, I didn't think much of the pianist. I'm sure you would have been much better.'

Marian Hughes was the beautiful wife of the local doctor, and the mother of a precocious son in Arianwen's class. She was from a wealthy Cardiff family and had never learned the tact necessary to survive village life. Seeing Arianwen during the interval she'd come over, confident and smiling.

'How is Stephen doing? I can see his reading improving every day. It's so wonderful for him having a young teacher with modern ideas. That old girl they had before taught as if it was still the 1920's.' Marian had a loud voice, and Arianwen noticed that people had stopped to listen to what she had to say. The woman was beautiful, opinionated, and came from Cardiff: not many reasons to like her.

'Well most of them left her class knowing the basics, and Mr. Jones, he makes sure they're learning. He believes in getting the best out of every child. That's what any teacher wants.'

'Yes, and he's such a lovely man, so much sex appeal.'

Certain chapel-going ladies looked shocked. They might be mothers, but sex was not a word in common currency. Arianwen tried hard not to giggle.

Tom came back with two cups of dark tea and a plate of cakes on a tray. Marian gave him the most beautiful smile, and walked off to look for further conversation and the fascinated crowd stood aside as if she was royalty. One of the drunken wags who had stood at the back, whistled and whispered something to his friend who laughed a loud artificial laugh and watched Marian's tightly clad bottom as she accosted the local vicar who looked terrified, especially as his cold faced wife was watching.

Arianwen was quite happy to watch this carnival of social life dancing in front of her, but Tom was in serious mood.

'Shall we go out for a breath of fresh air? It's ever so stuffy here.' He looked anxious, as if her answer was somehow significant.

'I'm fine here. It's not that stuffy.'

He looked hurt.

'Just for a minute then.'

She put the cup down on a nearby ledge, and Tom took her hand in a proprietary gesture. She couldn't snatch it away without looking rude, and as they walked hand in hand through the door Elwyn and one of his friends came through the door bringing fresh air and the smell of beer with them.

'Evening, you two. Sneaking out before it finishes then, not waiting to hear the best act on the programme?'

He looked meaningfully at their locked hands. She snatched her hand away. Tom looked cross.

He leant against the wall of the building.

'Somebody knows about us then. No bad thing. That Elwyn, He'll tell everybody. He always gets the women. Wonder he hasn't tried with you. But you're mine.'

And he leant over and kissed her on the cheek. It was chaste and she was moved by his diffidence, and she felt sorry for him and she was kind, and she let him kiss her on her lips.

PART 2

CHAPTER 18

The beginning of the school holidays and it was raining again as it had done through the second half of the summer term when the children should have been running about at play time, enjoying the sun and the fresh air, but the malice of weather had destroyed such hubristic plans.

She looked out of the kitchen window. There was a draught like November coming through, and she watched Tom's old tractor making a slow progress along the rutted lane to the road where the milk churns were left. It would have been nice to go to Carmarthen to shop and meet a college friend and have a good old gossip and a moan about teaching and buy something silly and frivolous to wear. But she never seemed to go anywhere these days

Life was different now. Occasionally, she still went to choir. Tom had given up, saying he was too busy on the farm, and often, after a day's teaching, and cooking a hot tea, and scrubbing the kitchen floor, a daily tyrant of a task, she was too tired even to think of taking her little car along the rutted lane with its hidden panoply of pot holes. When she did go, Elwyn was friendly, and made her laugh with his jokes, and even put his arm round her shoulders when she was glum, as if it was safe to do so now that she was a respectable married woman.

Yesterday she'd got stuck in the mud and when Tom came down from the hill from the sheep to tow it back, her car had a slow puncture and she was still waiting for him to repair it. Dad might do it.

They were coming for tea and supper. Ianto was bringing them. The thought of her parents cheered her up, but first a clean through of the whole house. Life was different now. How spoilt she'd been all her life. Her childhood had been so easy. It was only now that she was beginning to realise how hard her parents worked.

Now everything was so different. Tom was not an easy companion: a prisoner to the rhythms of the farmer's life. He was a taciturn man and sometimes over supper in the kitchen, which she tried to make cosy with a nice tablecloth and flowers on the table, he hardly spoke at all, his eyes filmed over with exhaustion. The kitchen was a huge depressing room. Nothing could mask the draughts of sadness which came through the window and the anger of the wind through the gap under the door despite the bright curtain she'd put up there.

Sometimes she planned her conversations on the way home from school, still exhilarated by the children and a political argument with Hugh Jones who was becoming more radical as he got older, and was still writing his poetry, and annoying his wife with his Romanticism and the fact that she was expecting a new unplanned baby.

'That Hughes boy, he's sharp as knives. You'll never believe what he said today about Winston Churchill. He might end up a politician himself. You never know, he's a right firebrand. His parents encourage him to express himself. I don't think he'll be a doctor like his Dad.'

Tom looked at her and leant over to give a bit of meat to Bess, the opportunist sheep dog who never left his side.

'Children are allowed to say what they like these days. No discipline. Wallop would do him good.'

'You know I don't believe in that, Tom.'

'If I have a son he'll get a wallop if he doesn't behave himself.'

The only topic of conversation he seemed to enjoy was talking about a son, a son cast in his mould who would run the farm when he got old, and would run the farm in the same way as it had been run for the century or so since his family had bought it.

After he'd taken the milk churns to the stand on the road, he came back for his breakfast. He only had a cup of tea with three sugars before he went out milking at six o'clock. Every day he had the same thing, a slice of the ham hanging like a suicide from the ceiling on hooks, ham so fat the pink was like thin veins, and two eggs fried till they were hard, all mopped up with the thick bread and butter he ate slice after slice. All in silence as she stood by the old range watching him as if he was a stranger to her. Every morning she said the same thing. She was, she realised, becoming a boring woman. What had become of witty, quixotic Arianwen of the dark eyes which sparkled? When she looked at herself in the mottled glass of the mirror of the dressing table there was a tired looking woman, a dullness in her eyes which was new like a new outfit she was wearing till she became used to it, but didn't really like.

'It would be nice to have the place modernised. You can get a grant for it. A lot of the farmhouses are being done up now, and this could be a lovely kitchen, nice new Aga would warm it and one of those fitted kitchen which makes everything look tidy and orderly. I'd paint the walls white and have blinds at the windows and do something about this floor, vinyl, easy to keep clean, and bright and cheerful.'

He looked at her.

'I need a new tractor, and the barn roof's got a leak. We're farmers, we don't need all that stuff in the house That's for people with plenty of money and too soft because they've never done a decent day's work in their lives. The milk cheque's good these days, but sometimes more money goes out than comes in.'

Worrying about money was habitual with him, as if he'd inherited it with the blood of his peasant forefathers. Though he complained about money he never explained anything to her, and expected her to use her salary to pay for food and the upkeep of the house. It was said that farmers were doing well, and she saw neighbours with new cars and their wives well dressed, but Tom was taciturn, turning himself away from her, more enclosed than ever in the turgid rhythms of his life.

Today she avoided her usual plea. Her parents were coming and she wanted him to be welcoming.

'Can you come in a bit earlier tonight? Mam and Dad are coming for afternoon tea and a bit of early supper. Can you do the milking a bit earlier?' He looked at her as if she'd suggested emigrating to Australia, as one of her college friends had done, and was now regularly sending her letters full of sun, and talk of beaches, and the infinite benefits of life in Western Australia.

***

Mam and Dad never looked comfortable at the farm, not that they came very often. It involved one of the taxis from Mam's brother, or Arianwen would pick them up and then have to run them back later, something she didn't like, reluctant to drive at night along the narrow unlit roads with the occasional sheep jumping out of nowhere, eerie eyed in the darkness.

Today they were being driven by Ianto, now semi-retired, but happy to get behind the wheel for special occasions like funerals and weddings, looking stately behind the wheel of the shining Rover, and when Mam summoned him, the most important of occasions. He enjoyed tea and supper, and the one pint of home brew he allowed himself when driving. He was little changed apart from his white hair and a bit of a stoop. He was, for Arianwen, the essence of childhood: Friday and Sunday drives back and fore from Cardigan, the songs they sang, and the gossip, and tales of his bad behaviour at the village school in long ago boyhood.

Once Mam had had a cup of tea and a glass of sherry which she feigned to despise, she seemed to relax. Dad sat at the edge of the settle in the kitchen and looked as if he was desperate to be back in his shed with its smell of oils and long burnt out echoes of soldering, and strange unrecognisable bits and pieces which would be used to repair radios, and, increasingly now, more sophisticated pieces of household equipment, cheaper than taking them to the electrical repair shop in Newcastle Emlyn.

'Shall we sit in the parlour? I've lit a fire in there.'

'Have you had that chimney cleaned yet? Still blowing back the smoke is it? I'm quite comfortable here, thank you.' And Mam looked round the dark kitchen with its smoky walls, poor light, and the floor which defied all cleaning, always smeared with mud, and however much she opened the windows to let in the moorland breezes the indomitable smell of the farmyard, mingled with the musk of damp. Outside it was July, albeit a damp one, but in that kitchen it was a perpetual damp November.

After the obligatory half hour Ianto knocked the door. He always allowed the family half an hour on their own before he appeared for his cup of tea, and his appearance was welcome, lessening the tension which palpably filled the kitchen.

He came in sniffing the air. He looked longingly at the griddle on top of the range and the plate warming on the hearth.

'Cup of tea, Ianto?' And she buttered the Welsh cakes and handed the plate and cup to him. He sat at the table. Like Mam he looked round the kitchen, not with such contempt, but he was obviously comparing it to his own trim little cottage, always freshly painted. Mrs. Ianto loved the women's magazines and within her budget kept up with modern trends.

Ianto looked at Arianwen.

'Champion Welsh cakes, cariad,' and she felt eleven again, but he was looking at her with the same sharp appraising look as her mother. Her mother saw that look.

'Arianwen's looking tired, isn't she? I keep telling her she'll have to give up teaching. It's too much for her, all day with little children and then coming home to the cleaning and the cooking and the washing.'

'Well, she'll have to give up when the babies come,' Ianto pronounced. Dad looked embarrassed, Mam glared at Ianto as if he'd stolen her lines.

Arianwen tried not to think of children. There were times when she felt that nothing would make her happier, after all she was an expert on little children, but they weren't her own, and she'd never had much to do with babies, apart from Doris's.

When she tried to talk to Tom about it he looked uncomfortable, almost frightened, as if she was suggesting something outrageous, something beyond plausibility. The son, apparently, would appear through an immaculate conception, fully fifteen and ready for a life of hard work on the farm and most nights he lay well away from her in bed, as if she shouldn't really be there. There were times when she felt that what he wanted was a more efficient housekeeper than the one he'd had to pay for.

Ianto had finished his cup of tea.

'Try a bit of Tom's home brew?'

'Just the pint then as I'm driving. I'm not used to these sheep jumping out all over the place at you.'

They all knew that once started he would be tempted by more, but he was the safest of drivers.

'Dad, will you try some, and Mam will you have another sherry?'

When Tom came in, bringing with him the whiff of cows and warm milk and accompanied by Bess, they were a cheerful little party: Mam pink with sherry, important with gossip from the village, and Dad and Ianto talking about car engines and bits of wireless.

Ianto had just asked Arianwen for a song. Beer and music went so well together. He and Arianwen were having a happy little argument about what to sing, a hymn or something from one of the shows.

Tom stood inside the door, a diffident smile on his face, and she felt a great pity for him. 'Cup of tea, cariad, I've made some Welsh

129

cakes, your favourite. We're going to have an early supper. Ianto doesn't want to be driving back too late.'

Tom looked tired, as he always did, and always that worried look on his face. Even on the day of their wedding, when it was all over and they were driving away from everybody to their hotel near Bala, his face was full of anguish, as if the happiest day of his life was full of terror.

The jolly little party lost its momentum. Ephemeral happiness escaped through the gap beneath the door. Bess went to her mat by the range, and Ianto fed her a couple of Welsh cakes.

'Mam, let's lay the table for supper. Tom, do you want to have a wash first?'

Mam looked at him for the first time.

'How are things on the farm, Tom?'

'Not too bad,' always the same answer, and then he seemed to turn in on himself as if embracing the exhaustion which assaulted him. When they were on their own, after a cup of tea, he would sleep in the big chair by the range, Bess with her head resting on his stockinged feet, and she felt obliged to turn the wireless off and had learned to move in silence, and these days she seldom sang, except when she had company.

It felt as if she was destroying an important part of herself. Sometimes she would put an old rug over him as he slept, but usually he pushed it off, looking angry in his sleep.

As she and her mother laid the table with the crockery an aunt had given her as a wedding present, she didn't listen to her mother's gossiping; mechanically dispersing knives and forks, she thought of the days before her marriage. It seemed such a short gap between starting her teaching job, and her wedding, as if her youth had been foreshortened. Those months when she first joined the choir had a ridiculously halcyon quality to them, an elegiac perfection to them quite irrevocable. Marriage kicked you into middle age. Had she ever been young?

She'd told her parents she was getting married before she took Tom home. When she thought of it now, it was a strange chronology. It wasn't, she was certain, how things were done. It was as if she needed to warn her parents.

It was the weekend after she'd accepted Tom, a hurried proposal in the car, just before she ran up the path to the manse in one of those sudden downpours when the sky appeared to be draining itself of all moisture. It had been an exhausting day, windy, the children excited and silly, restless in the classroom, and at the choir practice Elwyn had been all smiles with a new member who had long black curls and a figure like a Hollywood goddess. Nobody knew who she was, and she was creating a stir amongst the tenors and the basses, and, as always, Elwyn had been the first to talk to her, all flashing eyes and ready witticisms.

The proposal was without drama when it came, and she assented her life away, she sometimes felt, because she was in a bad mood, and felt sorry for Tom. And after that she had to convince herself that she loved him. Sometimes, that was easy. A long walk along the beach at Newport on a mild day, Bess barking at seagulls and picking up pieces of driftwood they threw for her, and afterwards sitting in a café with mugs of tea and great slabs of fruitcake, exhilarated by the walk, and Tom, relaxed, his face lit with joy, and taking her hand with that gesture of gentle possessiveness and she felt that this was what she wanted, and, briefly, the doubts dispersed on the breeze and the sounds of the sea.

Mam had been pleased that she was going home that weekend.

'There's a special concert at the chapel, with that soprano from Carmarthen. I'm helping with the teas, and I'm doing dinner for the visiting preacher on Sunday. You can do the Yorkshire pudding as yours always turn out better than mine. And you can drive him back and fore to Aberporth. It will save one of the taxi drivers having to turn out on a Sunday.'

This was the kind of conversation which reminded her that not living at home was such a good idea. Mrs. Richards was a bit inquisitive, but at least she didn't boss her around! Nobody knew, as yet, that she and Tom were getting married. Mam and Dad had to know first, and no engagement ring was to be bought before then. Every time she returned to the manse Mrs. Richards looked expectant and took subtle looks at her left hand. The whole manse, apart from the Reverend Richards and his study, pulsated with a sense of expectation.

She found her opportunity on Saturday morning. Dad had been called in from the shed for his elevenses and Mam was icing a Victoria sponge. The kitchen was warm with steam running down the windows.

'I've got some news for you, Mam.'

She put the knife down on the table and looked at Arianwen with the sharp look she used to give her when she was a child.

'What's wrong?'

'Nothing's wrong. I'm engaged, getting married.'

Her mother picked up the knife and stared at it.

They listened to the creaking of the floorboards as Dad came in, changing into his slippers in the hallway.

Her mother called out. 'There's some news.'

Her father came in, the usual look of concern on his face as if he was wondering what the two women were up to now.

'Tell your father the news.'

'I'm engaged to be married.'

'Duw bach.' And he sat down on the chair. 'Where's the sherry? Not tea when our girl is getting married.'

'Is it that farmer?'

'Yes.'

There was a smile of satisfaction threatening on her mother's plump little face.

'You're going to be a farmer's wife then are you, my girl?'

Her father got up and kissed her on both cheeks. Such a histrionic display was quite alien for a shy man of quiet movements.

Her mother was bending down getting the sherry out of the cupboard, her round bottom like a neat cushion in its flower sprigged overall. She looked up.

'Get the glasses, Arianwen, don't stand there like a village idiot.'

As they drank their sherry and nibbled at shortbread Arianwen's hands trembled. Her parents looked quite calm and she could see her mother's eyes shining with plans.

'Bring him home next weekend. I'll get the spare bedroom ready and he can sleep there. I'll order an extra big joint from the butcher's, and make my apple and blackberry pie. I've still got plenty of jars left.'

'Mam, you know farmers can't just go away for a whole weekend. I'll bring him to Sunday dinner, and I'm sure he'll appreciate your lovely cooking and then we'll have a cup of tea before going back. He'll have to be back for the milking and I like to have a couple of hours on Sunday evening to prepare my lessons for the week.'

'No chapel then?'

'No, only in the morning.'

'We look forward to seeing him, cariad,' and she watched as her father tried to make the wiping away of a tear look like swatting a pestering fly.

***

The day she took him home was the stormiest day of the year. The wind had howled across the village all night, and in the morning when she walked over to the chapel with Mrs. Richards, the salt smell of the sea was strong as if the wind had swept over the high tide and picked it up. The rain came down like doom and they held their brollies against the wind.

The chapel smelled of old damp and of mackintoshes and the women's hats dripped on to the pews. The lilies on the table, round which the deacons sat, scrubbed to Sunday holiness, smelt of death and funerals, and the old chapel's echoes had a watery timbre. As the rain hurtled against the high windows, which let in little light, they felt they were at sea in a perilous and fragile boat, and in later years Arianwen thought of those last years of chapel going, before West Wales turned to modernity, and the battle for chapel traditions was almost lost, and she felt that with her music making and entertaining of visiting ministers she was fighting against a great storm.

Tom did not come to chapel. During their courtship he had not spoken of faith. His was a hard and practical life. Arianwen would soften his life. She planned it at night lying in bed searching for the happiness which she expected, but, somehow, could not find, as determinedly errant as some irritating household item. She had been shocked by the bareness of the old farm house, nothing changed since his grandfather had come here: a house built open to the elements, a courageous fighter of a house, high on the hill, taking on the storms, not sheltering at the bottom of a hill, or an accommodating little valley, where you could enjoy the first warmth of spring. Tom had watched her anxiously as she looked round the unwelcoming kitchen with its smells of old soot and old meals, and the uncleaned windows and the table covered in papers. At least he was honest, and hadn't bothered to tidy too much, although the piece of sacking inside the door was new.

Now as he drove her towards her home, he was quiet; nervous, she supposed.

'You'll like my father. Ask him to show you his shed. He'll like that. He'll talk all day about his old wirelesses.'

She didn't mention her mother, he could judge for himself.

As she directed him to the lane for the mill, she realised how different was her childhood landscape from his, the openness of the moorland, hers, this enclosed valley, an untrodden world of secrets, she'd thought as a child. You could so easily pass the lane and not know it was there. She was proud of the mill, its lovely setting, the stockade of trees, the calmness after the turbulence of the storm; here the only remaining sign of the storm was a slight agitation at the top of the trees. At the last bend she looked at his face for the look of awe and surprise and delight she'd seen on the faces of first time visitors over the years. His face registered nothing, he said nothing, not even when he saw the wheel turning, the great whoosh of the water, and the size of the mill, and the flight of steps leading up to the front door.

'That is really so romantic,' one of her college friends had said. 'Lucky you, living in a place like this, not a boring little house in Swansea with a pocket sized garden!'

Dad was standing at the bottom of the steps with an umbrella, as if awaiting royalty. He'd probably been posted there for the last quarter of an hour, his old mac reaching down to his ankles, his cigarette becoming soggier and soggier. The dog was by his side, her tail wagging as it did for all visitors.

'We park here. We walk the rest of the way.' The man and the dog walked towards them, her father reluctant, the dog hysterical now that she saw who it was.

'Nice sheep dog. Do you show her?'

'No, she's too daft. Tell her to go in one direction she'll go in another, or go chasing a sparrow.'

Dad, she was so proud of him, so ordinary, so natural, Tom might have been a neighbour bringing a wireless to repair. Inside, her mother would be waiting, gracious, and determined to impress.

'Dad, this is Tom.'

'Hello, bad old night wasn't it? Heard a couple of trees crashing down in the woods. Go over there later, some nice logs for the fire. Ash. They burn lovely.'

'Don't have too many trees where I am. I get coal delivered for the range.'

Mam was standing at the top of the steps, five foot of regal inquisitiveness. The beef would be roasting in the oven, and all the vegetables boiling for twelve thirty dinner, and the best tea set laid out on the little table by the hearth for a cup of tea at three thirty. The old oak dining table would be opened up by the window looking over the millwheel, all damask cloth and table napkins and they would sit there trying to make conversation to hide the noises of eating.

'We'll have dinner in the kitchen as usual, Mam,' she'd said over the phone. 'It's so nice and cosy in there.'

'Dinner in the middle of the saucepans, and the smell of food, don't be so silly, girl, what would your fiancé say?'

Mam had not used his name as yet.

They sat to dinner at 12.30 precisely. The meal was perfect, testimony to Ma's efficiency and planning. Topics of conversation were equally regimented: sermon, in both chapels, teaching, behaviour of children, mild gossip from the shop, not an exciting week, no deaths, no unwanted pregnancies, no births, only the animal world had recreated itself.

Then she got down to business, her deep set little eyes sparkling.

Mam had money, and now she was going to spend it on her daughter's wedding, as she had been planning since Arianwen was born. She had hoped for a minister, doctor, vet, teacher or gentleman farmer, not in any order of preference. Tom was not a gentleman farmer, he was obviously of hardy Welsh peasant stock. Arianwen had seen all of this in her mother's face in the first perusal, as she took his coat off him in the hallway, and checked the quality of his shoes. Mam reckoned that you could tell the status of a man by his shoes. Arianwen had looked down at Tom's: highly polished for the occasion, but shabby.

'When will you be getting married?'

'Oh, quite soon.'

Sharp look, Mam's spoonful of blackberry and apple pie stopped mid plate and mouth.

'Next summer, at the beginning of the school holidays, then some of my college friends could come, and I'd love Arwyn Morgan to play the harp, and it gives Tom time to organise somebody to do the milking so that we can have a few days' honeymoon. North Wales would be nice.'

The spoon resumed its journey.

'You'll have to make a guest list.'

'Well we want to keep it small. Just friends and family.'

The look on Mam's face told her exactly what she thought of that.

Tom looked out of the window at the wheel's turning, seemingly mesmerised. Her father was feeding bits of pastry to the dog.

'That dog will have indigestion.'

'That was lovely, Mam, I don't think Mrs. Richards does such good roast potatoes as you do, and the pie was lovely.'

Arianwen looked at Tom.

'Lovely dinner, Mrs. Evans.'

Mam tried to look modest.

'Take Tom for a walk by the river while I clear up.' She nodded to her husband, 'You'd best take that dog for a walk before it disgraces itself.'

'I'll go with Arianwen and Tom.'

'No, you go in another direction. The young couple want to be alone.'

The valley was not looking its best, the storm was now spent out like an over active child and the valley was asleep like an exhausted reveller and its stillness was somehow disturbing.

They stood by the stream, feeling the damp rising through their shoes. In the distance they could hear the dog barking in excitement, and her father calling.

'It's beautiful in the spring, with the first flowers coming through, and when you have a really hot summer day, you can paddle in the stream, and we used to have picnics here, the three of us, and Dad used to make daisy chains and put them round my neck and call me the queen of the valley.'

He smiled and leaned down, as if to kiss her on the cheek. Then he touched her face with his finger. Then silence, as if he was trying to say words which would not come.

'I've never heard you say much about your parents, Tom. Did they ever take you up the mountain for picnics? I've been lucky, Mam is bossy, but kind, Dad is Dad, wonderful. I know I'm always loved.'

'My parents worked too hard for picnics. That's what it's like on the farm. Dad never stopped working. He used to come in after milking, have his supper, sometimes his head was down on the table before he'd finished eating properly.'

'What about your mother?'

'She had her hands full. A farmer's wife doesn't just look after the house and the children, you know. She has chickens, eggs to collect, help with a difficult birth, gather up the lambs in the spring, feed the orphans. My Mam had a hard life. She never went out very much after my brother died. Something died in her as well.'

'I didn't know you had a brother. You've never told me.'

'Killed when he was eight years old. She worshipped him She was never the same again.'

'You never told me.'

'Time we were getting back. Your Mam will be making the tea.'

She stumbled trying to catch up with him and it wasn't until he was standing at the top of the steps that he looked back to see where she was.

Mam had been baking.

'Just a cup of tea, Mam.'

'You'll have to take some with you, your Dad and I can't eat all this.'

'Mrs. Richards would be very hurt if I turned up with cakes. She wins prizes for cakes. Tom will take some home with him.'

There was no more time for wedding planning as Tom was looking at his watch and looking uncomfortable.

They drove back in silence. She expected him to talk about the mill, or just something about what a decent man her father seemed. There would be no mention of her mother. She was quite used to that. Her mother always overwhelmed first time visitors. A first encounter with her particular brand of bossiness was always disconcerting, but those who returned acclimatised to her, as they did to the silence and the stillness of the valley, its strange air of otherness as if you had suddenly stepped through one of the copses into a little world abandoned by the twentieth century hurtling along in its race for progress. Already the mill was an anachronism, its wheel turning aimlessly, an architectural feature, a novelty, especially in later years when the mill was converted into holiday rentals.

Her mother had kept some of the old blankets made in the 19th century, they sat like great monoliths on the top of the chest of drawers in the spare bedroom.

For many years she would look back at that day, perhaps the last day of youth, of possibilities and choices.

She'd watched him drive, a careful man, his head close to the windscreen as if waiting for some great sorrow to fall out of the sky. Dusk was beginning to fall and the sun was brooding to the west and they followed it along the moors beneath the hills till they were in the open landscape of the village.

The school was grey, growing out of the field, a little building which looked as if at any minute it could be swept away by the enormity of pulsing life about it. The sky was the deepest grey and looked like a great weight on the little building, threatening to crush it; a sliver of fading light lit the slate roof with its growth of moss. The schoolhouse lights were on, and she could imagine Hugh Jones sitting by his fire, long legs stretched out, reading, writing a poem, or planning the week ahead.

Mrs. Richards was waiting by the door. Eager, psychic. Her infallible instinct for news and novelty had told her that it was a momentous Sunday and when Tom, for the first time, waited at the door instead of going straight back to the car, all her hopes were realised.

Before Arianwen could say anything Tom spoke.

'Mrs. Richards, Arianwen has consented to be my wife. We would like you to be the first in the village to know.'

There was in his voice the pride of possession, the triumph of success, and the language like something out of some ghastly romance. She was torn between amusement and irritation. She was not a prize.

'That is such lovely news. Come in, we'll have a nice glass of sherry. I keep it only for the most special occasions. My husband does not really approve, but the world moves on.' A little gleam of rebellion on her plain little face.

'Sorry, Mrs. Richards. Milking. I'm late already.' He turned to Arianwen and kissed her lightly on the cheek.

Mrs. Richards was smiling beatifically. She watched him hurry to the car.

'Let's go and have a little glass of sherry in the kitchen, cariad fach. We'll celebrate. Samuel is having supper with John Daniels.

Discussing chapel finances,' she said, glowing with anticipation and daring as if proposing a drunken orgy.

'Just one. I've got to go and prepare my lessons for the week.' She was exhausted, the survivor of an arduous journey, a pilgrim's progress of a journey, one beset with terrors and trials.

'You'll be giving up teaching when you get married. You'll have far too much to do on the farm. I hear it's a bit run down.'

'No, I want to carry on teaching, I didn't do all that training to give it up so quickly. We'll have to renovate the farm, make it easier to run.' Her landlady looked dubious.

'Farmers don't like spending money you know. I thought women teachers had to give up when they marry.'

'Not any more. Although, we still don't get paid the same for doing the same work.'

'Oh, you're not turning into one of these angry women are you? Tom wouldn't like that.'

Arianwen put her empty glass down.

'Another one, cariad.' Mrs. Richards was quite iridescent with excitement. 'Let's hear about your plans. Oh it's so exciting. What colour are you having for the bridesmaids? How many flower girls are you having?'

Arianwen hid a yawn with her hand.

'I'll be saying goodnight then, it's been a long day.'

'What about your supper? Shall I bring up a tray?'

'I'm still full after Mam's Sunday dinner.'

When she went over to the school the following morning, some of the mothers delivering younger children were already waiting for her. They all smiled at her as if they already knew, a few of the bolder ones taking speculative looks at her waistline. Oh dear, she had put on some weight because of Mrs. Richards' over generous meals. Diet from today or a notice in the shop: 'Miss Evans is getting married because she's getting married not because she's expecting.'

Nothing was said, but she tried to look brisk and professional, adding to the effect by shouting at one of the older boys who was making rude gestures behind the very large Mrs. Hughes the cook who was waddling across the playground looking cross and important.

Inside, Mr. Jones smiled.

'Well I hope the approaching nuptials don't mean that I'm going to have to start advertising again.'

'I'm staying. You're not one of those heads who don't like married women are you? And how did you know?'

'I don't have to remind you of the extreme efficiency of village communication! Of course I don't mind married women teachers. Congratulations, and don't let the babies come too soon. I think that was the mistake we made, children too soon on a teacher's salary. Penury my dear. I've been asked to invite you to come to supper as a little celebration on Friday evening. We'll put the ghastly children to bed.'

'Can I come on my own? Apart from choir, Tom doesn't like going out in the evening very much. He says that once he's done the milking and got himself some supper, he's tired out.'

'And soon he'll have you to cook and look after him. Arianwen, my dear, please forgive me for this, but are you quite certain?'

He bent down, his dark serious eyes searching into her spirit, searching for the little serpent of doubt even now unwinding itself and threatening a journey through her blood to the plains of consciousness.

'You are very young. Youth is very brief, and then you have the rest of your life for regrets.'

He looked at his watch.

'9 o'clock.'

'I'll look forward to Friday.'

'It'll probably be shepherd's pie. I'll go and ring the bell, let the savages in. Let the week commence.'

By choir night, the whole village knew, every choir member, and, probably, every sheep meandering by the streams had bleated the news.

Arianwen tried to look as normal as possible, although the ring, tiny and insignificant, bought one Saturday morning at a jewellers in Haverfordwest, was like a rock on her finger, weighing her down with its importance, and screaming its symbolism. She didn't bother to change from her dowdy child resistant daily uniform of checked skirt, and long cardigan and sensible shoes to fight off leg exhaustion, and the varicose veins, which looking at older women teachers' legs, appeared to be an inevitable part of the pension deal.

Perfectly aware that she looked dowdy and school-marmish, she took her time, yet, as always, she was eager to see Elwyn, even though he'd be telling jokes to the men or talking to some pretty woman who'd be laughing, with her head thrown back, and a hip sticking out in invitation. Arianwen's hips were acquiring an extra burden of fat as the weeks went by. She was still so young, but she felt middle age was kidnapping her and she didn't have the will to resist her powerful captor.

Tom was waiting outside as if waiting to escort her. She fought down her irritation. Would she never again be allowed to be alone? Perfectly aware that she was being petty she smiled her most radiant smile at him and it was in that deceptive pose that Elwyn slipping out for a quick fag, frowned upon by the choirmaster, found them.

'It's the happy couple. Well done, Tom, never thought you had it in you, boy,' and he banged him on the shoulder, gave Arianwen a light kiss on her blushing cheek and stood against the wall, one leg bent, smiling at them through the smoke.

'Tell Adolf I'm on my way, just getting a breath of fresh air before we start.'

Inside, Tom was met by further back thumping, and Arianwen was surrounded by women, feeling rather silly, holding out her hand to show the ring.

Hannah, the daughter of one of the wealthier farmers who was marrying an auctioneer looked at it with a smug smile.

'Really dainty, isn't it? Really suits a little woman like you,' looking complacently at her own huge ring and pulling her expensive dress down over an expansive bosom and subtly rounded hips, she wiggled away.

Her loud self-satisfied laugh could be heard across the room. Arianwen looked round, she was in the group of men congratulating Tom, her bosom sticking out at the front, and her bottom sticking out at the back, a perfect seductive shape against the huddle of flannels and jumpers.

It was a bad tempered rehearsal; the sopranos couldn't concentrate and the choirmaster was at his spluttering, bullying worst, and the tenors and sparse basses didn't appear to have recovered from a story told by Elwyn which had rambled on beyond the official starting time, and then the choirmaster had dropped his sheet music and it took him a long time to put them together again.

After tea and biscuits, they were calmer. At the end they sang a favourite hymn, *Gwahoddiad* with such sweetness and harmony and love, that the choirmaster felt the pricking of tears in his eyes, and even Elwyn, as his voice soared into the shabby ceiling, was solemn, and when Arianwen turned round, quite instinctively as she always did to perfect sound, he was looking at her, he didn't even wink or make a silly face, but looked at her as if the song with its words of existential yearning was all for her, and she looked down at her little ring, tiny, even on her little peasant hand, as if to remind herself that this was the world she had chosen.

Thursday afternoon was one of those misfit early winter days when the warmth of the sun reminded one of summer, as an actuality, not just a remote dream. After school she had a cup of tea with Mrs. Richards.

'It's such lovely weather, I think I'll have a walk before dark.' Mrs. Richards looked disappointed. There was a catalogue of wedding dresses on the table. She'd promised her mother that she would discuss wedding plans at Christmas and had no intention of doing so before then. The wedding would be the first week in the summer holidays, the chapel was booked, and a country house hotel near Llechryd with views of the Teifi for pictures, and Mrs. Richards had deemed it a great honour to be asked to make the cake. Enough for now. Before then the school Christmas concert, quite a challenge for a new teacher and the choir's Christmas oratorio with carols at the chapel and, in a moment of glory, the big church in a neighbouring town.

'Don't you go stumbling around in the dark now. It's so easy to fall over one of those silly sheep.'

Mrs. Jones was sweeping outside the shop. She was always sweeping around the shop if there were no customers, as if the motion of the broom would sweep up new customers and the tales which her inquisitive little soul craved.

'Such lovely news, cariad. Let's have a look at that ring. Oh, lovely. It really suits a little thing like you. You'll be living on the farm then. Having it done up are you? I hear it's a bit rough. Poor Tom, he needs a good woman to look after him. Where are you going on your honeymoon? White wedding with all the trimmings is it?'

Mrs. Jones had a strategy. Ask a number of questions in quick succession and a certain ratio would be answered. So Arianwen gave her the honeymoon: North Wales, which if not sufficiently exciting would be transmogrified into somewhere more exciting. Like the more salacious Sunday papers, Mrs. Jones never allowed the truth to spoil a good story. Soon certain sections of the village would know for certain that they were going to Italy and sailing in a gondola. Bala, with its little rowing boats, faded into shabby ignominy.

They were interrupted by a young farmworker ringing the bell of his bike to warn them to get out of his way.

'Hello cariad, Miss Evans has been telling me all the details of her wedding. Isn't it exciting?'

Arianwen smiled a grateful smile at the young man and escaped.

By the time she got to the little path which climbed above the village and the spot where you could look down at it from a convenient piece of ancient rock, it was almost dusk, and the sheep were already lying down in dirty woollen clumps in the grass. Already, she could see the mountains of cloud battling in from Ireland. The glorious day was gone, and by the time she opened the door to the manse, it was dark.

By Friday afternoon she was exhausted, but was looking forward to an evening with the Joneses.

She put on a pair of trousers she'd bought during college days, and a red sweater with big sleeves which gave her a rather Bohemian look. Sal, the Head's wife, was quite racy in her style of dress and often wore trousers. The sight of her large but well-shaped bottom was much appreciated by the local wags, and the old boys who sat on the bench in the middle of the village and smoked and gossiped away their days.

Hugh Jones was laying the table in the kitchen when she arrived. Sal was looking tired, and already her bump was visible beneath a thin dress covered with huge flowers, somehow inimical to an evening of cloud and the rain just beginning to hurl itself at the steam covered kitchen window.

'Hugh's special dish, shepherd's pie. Hugh's only dish.'

Sal sat down in one of the chairs by the stove, and lit a cigarette, and blew it over her husband as he polished the cutlery before carefully laying it out on the table.

'Where are the children?'

'Bed at seven. They need their sleep.'

Hugh looked up. 'They wanted to stay down to see you, they were going to sing to you, a special song they've been practising.'

'I don't believe in children intruding on adults, Arianwen. Hugh would have them stay down with us if he had his way.'

'They're eleven and twelve, Sal, and it's Friday night. We've got to allow them to grow up a bit.'

'Hugh has more modern ideas about child rearing than me; to be honest, children bore me, even my own, and now as you've noticed,' she patted her stomach, 'another little blighter on the way. Pour us a sherry, Hugh.'

Arianwen sipped her sherry as Hugh tidied around her and Sal lit one cigarette after another, till the little kitchen was grey blue with smoke and the steam from the vegetables boiling on the hob. At home she would have opened the windows to let in the air. Here, where you could smell the sea and the salt on it when the wind was in a certain direction, she felt a yearning for its cleanliness. Sal poured herself another sherry. As she smoked and sipped she created her own world, alienating Arianwen and Hugh, and her thoughts meandered up to the ceiling with the cigarette smoke.

As they ate, and the shepherd's pie was excellent, Sal relaxed, even though she ate little and sipped anxiously at her glass of water.

'So, Arianwen, you're getting married are you? Congratulations. Young aren't you, as we were. Hugh had only just finished his teaching qualification and I was still doing my degree at Aberystwyth. Never finished it. I was doing languages. When I started I had it all planned out: first class degree, then work as a translator. See a bit of the world. Now look at me: fat housewife in West Wales. I wanted to get out of the valleys, education was the great escape route, and I've ended up like my mother.' She reached out for her cigarettes.

'There's no pudding, I forgot to make it. Pregnancy affects the brain. Get some fruit Hugh, if the children haven't eaten it all.'

There were footsteps on the stairs.

'I told those children to stay in bed.'

Ellen, the daughter, walked in. At eleven, already tall, she had her mother's indolence of movement, and her long sculptured face, but her eyes were her father's, sharp and full of humanity and a comprehension of the world.

'I can't sleep, the rain's making so much noise on the roof, I keep thinking it's coming in and drowning me.' She rubbed her eyes and threw her long hair back from her face, and already she was a young woman aware of her beauty.

'Emyr is fast asleep. He sleeps like a pig, all noisy and snorting. The roof could come in and fall over him and he'd still be there snoring.'

She looked at her father.

'Can I stay down for a minute?'

'Just a minute then, cariad,' and she went to sit on her father's lap as if she was a much younger child.

'You spoil your children. As a schoolteacher you should know better. I wouldn't have dared come downstairs after being sent to bed.'

Ellen glared at her mother, then ignored her, then stared at Arianwen with those huge all-knowing eyes.

'You're getting married. Mother says you're a fool to get married, although she got married to Dad. I won't get married. Ever ever.' She glanced at Arianwen's ring, then looked away as if it was not worthy of comment.

'I've written a poem. I'm going to be a poet. Shall I read it to you? It's as good as yours, Dad.'

'Tomorrow after school, cariad.'

'Promise.'

'Yes, I promise.' She kissed her father and ignored her mother, smiled at Arianwen, and in silence they heard the slap of her feet against the stairs and a rhythmical enunciation like the whisperings of a ghost.

'She's reciting a poem, she loves poetry.' He smiled the smile of a proud father.

'I don't know why you encourage her with all this poetry. All this Celtic twilight stuff, Hugh. Encourage her brain and if she wants to be a writer encourage her towards prose. There's no rewards in poetry. What does it achieve? If she's got a brain steer her towards something that moves the world forwards, not all this retrograde navel gazing. Make us some coffee. There's still a bit of brandy in the cupboard.'

Their conversation drifted towards safer territory and Sal, humanised by alcohol and nicotine, reported gossip from the village shop, and the story one of the farmers told her about a fight behind the pub in Eglwyswrw one Saturday night, over a girl who'd been two-timing two volatile young men. Best of all, she'd turned out to be the daughter of a Pentecostal preacher and was pregnant and didn't know which of the young men was the father of the baby.

Hugh walked her back through the rain and smothering darkness to the door of the manse.

'I'm sorry about Sal. She gets so bitter about the way her life's turned out, and this new baby is making her feel worse. She's not a naturally maternal woman. The children love her, though she and Ellen clash all the time. I might look for a post in a town where there'll be more women like her, educated women with opinions. She needs something to fight for, but she's lazy. Gives up easily.'

'She's a lucky woman to have such a kind husband. And you can cook as well. I don't think my father knows how to fill a kettle. Repairs wirelesses like a demon.'

'Tom is a lucky man, you'll be very happy together.'

She watched as his tall figure vanished into darkness and waited there in silence for her future.

There were so many times when she returned in her mind to those days, days which were not bathed in Wordsworth's celestial light of glorious youth, but a time she remembered an innocence in herself, a naiveté, as if some great epiphany awaited her: the truth of life. And as she thought about her visit to the Joneses, the celebratory meal which had turned to bitterness, she felt that she had entered a new world, so used was she to the amiable equilibrium of her parents' life with its harmony and certainties, its coherent boundaries. And marriage was a strange land full of dangers, of words unspoken and the electric power of hate and love.

***

After her parents had gone, after the early supper of ham and eggs and chips, her mother picking at it, as if the range on which it was cooked was not to be trusted, a breeding place for germs and stomach curdling disease, she sat at the kitchen table too tired to clear it. There was still the smell of frying, and though the room was draughty and the windows badly fitting, cooking smells dispersed slowly, and she felt the palimpsest of smells of meals cooked over a century, the fumes seeping into the porous stone and sliming the ceiling. There was no comfort, physical or spiritual, in this place.

As they left, as Ianto fussed round the car as if it was a recalcitrant animal to be pacified, and ran the engine 'to warm it up a bit,' she kissed her father on his warm cheek and smelt the home brew and Woodbines on his breath, she felt the most dreadful yearning. If only she could get in the car, cuddle up to Dad and then they'd all sing, even Mam after a bit of desultory tutting for show. Once a year they'd had an outing to Aberystwyth and even Mam laughed as they walked along the prom towards Constitution Hill and Ianto with one of those silly hats, and she with ice cream and toffee apple after fish and chips in the café on the front with the big steaming windows, and Dad drew a picture of her, a big round face with curls growing out at right angles, and then the journey home and she full of food and her skin tingling with salt and sun and the once a year joy of the sea, and how they'd all sang.

Those days were gone never to come back again.

The men got into the car. Her mother held back, and did something she never did, now that she was a grown woman, and married: she held her and looked at her face as if looking for secrets and pulled her towards her, and smelling of Mam smells, the powdered skin and lavender and cleanliness, kissed her on each cheek, whispered, 'You look after yourself, and remember how we love you.'

'Tom loves me,' she wanted to protest, and he did. She remembered the adoration of his patient courtship, the way, even now, in company, his eyes looked at her as if she could reassure him, 'All will be well, life is not an enemy it's a friend, use it, make of it what you can.' There was a fear in him she didn't understand, and the dark moods he had hidden so well, they frightened her. Always, she had lived her life in the sunny byways of the world. Even at the Daniels' house there had been Doris and giggling, and the top of the house picnics and the certainty of Friday and a good laugh and a tune with Ianto. Now the weeks passed and with Friday came exhaustion and two days without the children to lighten her mind with their demands, and their youth and energy which she absorbed like rations to sustain her.

She stood up to clear the table. The dog moved and she fed her some scraps. Tom slept on, he had been asleep before her little party left. When she went to wake him her mother intervened.

'Let him sleep, the poor man's exhausted. Can't he have a man to help him?' Mam, who had never really known poverty, never known what it was like to worry about money day after day. Tom was better off now, as were so many farmers in those years after the war, but like so many of them he could not recognise it and mistrusted it; ingrained in him was not a meanness, but a care which tyrannised his days and made him work himself into daily exhaustion. Even on their honeymoon when, sated with love he would sit on the side of the bed, his eyes were brooding, and every night he carefully counted the money in his wallet, and the loose change in his pocket.

She moved quickly around the kitchen, tidying and clearing. He slept quietly, only the occasional snore breaking the evenness of his sleep. Under his eyes were the dark bruises of the permanently tired, and his jaw was dark with two days' stubble.

She remonstrated with him about this.

'What's the point of shaving? Nobody sees me, only you and the dog and the stock. I shave when I have the time, and when we go out.'

'We never go out,' she wanted to say. Not quite true. She still went out; Tom had left behind the choir, chapel, village events and as she did the shopping, he didn't drop into the village shop for the obligatory gossip.

Even that morning, Mrs. Jones had asked after him.

'Tom's quite a stranger these days,' she'd said, the light of inquisitive mischief in her eyes. 'Keeping all right is he? It must be so nice for him to have a good wife to look after him. You're not looking so bright,' looking meaningfully at Arianwen's waistline, desperate with the desire to be the first one to give the news.

'Tom's wife's expecting. She'll have to give up at the school. Oh, it'll be nice for that old farmhouse to have children's voices in it again.'

Arianwen was perversely pleased to disavow her of any coming confinement.

'Just a bit of a cold, and it's been a long term. This Christmas term is always a long one.'

And this time last year she'd only started teaching and life was something shining and bursting like a spring after rain.

'Oh, and looking after that old farmhouse, nothing's been done to it for years. I thought a modern young woman like you would be changing things by now. Bit of modernisation, you could turn it into a fine place.'

'It'll be done in time. Good afternoon, Mrs. Jones.'

As Tom was still sleeping she sat at the table with her little notebook and made a list of what could be done: the magazines were full of these new fitted kitchens, she'd keep the old dresser, stain it a lighter colour, some nice china on it, scrub the old stones of the floor, colourful rugs, and have it painted white, every bit of wall, and bright curtains at the door, and put in a new bathroom, oh she had such plans, the house would be beautiful, a place to bring up all those little dark haired children, and a piano in the parlour, and one day, for a little girl quick and dancing as a sprite, her dark eyes full of music, a harp in the corner of the kitchen, and a boy clever, quiet and studious over his books at the table. She smiled at her dreams, and the light of the lamp eased the strains in her face, the lines which came with tiredness and the loss of joy.

As Tom woke up she tried to hide her notebook.

'What about a cup of tea, Arianwen? I'm parched after that home brew. Your father's partial to it isn't he? Best part of three pints he drank, and that Ianto had more than the half pint he promised himself. Hope he doesn't go over the side of the road.'

'He's been driving for years. Best driver in West Wales. I'll put the kettle on.'

She watched him pick up the notebook.

'What's this then?'

'Oh, just some plans for what I'd like to do the house. It could be a lovely home. We're a modern couple and we should have a modern house. Look at the kitchens in here,' she picked up the magazine. 'This is a big room. It could be lovely.'

He glanced at the magazine and put it back on the table.

'My mother liked it like this, she never complained. I'm just a simple farmer, I've no time or money for all this nonsense. We're comfortable like this.'

And in answer the wind gusted down the chimney and the bright hopeful rug she'd put by the door undulated as the draught lifted it. And the windows which were loose in their frames clattered in a harmony of discontent.

Arianwen knew nothing of argument. All her life, apart from her adolescent skirmishes with her mother, life had been without disagreement. These discussions with Tom tired her, she didn't know how to persuade him towards an easier life. He was reluctant to change the pattern of his life, content to follow the unquestioning path of his parents' life. She was not a woman for sulking, for the use of feminine wiles.

There was a pattern to their disagreements. He would not argue or shout, merely turn away or go to sleep, and after she made his cup of tea, he went back to his chair by the stove, drank his tea quietly, and then went back to sleep, closing her away from him. She knew that other women would have screamed, shouted, made a drama of it all, but it was not her way. If she ran out of the house where would she go? There was a farm track down to the road, usually thick with mud or cow shit. She would only make a fool of herself, floundering around in dark and mire. There was now a sadness to her life which she had never encountered before.

And the man who created that sadness was in his chair, snoring slightly, his mouth twitching, and his face a worried question mark. Occasionally, aware of her disloyalty to a man who, undoubtedly, loved her, she thought of Elwyn, laughing at the world, and how, perhaps, if she'd married him life would have been fun. But then she laughed at herself, he'd never really shown any great interest in her. She was only one of many, caught happy, in the broad illuminating sweep of his smile.

She sat at the table, the notebook closed and the magazine closed. Then soon after 10 o'clock she shook Tom awake.

'Time for bed.'

And like his father and his grandfather, he locked the door, wound the clock, and she listened to his footsteps, slow and heavy, climb the stairs, and she laid the table for his early cup of tea before milking, set the teapot warming by the hearth, a plate for his bread and butter, and filled the kettle as his mother would have done and his grandmother would have done.

By the time she went upstairs, he was already fast asleep, his face turned away from her.

When she went down next morning, two hours after he'd gone out for the milking, to put the bacon in the pan for his cooked breakfast, her notebook was gone, as was the magazine. She looked round the kitchen at the dank walls and the curtains blowing in the draught and decided that something must be done.

CHAPTER 19

It was one of the choir rehearsals, when everything was right. Their voices soared, nobody coughed or missed a note or a cue. The choirmaster was in a fine mood and used his baton with great aplomb and expertise. There was a great humour that soared into the tin roof and their voices invaded the complacency of a wet and windy evening.

Arianwen was on the tea rota. The men were milling around the hall. Men never made the tea. Something, she decided, would have to be done about that.

She could hear the laughter of the men. And she felt a happiness she hadn't felt for a long time. It was music, always music, it helped always, and singing in the choir she could forget the uncomfortable farmhouse and Tom's sadness which she could not cure.

Music transformed her. She was a very ordinary singer, but she could reach the notes. She could play the piano, and the children enjoyed the music lessons, such a welcome change from sums and writing and Scripture and history. Music could transform their lives too. She allowed them to make as much noise as they liked and, tolerant Hugh Jones, hearing the row through the thin partition, never complained.

'Plenty of music, good for them.' And on Friday afternoons she took his class for music, and the older children went home singing to shabby farm houses at the end of shit spattered lanes, and he told stories to the little ones.

'They love the Mabinogion and Gelert and Llywellyn. The stories I used to tell my own when they were little. They particularly like Bendigeidfran. There's a little dark haired boy, sits in the front, great solemn eyes taking it all in.'

'That's Ben.. He'll go far that boy. Sharp as a knife.'

She carried the heavy teapot into the hall.

Elwyn, face flushed with laughter, was standing by the door.

'Let me help you with that, too heavy for a little lady like you.'

She passed it to him.

'I may be little, but I'm pretty tough, and stronger than I look.'

'I'm sure you are, I've heard you're pretty fierce with those little children you teach. I also hear that you're very good and Mr Jones is very pleased with you.'

'Who told you that?'

'Never you mind. You know this village. Gossip flows in the breeze. Even those sheep out there, they carry it in those damn great fleeces of theirs. Sorry about the damn, chapel-going girl.'

'I've heard plenty worse. Don't you treat me like a prig. I'm not one.'

'You're a respectable married woman now.'

He made her feel uncomfortable, but, also, somewhere beneath the discomfort a little flutter of happiness was pushing at her innards, a resurgence of youth, an assertion which had been lost for so long, and she smiled.

'Time I poured the tea. It'll be getting stewed, and everybody will be complaining, especially you men, who don't even make the tea. Next time we do the rota, I'm going to put some of you men on it.'

'A revolutionary spirit. Quite a girl, aren't you? Right, you put the milk in and I'll pour.' They smiled at each other in a kind of recognition. Two women coming out of the kitchen with plates of biscuits, saw them laughing together. One of them remembered it for a long time.

She drove home through the darkness which no longer threatened, quite used now to open spaces, not missing the presence of trees, their familiar shapes, each one marking a different progress, as she and Dad or Mum walked down the lane to their valley, their torches making a shining path in front of them.

At the end of Tom's lane, now her lane, the milk churn was ready for collection. She noted that, and when the time came, remembered. The track was unwelcoming as ever, rutted, the tyres of her car sliding over the surface slime, the high hedges oppressive, all life suspended till morning, except for nocturnal creatures. Sometimes she might see a slinking fox or the pale splendour of a swooping barn owl.

That night was wet and wild. There was nothing to see except the rain and the manic windscreen wipers. As she drove she smiled, because it had been that kind of evening, Elwyn teasing her, talking to her, not one of the splendid big women he usually chose: all bosom and perfect hair. And the music had been perfect, as perfect as could be expected from a little village choir, but the singing was full of love, and had ignited that strange yearning which she had experienced for so long. Perhaps it was time for a child. A child would brighten up that dreary farmhouse more than any decoration. Tom would be pleased. He wanted a son to run the farm, but sons didn't always want to farm these days. So many opportunities now, university, even the children of the poor could be well educated. And quite right too. Embrace the future, she thought. As teacher and mother she would look to the future.

The light was on in the kitchen, and Tom had remembered to put the outside light on, so that she wouldn't trip as she walked from the car to the door. He was thoughtful in that way. The house was dreary in its grey stone, almost black in the car light, and the sheds and the outhouses were ramshackle and the tinned roofs were sagging, the guttering over the porch was leaking. It didn't look like a well-kept farm. It looked as if there was no love for it, yet Tom loved the farm fiercely, he lived for it, loyal to the precepts of his father and grandfather. The farm would endure, yet he did nothing to improve its structures. He had no time for aesthetics, the man who would tend a sick cow all night, never saw the shabbiness of it. And he was right, she knew, but she was a woman used to comfort: the cosy eccentricities of the mill, always warm, served inside by her mother and outside by her father.

As she unlocked the door, the lightness of mood left her, and again she felt the dullness which had prevailed for so long fall again, like rain, on her shoulders. A cup of Ovaltine and a nice buttered Welsh cake would lift her spirits, and she'd poker the range back to life. Tom would probably be asleep by the fire and she would tell him about the choir, the hwyl they'd found tonight, and the rare good humour of the choirmaster, and a few snippets of gossip from the matrons of the village.

The kitchen felt cold, as it always did when nobody raked the stove up and added a log. She took a log from the basket by the door. It was a log only recently brought in, slightly clammy to the touch. It would make the range smoke a bit, but she needed a hiatus before going up. Tom must have gone to bed. He must have been particularly tired. Usually he stayed down if she was out, as if his staying down was a talisman against fate, to help her arrive home safely. Bess was lying in her usual place by the stove. She wagged her tail and looked at the cupboard where her biscuits were kept and Arianwen fed her.

'Master gone to bed and left you Bess, poor old girl.' She rubbed the dog's ears and stroked her, but the dog looked bereft, as she always did when Tom was gone.

'I'll do an extra Welsh cake for you, girl.'

The dog wagged her tail, but with no great enthusiasm.

The kitchen table was clear, and there was no crockery in the sink. Somehow this touched her, although Tom had cooked and cleared after himself in the years after his parents died. That woman he'd employed, she'd only done the washing and what might be called cleaning, leaving the windows smeared and the crumbs on the kitchen floor swept into the dark corners, and the cobwebs left to hang like eerie decorations.

By the time she'd warmed the milk for her Ovaltine, and buttered her Welsh cakes, the log had ceased its spluttering and the fire was burning well, and she sat by the fire bent towards it like an old woman, and thought of the evening, and Elwyn, witty and sharp, and Hugh Jones, kind and clever, and the different kind of life she might have had with such men. It was almost midnight when she rinsed her cup out and laid the table for breakfast and thought about what she was teaching in the morning. They'd have music before sums, that would put her and the children into a good mood, and definitely she was going to do one of those songs from one of the American shows with the older ones on Friday. Humming the song, she went upstairs to her bathroom, smelling the odour of old dust in the old carpet with every step on the stairs. Looking at herself in the mirror in the cold bathroom as she cleaned her teeth, she decided it was definitely a time for change.

It was dark in the bedroom, but she was used to undressing and fumbling for her nightdress in the dark. The room was silent, no breathing or snoring, not like Tom to sleep so quietly. She put the light on. The bed was empty. Must be with a sick animal, not unusual, but he hadn't said anything and there were no calvings due, and it was too early for the lambs.

She looked out of the window, no light in the cowshed, but a faint light almost like a remnant of day in the big barn where he kept the farm implements and the tractor. Even in her thick dressing gown she shivered. In the kitchen, all was normal. Bess wagged her tail at this unexpected nocturnal interruption.

'Come, girl.' Bess didn't look too enthusiastic about a late night walk, but trotted happily behind the master's wife.

Outside it was calm, the wind slowed to a mere breath, the rain gone, that faint smell of the sea from the coast, and that faint teasing light as if the waves were reflected in the sky. The dog padded quietly beside her, snuffling at the night air. The barn door was heavy and as usual she struggled with it. The dog was whining slightly now and her tail drooping. Arianwen put her hand on the dog's head and kept it on the warm fur.

The barn was warm with the smell of stored hay and the unique pervading cattle feed. At the far end of the barn, there was the source of the faint light, the hurricane lamp. She could smell its oil, the smell of its burning, it was spluttering, the oil running low, and there was movement and another smell, and her breath like an attack and she held the dog to her and there was a movement and horror and darkness.

CHAPTER 20

Arianwen was too busy in her later life for reflection. In the huge happiness of her second marriage she embraced the pleasures of suppression. The dreams were gone. The long period of darkness was a memory she did not allow herself. And we'll never know whether in her last moments she remembered that time.

In a small community you are never allowed to forget. People look at you with sincere concern, curiosity. She was the woman whose husband committed suicide. Why? The question was in their eyes, even at the funeral. She was loved by the community, of that she was quite certain, but why does a man, not long married, take his own life? He was a peasant farmer, as were so many of them. Life was hard. You knew that, you endured with the gorse and the buzzards and the cromlechau on the hills, and the Carns, enduring the harshness of climate for millennia. Your forefathers battled with the earth and sickly animals, and you were never rich, but you carried on. For that you were born. Tom had not conformed. At the end he'd rebelled. All his life he had done what was expected of him: worked on the land with his father who had taken over from his own father who when he could work no more, sat in a dark corner of the kitchen chuckling to himself and causing no trouble, dying quickly with no fuss, and when his parents died, Tom served the years of loneliness and found himself a wife, and then he confused the woven pattern of country life. He did not endure. He did not endure. And she had not seen the sadness in him, the timidity of his existence.

Never had she felt such anger, at herself, at a world which allowed such things, at that dictator God she'd been trained to worship. And at Tom. To put her in this horror, a spectacle; to be the object of stares as if she'd committed murder. She saw it in their eyes.

Reverend Richards wanted her to pray. 'No, no,' she wanted to scream, she wanted nothing to do with this punishing God. Obediently, as if she was nine years old and chanting her times tables, she sat in the study with him and bowed her head till it ached and recited the Lord's Prayer and she walked in the shadow of death. It was the shadow she'd seen first that night, moving slightly like a tall plant in the faintest of breezes, holding the dog back as she barked at her master, then whined in her confusion at his swinging body.

The postman had found her the next morning in the yard, soft rain falling, in her wet dressing gown, holding the dog shivering by her side.

'They were like statues, her and the dog,' he said. 'Not moving. She could hardly talk. When I spoke to her she just pointed to the barn.' And in memory his ruddy countryman's face paled and his bulky body shook, and he accepted the fifth cup of tea of the morning from one of his regulars as he handed over the bills.

Looking back at those days she wondered why she went back to the village during those early somnambulistic days. The farm was sold, for a good price. Poor Tom, had he really not realised? Times were good for farmers. English people bought it. They made a mess of it. Local farmers enjoyed their little frisson of schadenfreude. It was expected that the English would make a mess of farms. It was then she should have gone away: to a big school in Swansea or Cardiff, made a city woman of herself, exhausting her body and restless mind with huge unruly classes. Sleeping and teaching, living and half living.

For a long time she was at home with her parents, her mother not knowing how to cope with her, how not to fuss. Her father accompanied her on long silent walks, exhausting walks through the trees, avoiding the village and the diffident smiles, the averted eyes, the helpless mute gazes, and followed the course of the stream as if to its source, looking for its deep underground beginnings, as if somewhere there was that deep cavern where all time began and there would be answers to all questions.

Her mother would take her a cup of tea in the morning, then come back an hour later, finding the tea cold and filmed over, and her daughter lying wide eyed on the bed, or sitting by the window, which was always slightly open as if she could escape at any time, listening to the sound of the wheel and its susurrations as it turned in its pointless round.

'Are you going to have breakfast, cariad?'

Arianwen would shake her head. Her round little daughter was thin, her eyes vacant as an old woman's, deep shadows beneath the eyes and beneath the cheek bones, and her lips were set hard with hopelessness.

'You've got to eat.' No answer.

And, always, the untouched food. And then in the middle of the night she'd find her in the kitchen, looking mad, with a knife, hacking away at a loaf of bread, eating a great untidy slice of unbuttered bread holding it in both hands, like a child, gobbling at it like a starving peasant.

They got used to the sound of her feet on the floor boards, the slight slither of naked feet on wood and rug and the creaking of the old floorboards. And they could see in their minds the tiny figure moving down the hallway.

The doctor came, sleeping tablets prescribed. She kept the bottle under her pillow, never took them, sleep was nightmare, and waking up with tears and shaking, and the moon's evil light through the trees a beckoning monster wanting to take her back to that place. When day came she wanted to sleep, reassured that there would be no nightmares in benign daylight. Her mother took back untouched trays, was frightened of her, of the blue bruised eyes which would not look at her, the despair in the long lines about the mouth where there should be plump youthfulness. The days became weeks, and there was Christmas which they ignored. Her mother went to chapel. Her father sat on that damp day, at the bottom of the steps, with his Woodbines, quite dumb to speak or help.

In the way of country mourning, the people came bearing cakes like votives; those who'd known her since childhood, the blessed little girl with the sweet voice and the smile and the laugh, hand in her mother's, and then giggling with the others outside school and telling secrets. The girl who'd come back from Cardigan changed, but no side to her, confident, but not too big for the village, and always laughing, and now there was a woman sitting by the window who looked as if she would never laugh again, all joy bleached out of her, like an old tree, dead.

There was so much kindness, and a natural curiosity. They whispered with her mother in the kitchen.

'How is she? Shall I cut the sponge? Sandwiches? Shall I slice the ham? How many spoonfuls in the pot? Oh what a pretty jug. I've got one similar, but not so nice.' And then faces would crumple.

'Oh, Arianwen fach. What can I say to her? That poor girl. That poor young man. What made him do it?'

'What made him do it?' Arianwen let the question tangle like vipers in her mind.

Would they blame her? She had tried so hard to make him happy, but had there always been in him that deep despair, some memory reaching back to the dark ages of poverty? Money? Surely not? She had enough. She would have paid for the improvements, money left by an aunt. She'd told him. And these were good times for the farmers. The milk cheque was regular. He was a good, efficient farmer. Had he been happier, a single man, with his sluttish cleaner? He came after her. He had wanted her so much. And then he hadn't, escaping in the most effective way he could.

The ambassadors from the ordinary world came to pay respects: men shuffling their feet and looking down and muttering, the minister with a prayer, the women carrying plates from the kitchen like maids, with diffident smiles, as if the power of her sorrow could destroy them.

'Arianwen fach,' and then a kiss, and a taking of the hand and silence.

They would sit for a while, all quiet, a muttering now and then, the litany of West Wales in the face of sorrow: 'Yes, that's how it is,' the acceptance of the peasant who expects nothing, and they would go away again and then others would come, and like the obedient little girl she had always been, she sat there and listened and nodded, not looking at them, looking to the wheel turning, a constant background to her sorrow.

Days were meaningless, weeks or days, time lost its tyranny. On the day of the funeral Ianto came, not her Ianto, but a serious man in a dark suit and black tie, not a singing Ianto, and he helped her into the car as if she were an old woman. Her mother travelled with her, aged in black, and her father went in another car, sitting in the front with the driver, smoking, looking small in the suit he hardly wore.

She looked out of the window at the countryside, so familiar, fading like film from trees and streams, to open moorland and wide views, and the Carns like old friends: 'I will lift up mine eyes to the hills,' she thought, but there was no comfort in a washed sky and racing clouds and the hills were unfriendly blank faces. This route was so familiar. She had driven this way so many times in her little car, singing something silly, pleased with her freedom, and now this dreadful, dreadful journey.

As is the way with country funerals the chapel was full; Hugh

Jones and a couple of the oldest children from her class stood outside the chapel waiting for her. The children looked at her. It wasn't Miss, it was an old woman. Where was the smile to make them better when they fell in the playground? Where was angry Miss when they were naughty? This woman was terrifying. Miss was coming back Mr. Jones said. 'In good time.' That's what adults always said when they didn't want to give you a proper answer. The older ones knew what had happened, awed by something beyond the day to day tragedies of their lives. Death happened to the old like grandparents, not to the husbands of lively young teachers.

Hugh Jones came up to her and shook her hand. The children stared at her, and stood straight.

The Welsh are good at death, nothing like a funeral conducted in the language of heaven.

They were all watching her, waiting for tears, which would be expected in the circumstances, controlled sorrow, nothing uncivilised, not the ululating despair of the savage. And she sat, her face tight with despair, frozen, unable to blink or frown.

And the hymns were beautiful, all the nation's songs of mourning, and then that hymn sang at all funerals: *Gwahoddiad*, and the first verse was sung by a soloist, a lovely tenor voice calling to the hills, through the open door of the chapel to those standing outside, and it was Elwyn. And then she cried, and her mother, waiting, passed her a handkerchief and took her hand and squeezed.

***

On the first day of the new term she sat on her bed in the manse, terrified. It was like being a new teacher all over again.

The day before she'd put the farm in the hands of the local auctioneers. It had been cleared, Arianwen would have nothing else to do with the place. A local building contractor had been ordered to demolish the old barn and put a modern one up in its place.

'That is not a good idea,' the auctioneer told her. 'The money you'll spend is just waste. It won't make a difference to anybody who wants to buy a farm, you can't ask for an increase to cover the output. You're moving out.' Then he looked embarrassed and clutched at his trilby, red faced, wishing he was in the pub with some mates instead of standing here in this bleak farmyard with this serious and distant young woman.

'You can't stop me. It belongs to me until it's sold. If I have to

I'll get a can of petrol and burn the place myself. Good day, Mr. Price. Let me know when the sale's gone through.' And with unspeakable dignity she walked to the silly little car and drove off down the pitted lane, mud and cow shit splashing behind her. He watched her, shrugging his shoulders.

'Little thing, fierce as a lioness,' he told his drinking mates later in one of the pubs in Haverfordwest as they waited for their Friday dinner of pie and veg and mash. 'Wants the old barn where she found her husband pulled down and another one built. Waste of bloody money. Won't listen. Says she'll torch it herself. And do you know, I think she would. Determined little thing she is. Poor woman.'

And they all sighed and watched the pretty waitress bring their tray of food, and joked with her, and then talked about the mart and the price of lambs.

Mrs. Richards was standing by the Rayburn in her warm kitchen. Rain against the window pane, wind in the chimney, sound of Rev Richards talking to a parishioner in the hallway, a tractor passing. Nothing changed. All changed.

'Good morning, cariad.' Her face was anxious. This was a new Arianwen, carrying with her the burden of tragedy. What language is there to say what is in your heart? What language can assuage the hurt of this young woman who she sometimes believed was her daughter, not of the plump little woman who looked a bit like a cross Queen Victoria. If only she could suffer for her, an old childless woman like herself, no use to anybody, and her husband remote with his God and his unreadable books and his parishioners and his meetings. If only she could take that burden from this girl, and, somehow, make her happy again. She'd watched mothers take crying children, kiss them, wipe a nose or a cut knee and all was well again. If only she had such power. And this god who lived in that miserable little chapel with the damp and the mice and the creaking organ. What good was he?

'Terrible morning, make sure you take a brolly with you, or you'll get soaked just walking over to school. Such rain in the night. Did you hear it?'

All night she'd heard the girl pacing her little bedroom, trapped like an animal, and wished she had the right to go to her and hold her and let her cry.

161

'There's a cup of tea, bit of toast in a minute, and some of my marmalade. You used to like it.' But there is no connection between what was then and what is now.

The girl sat at the table, nodded, took the tea. The toast was put in front of her and was ignored.

'I'll walk over with you. I've got to get some messages from the shop.' When she turned round from the sink Arianwen was gone. Out through the back door to avoid Samuel and his parishioner. So insubstantial was her presence that Mrs. Richards wondered whether she had really been there. The hall door slammed. Samuel Richards came in.

'Arianwen gone? Bit of an ordeal for her, first day back at school. I was going to have a little prayer with her before she went, but Mrs. Eynon, Pant y Ffin called about the Band of Hope meeting. Just an excuse. That woman is a nuisance.'

Prayer, as if prayer would help Arianwen. Only life would help, day after day, relentless, the passing of days, day and night. There was only that. Endure.

She loved having Arianwen back, but her sharp pragmatism told her that Arianwen should move away, a busy school in a city or a busy little market town, where in time, she hoped, Mrs. Richards, secret reader of romantic fiction, Arianwen would meet another man. What was there for women other than marriage? Even though it was not always completely satisfactory. The Arianwen of brightness and music and joy could not be completely destroyed. Who would she meet here? In a little village at the back of beyond, half way into the cold Irish Sea.

It was a short walk, but endless. Arianwen had not been back to the school at all. Hugh Jones had arranged for old Miss Davies to come back to the classroom for half a term, but no more.

Mrs. Jones was outside the shop sweeping leaves even though it was February. She stopped when she saw Arianwen, and leaned on her broom, like one of the roadmen, smiled her ingratiating smile, remembered that it was not appropriate. Mr. Jones, coming out to see where she was wasting her time, saw Arianwen and quickly went back inside.

'Cariad fach. How are you? Terrible day.'

Arianwen walked past her as if she wasn't there.

As it was raining, the children were already indoors. They were allowed to talk until the bell rang.

Merfyn Price, a self-important little boy who would become a bank manager in later life and never marry, was already standing in the entrance with the bell which would be rung at 9 o'clock precisely even though there was no one in the playground.

'Good morning, Miss,' he said already displaying signs of the unctuous man who he would later become.

In her classroom Mr. Jones was standing talking to old Miss Davies who looked older than ever in one of her droopy skirts and quaint old mac which she used to cycle the mile to school.

The children were silent. They were not meant to be silent till 9 o'clock. There was still five minutes for noise.

'Please be yourselves,' she wanted to scream at them.

Then when they saw the adults were talking, they gradually started to talk again. Clutching her big work bag as if it was her only connection with the real world, she looked at her class after a term's absence.

They looked blessedly familiar. Two little girls sat in the front looking smug and superior as they always did. Peter, the garage owner's little boy, had a runny nose as he always did.

Little Catrin from one of the tumbledown cottages at the edge of the village, who would always remain the little savage she was born, came to the front, a wide smile on her dirty little face. Nobody would ever tame her. She was tolerated, sometimes bullied by the other children; Miss Davies had been quite unable to make her sit up straight in the good old fashioned way. She didn't like Miss Davies. Proper miss, she liked, little miss with the dark eyes who smelled of flowers and let her sing songs, with nobody swearing at her, or lashing out or telling her to shut the fuck up.

Her miss was back and she came up to her and took Arianwen's hand in her own grubby one and looked up at her

'Are we doing singing?'

Merfyn rang the bell. Far longer than was necessary. The day had begun.

Miss Davies clapped her hands for the children's attention. They sat staring at Arianwen, confused by the choice of authority.

'This morning you will practise your writing. Open your exercise books and copy the letters on the board.' This was obviously a frequent exercise. The Welsh alphabet decorated the blackboard in Miss Davies's immaculate printing. The children, she'd forgotten what babies they were, looked bored, and stared at her expectantly. They'd always started the week with a song, allowed to make as much noise as possible, even banging the desks if they wanted to, as long as it was in time to the music.

They picked up their pencils, all fresh and sharpened by Miss Davies for Monday and started their laborious copying.

Let the children sing. That voice from the past, from the life of that other person, now lost to darkness, called to her.

'Thank you, Miss Davies,' she whispered to the older woman. 'You've done wonders, you can go back to your well-deserved retirement now.' The older woman shook her hand, smiled an embarrassed smile.

'Goodbye. My very best wishes.'

Behind her Mr. Jones smiled a smile of approval, and then escorted Miss Davies out to her bicycle.

Later, at morning break they stood in the porch sheltering from the strong wind which was driving the children exuberantly mad. The rain had disappeared with Miss Davies and her bike.

'She insisted on coming in this morning, convinced that at the last minute you wouldn't come. I knew better. Poor old girl, she's done her best, but she's found it hard. She's not criticising our more enlightened methods, but education, as far as Miss Davies is concerned, should never be entertaining or even enlightening. Noses to the grindstone. I think she found it hard work, but she did her best, but I'm so glad to see you back. I won't insult you by asking how you are. You can never tell me how you are after what you've been through.' And then he walked away.

It was a long day .Her legs ached by three o'clock. Mothers smiled their uncertain smiles as they collected their children. Somebody took her hand, but never spoke, quite inarticulate in the face of sorrow.

In the kitchen Mrs. Richards waited with the teapot and anxious eyes. In her room she sat at her desk staring at the wall. How could she go on living? Were there codes for the wives of suicides? How do you conduct the rest of your life without giving in? How had he felt that last night? Was it sudden, that desire for death, or did it come long and hard, hidden like a tumour in the darkness in his heart? And did she cause it? Always that question, that unyielding question.

The prospect of the long summer holiday frightened her. How would she use up all those empty hours? She'd always looked forward to those glorious six weeks. She'd talked about it with Tom, but for Tom it never came.

'Just a week away, surely you could pay for somebody to do the milking for a week. We hardly see each other. You're asleep every night after supper.'

'That's a farmer's life. It's the way it's always been.'

'The world's changing. We should be changing with it.'

'You're a farmer's wife now, you have to get used to the way we live.'

'It's not the way I was brought up. There's got to be some pleasure in life.'

'It was different for you, plenty of money in your family, you were a privileged child, not like me.' It had always been the way, so many discussions, and it had led to this. She could have been his salvation. It hadn't worked out that way. Why had he married her? At night she lay awake as the questions charged at her. She interrogated herself in the strong light of her self-hatred and despair.

Their discussions had always come to nothing. As an only child she was unused to conflict, had no practise in negotiation. They always let a topic fade away, and in the mornings, after the evenings of inconsequential meanderings, pursued the business of life.

Let it be, and then she had let it be for too long. No resolution; only a dark shadow swinging in a barn, and holding the dog's warm neck and the long night, cold as death in the farmyard, and in the morning the cows bellowing for milking.

Now the summer term was over. Her first in that new unwanted life. Such a blissful term it had been that first year, taking the children for walks up the hill behind the school, giving names to the wild flowers they never noticed, the novelty of looking down at the school house where Sal Jones was hanging out her washing, and the postman on his bike, small as a toy, the bleating of the sheep as the children walked past them, the summer concert, proud parents, and cups of tea in the hall, cakes and excited children, walking home through a warm dusk and the scent of unseen flowers, and walking back to the manse after school, lemonade with Mrs. Richards on the lawn, watching the sun set before supper.

This past term was without such memories, a mere passing of time, no rehabilitation. She was a sick patient who could not heal. There was constant tiredness, and temporary escape in the sound of children. There was the mechanical smile, the lesson taught with no memory of it afterwards. The children thrived They learned to read, little fingers following print along the page, the shapes made sense.

At the end of term she drove home. Her mother was expecting her to stay for the whole six weeks, but she knew she couldn't. That morning a letter had come from Angharad Morgan inviting her to stay.

'Dear Arianwen,
Come and stay for a week. I'll let you be what you want to
be. It would be good to see you.
Angharad x

When she got home she wrote a letter of reply, telling Angharad that she would come.

She walked up to the village to post the letter. She could have phoned, but conversation with adults came slowly, as if she was out of practice. The only people she spoke to regularly were Hugh Jones and the Richards and the occasional parent.

When she told her mother she could tell she was upset.

'It's only for a week, and I'll go to see Doris while I'm there.'

'Are you sure you want to stay with that family with their strange ways, and those children are so exhausting, so peculiar.'

'It might do me some good, and they were always so kind to me.'

How could she tell her well-meaning mother, desperate with the need to help her, that she could not bear her, that she needed to get away from her sadness, and the eyes that followed her every move, her every expression.

Her father understood.

'Good idea, you need to be with somebody other than us. I think we love you too much to help you. You need to be with those who are fond of you, but don't love you like we do.'

Coming from her father, this was strange, the silent man, the man who communicated his feelings through the currency of practicalities, the kindnesses of repairs and common sense. She was infinitely moved, and kissed him on his grizzled cheek,

'You smiled, girl. Good to see that smile.'

Angharad was standing in the doorway waiting. As ever, she looked as if she was waiting for something unworldly, some being from another world. As usual she was wearing a strange combination of flowing clothes which on another woman would have looked shabby, deranged, but gave her a strange romantic glamour, that glamour which made people stare at her in the street, whispering, laughing, disturbed by her lack of convention. A thin grey skirt reaching her ankles, a black top, a hint of mourning to it, a dustiness, enhancing her wan beauty. She had aged a little: a loosening of the skin around the jaw, little pockets of blue flesh beneath the grey-green eyes, some grey in the hair. Her feet were bare, veins standing out, but her smile, diffident, uncertain, was beautiful as ever.

'Cariad.' No conventional statements of regret, just that smile, which spoke of everything, of all loss, of all the cruelties of the world.

A light kiss on the cheek with cold lips, a pressure of the hand, the perfume of wild flowers from her hair. Angharad was still the same, though the world had changed.

'Cup of tea, and I've made a sort of cake. There's no name for it, I put things in a bowl and mixed, and put it in the oven and it came out looking quite nice. So we'll have some.'

Still holding Arianwen's hand she took her into the kitchen. Touchingly, there were signs of an attempt at order, and the house seemed to be in a state of shock as if a storm had attacked it, but only a little ineffectual storm. The kitchen table looked as if the usual debris of papers and sketches and crockery had been swept to the one end. The harp was gone. The kitchen floor had been swept. A dog lay on the rug in front of the range, and a tiny kitten slept in the dog basket.

'New dog called Bendigeidfran. He's very quiet and sane, and the little bundle of fur is called Pws. Blodeuwedd's knowledge of the Mabinogion came to an end and she no longer has time for whimsy, so the little cat is a sacrifice to common sense, something which is in short supply in this house. Now, tea.' She moved about the kitchen in her usual vague way, filling the kettle, then turning to the window, picking up a pine cone from the window sill, running her long fingers over it to probe its surface, then dropping it on to the floor.

Arianwen went to the chaotic crockery cupboard and picked out the cups and saucers, and found the teapot in the sink still full of cold tea from breakfast.

'Where's the tea caddy?' Angharad waved to an open cupboard. There was a half empty packet spilling out its contents. She made the tea as Angharad stood by the open door to the garden, a warm breath of breeze flowing around her.

Arianwen realised that this was the first time she'd done anything practical since Tom's death. Tom was dead. She really must learn to live again.

There was always somebody fussing over her. She could see why. Helpless in every other way to mitigate her grief, they made her cups of tea and offered her bits of food she didn't want, and nobody, ever, said: 'Tom is dead, and you have to live, and it goes on, and that terrible truth will always be with you.'

Reverend Jenkins had offered prayers, and she'd closed her eyes and bowed her head and seen and felt nothing. She did not curse that God, that rather angry God who had been offered to her throughout her life. There was no time for God now. She had to lead her life.

'Arwyn's gone.'

A coldness. Not Arwyn, too. Nobody had told her. The world had moved on in aeons while her world turned slow.

'What happened?'

'He's not dead. Easier if he was. Oh no, I'm sorry Arianwen, that's one of the glib remarks I make to myself and the children, so silly. I shouldn't have said that, I'm a silly insensitive woman. Everything I say is wrong. I'm sorry, I didn't mean to upset you.'

'Upset? I don't think that word has much meaning now. Upset is a silly little word for silly little feelings. Nobody talks to me about death. They avoid the word. They can't talk to me. Nobody's normal with me. I've got to go on living, Angharad. It helps if people treat me as they always did. I'm still Arianwen. I had a husband. Now I don't. I'm still the same person. Where's Arwyn gone?'

'Another woman.'

'A young woman?'

'No. Why would a young woman want an old man like Arwyn? That Siwan. She wouldn't want him now. She's done well. Well known Welsh artist. That's what I wanted to be: pictures in

London galleries, the Royal Academy. Your pretty friend lives my life. She was a very long time ago.'

'So where is he?'

'The world's dullest woman. He lives with her in a neat little bungalow somewhere on the way to Aberystwyth. A widow. He's been going round the county giving piano lessons and he taught this woman's ghastly daughter to play. Badly, I'm certain. Nothing that came out of that woman would ever have any talent. She's plump as a pigeon, corsets and navy costumes from the drapers, and she's got him in sports jackets and suits like a bank manager and he's shaved off his beard. He now gives piano lessons in her horrible parlour full of brass ornaments and hideous photographs.'

'How do you know that?'

'I went up there and pushed my way in and swore at her and asked for my husband back, and she wouldn't give him back to me.'

The lovely face puckered in anger. She looked like Blodeuwedd when she used to have her tantrums, defiant and beautiful, self-absorbed, inhuman.

'It's probably one of his little episodes. Let's go into the garden. Such a lovely day. Bedwyr will be home soon. He's working at the book shop in the morning to earn some money. He's home from Cambridge.' She smiled proudly. A mother again.

'How is he enjoying Cambridge?'

'I don't know, I don't think enjoyment is something which Bedwyr regards as important. They work them very hard. He approves of that. When I ask him questions he gives me one word answers. He thinks I'm so stupid that there's nothing he can explain to me. He's studying Mediaeval History. All that past. I don't really see the point. Now let's talk about you.'

And then she stopped. Like everybody else she couldn't find the right questions, and Arianwen could see her face working its features to the appropriate expression, a widening of the eyes, a tightening of the lips, and adjusting the smile to the right width for mourning.

'I remember reading the line somewhere or hearing it. 'Living and partly living.''

'T.S Eliot.'

'Whoever it was he was right, that's how I feel. I'm alive, my body tells me, but nothing moves on. It's as if I've come to a halt. This

169

is what they call grief. All darkness. Blodeuwedd. How is she?'

'In the fourth form. A bit wild. I don't know what to do with her. All black clothes and red lipstick. Rebellious. Who am I to talk? She misses her father, blames me. Boyfriends. Some a lot older than her.'

'What will she do?'

'Wants to go to Art School. She has less talent than me. It's college life that appeals to her. She wants to go to college in London, to get away from here. Me all over again, but I'm not my mother. I won't oppose her. Sometimes she says she wants to go to drama college, but she can't act, she's too selfish and pig headed to put herself into somebody else's character.'

'She's young, give her time.' They sat in the garden till Bedwyr came. He looked just the same, just an extended version of his former self, taller, a wider jaw, still the air of intense personal conflict as if he was always at war with himself or the person he was trying to be. He was dressed in black with a heavy sweater and big black boots even though it was one of the hottest days of summer.

'Bedwyr likes to hide as much of himself as possible,' his mother whispered as he came across the garden towards them, trampling the long grass of the again neglected garden.

He stopped and looked down at them, uncertain of what to say to the two women.

He looked at Arianwen. He was in the face of her grief, a gauche boy again, uncertain how to speak to her, and she was no longer the happy girl who had been his friend and tolerated him when he felt his whole family had turned against him.

'Arianwen.' He blushed, and sat down on one of the broken-down chairs.

How easily she'd spoken to him, that young woman, now each word uttered was a painful stone dragged up from the depths of her throat, a knife scraping at her mouth. She could no longer make it easy for him. She couldn't think of any of the usual questions. There was no etiquette for the grieving, as there was none for the sympathisers. The silence between her and Angharad, the sun soft on their faces, was heavy with unspoken sympathies, but now there was a silence which scratched at their throats, demanding to be broken.

Angharad stood up.

'I'm going to see about some lunch. I'll call you when it's ready.'
It was already three o'clock. Not that Arianwen minded, but she was her mother's daughter, and even now the rhythms of daily life gave her purpose, even on the darkest days when she had sobbed all night and cursed the sight of daybreak.

Bedwyr looked at her, looked away then looked at her again, his eyes intense behind the glasses which masked his face and gave him a look of benign vagueness which was not his real self.

'My father's gone. Blodeuwedd cares, that's why she's even fouler than she used to be, causing trouble to my mother. Mother thinks he'll come back, as he always did, but he won't come back this time. He's become what he really is, an ordinary little man with no great ability. Mother realised a long time ago that she's no artist. But my father held on to the idea that he was some kind of musical genius, that he was going to be a concert harpist. And what's he doing? Teaching idiots the piano in somebody's front parlour. All the time, in school, he embarrassed me with the great Bohemian act and I had to listen to what they called him. I don't want him back. He can stay with that woman. Mamgu left a lot of money to Mam, Dad won't get a penny of it, and I get a grant. We don't have to live like this – ' he made a gesture encompassing the wilderness of the big garden ' – we choose to.'

'Tell me about Cambridge. I hear it's a beautiful place.'

And his face was young again, a boy's face, plain and skinny, lacking the handsomeness of his parents, and his sister's alien beauty, but lit with something like real joy.

'It's wonderful, I want to stay there forever.' Bedwyr, unlike his parents and sister, had made his accommodation with life and it was a happy one. 'I'll work hard to get a First, do a Master's and then do a doctorate. Then perhaps I can stay there. I don't want much, a quiet room and books. I don't care for company much, I only want peace and quiet. There never was any in this house. I'm happier now than I've been all my life. Childhood is so frustrating.'

He looked at her.

'Sorry, I've been talking about myself. That's what we Morgans do. I don't know what to say to you, so I won't say it. Forgive me.'
He wandered off towards the house and for a long time she sat there, quite numb in the warm sun, and realising that she might be hungry, headed for the kitchen. Angharad was standing holding

the kitten, and stroking it. The dog wagged his tail and went back to sleep.

There was a big loaf in the middle of the table, butter melting on a plate, a hunk of cheese and a bowl of tomatoes.

'Help yourself, cariad. I was going to go shopping before you came, and boil a ham, but I forgot. You know how it is, time crashes around you.'

She sat down and hacked at the loaf. Arianwen took the knife from her and sliced it neatly, and buttered it, slicing tomatoes and cheese.

'Go and get Bedwyr.' She filled a jug with water and set out plates.

This was to be the pattern of her week with the Morgans. Life was formless, the days amorphous, the children came and went. Blodeuwedd came home from staying with friends, and complained about her mother and talked of escape.

When she called to see Doris the children were home and her mother-in-law staying and now with the great obstacle of Tom's death between them, the two were quite unable to resume their friendship in the easy way they had always done in the Daniels household. They drank tea like strangers, and the children played around them. Doris was a plump matron. Where was the skinny little maid? Quite gone, quite gone, those two laughing girls.

She didn't stay for long. The mother-in-law kept sighing as if this was the only way to behave in the presence of the recently bereaved. Doris was uncomfortable, the children bored by their mother's visitor.

On the doorstep Doris kissed her.

'I'm sorry. It wasn't supposed to be like this. Mother-in-law said she'd take the children out shopping and for tea in a café but at the last minute she said she had a headache and couldn't go. Perhaps another time, when the children are back at school, but you'll be back at school then as well.' They both knew that something was lost, and would never be found.

Bedwyr walked her to the car on the day she left.

Angharad was still asleep. Blodeuwedd was at a friend's house.

'Sorry about Mother. She was very late to bed last night. She's worried that this friend of Blodeuwedd is a boy. It could well be, knowing my silly sister. She just goes from one mess to the next. Her last report was dreadful. This family is falling apart.'

'Are you staying here for the whole summer?'

'No, I'm going on a walking holiday in France with a friend.'

'I went to Paris once with a friend.'

'Not that Siwan? The one who caused all the screaming and shouting. I thought Mother was going to kill herself. I think I've hated my father ever since. I've seen his weakness and his posturing. I idolised him when I was little.' His bitterness made his face crease. He looked older, spent, as if the world was more of a burden than he had ever expected.

'Enough of my father, what about you? How are you going to spend your long teacher's holidays?'

'Home to my parents.'

'How strange! Just like a child again.'

'I've nowhere else to go. The farm's been sold.' She turned to her car and fumbled with the lock.

He kissed her on the cheek, the touch of his young skin a reminder of life.

'Look after yourself, Arianwen.' He turned away, and she watched his gangly figure walk up the weed ridden path, his shoulders rounded with sadness, Bedwyr who felt too much, too burdened with a helpless mother, his wild sister, and the absent father, Cambridge his only sanctuary.

And there she was, going back to her mother. So much sadness in the world. Nobody had told her when she was a child. Back to being a little girl again in her mother's house, but a little girl burdened with knowledge. The boy was right. There was no cruelty in him. It was his analysis of her condition, infantilised by her tragedy. He didn't hurt her. This was Bedwyr, candid, honest, and she rather loved him.

One night when she sat up with him, waiting for Blodeuwedd, he talked about his friend Andrew, a young Englishman reading theology, 'Decent for an Englishman and a God squad type, he's spending the summer volunteering at some home for disabled people. And people who've been dumped there by their families because they can't be bothered with them anymore. Perhaps we should do that with Blodeuwedd. Trouble is they'd soon send her back. The girl's impossible. I'm fed up with always being the good one.'

'Why's your friend spending his summer doing that?'

'Expiation of imagined sin, he tells me, guilt because he's so lucky. Feels the lack of tragedy in his life. Oh God, I'm so sorry. Mother says I don't think enough about others' feelings. Too many bloody feelings in this house. I am so sorry about my lack of tact.'

Blodeuwedd came in, bringing the scent of wildness with her, her eyes huge and black in her white face, her body swaying a little as if she was still dancing, the reek of cigarette smoke in her clothes, and the sweet smell of gin on her breath.

'Where've you been? Mother's worried sick.'

'None of your business. You're my brother not my keeper. Just because you're at bloody Cambridge you think you're so wonderful. I can't wait to get away from you all.'

'You're fourteen, you stupid girl. You should be at home doing your homework, not out till all hours. No wonder you're so useless at school.'

Upset by their bickering Arianwen went up to the little room where she'd always slept. For a long time, she sat on the bed and stared at the wall.

As she drove the few miles home, she didn't think of the Morgans, but of an unknown young Englishman atoning for non-existent sins by spending the summer with those 'less fortunate than himself'.

And she began a new pattern to her days: the walks avoiding the village, her only companion the dog, walking through the closed little valley, following the stream, often sitting by it for hours, looking unseeing into its cool glassiness, the dog restless by her side, and coming back to the house, to evenings of silence, and the long nights which she dreaded, pacing in her room, the dread as daylight came, and her parents' helpless kindness. And, always, her own darkness where no light came.

Yes, the organisation she wrote to would be most pleased to take on volunteers. The work would be menial, but perhaps she could read to patients, and there was one home not too far away who would be pleased with her help for a month.

She was assigned feeding duties: serving, clearing and washing up. This took up the whole day. Occasionally she read to a patient, but, mostly, there was no time.

'Why do you do this?' one of the cleaners, Mari, asked her as she washed up after lunch. 'You wouldn't catch me doing this if I didn't have to. Somebody said that you're a teacher, long holidays, you could be at home enjoying yourself.' She glanced at Arianwen's wedding ring. 'What does your husband say? Must think you're mad. You could be going away on a nice holiday somewhere. No kids, I suppose, not with that slim figure of yours.'

Arianwen turned away and reached for more plates to wash. Just a few days and, already, her hands were raw and red from the cheap washing up liquid. Each night she rubbed cream into them and wore thin gloves to bed, but at least now she slept, hour after hour, till her alarm clock woke her up and she'd look round her prison cell of a room, hear the birds singing, louder and clearer than she'd heard before, as if they were alien to her, or she was a stranger come back from another world where the birds never sang.

Mari was a decent enough woman, but she was nosy, and it grieved her when people didn't allow her into their world. Arianwen challenged her with her quietness, her sadness, the way she'd only talk about the work, which was not important, and avoided all the questions about herself. Mari watched her, knowing there was a story to be told.

A pretty little woman, well educated, a teacher, she'd found that out when she was dusting Matron's desk, did not come to work in this place for no reason. And what kind of husband did she have to let her come here, even if it was only for a short time? Alf didn't like Mari working here.

'Why don't you go and work for some posh women in their big houses? They might even pay you more. Why have you got to work with all those cripples? Sad, I know, but they're still cripples or loonies.'

He didn't understand that it was more interesting here, a big staff to talk to, not being alone in the house with some stuck up old biddy who'd only talk to issue the next set of orders or complain about something. It was the gossip here Mari liked. Always something going on. And those nurses. Quite racy some of them. And always one falling in love with a doctor and crying her eyes out in the kitchen. As good as those stories in the magazines, and Alf was glad enough of the money she brought in, a bit extra to spend down the pub.

Mari liked women who gave her something of themselves, smoked in the toilets with her, cursed anybody in authority. Bit of

175

a laugh kept you going. Not much laughing from this one.

She tried most days: 'How are you today, Arianwen?'

'Quite well, thank you.'

Didn't look well at all. Her face was thin, her hands were moving all the time, that pretty face set in strong lines. If she smiled a bit those lines would go. She'd be a pretty young thing again. Must have split up with her husband. Yes that was it. Get her out of herself. Night out with the girls.

'Gang of us going to the pictures in Carmarthen tonight. Want to come with us? It's *Roman Holiday*. Have you seen it?

'No.'

'Come with us. It's a lovely film. I've seen it three times. Oh that Cary Grant is so handsome, and that Audrey Hepburn. Imagine looking like that. I like a bit of romance,' and she looked despairingly round the shabby kitchen with its chipped cups and torn lino of indeterminate colour.

Jane, one of the other orderlies came in, buttoning up her overall.

'I was just saying to Arianwen, come to the pictures with us tonight.' They watched as Arianwen picked up the tray with the porridge saucepan and ten bowls and went out to the ward.

Mari rolled her eyes. 'Bit stuck up really, isn't she? Because of her being a teacher, and too good for us. So why is she here then? She's not one of the religious types doing it to be a good girl for Jesus is she? Strange.'

'Leave the girl alone, if she doesn't want to tell you, that's her business. C'mon, time for a fag before we get started for the day. Matron's talking to the gardener so she won't be round for a bit. Look who's here then. God's gift to women.'

Dr. Price was good looking and loved himself for it. The nurses loved him and he broke hearts: a perfect stereotype in white coat and stethoscope and boyish lick of hair on his forehead. Arianwen was a disappointment to him. The little woman, hardly more than a girl, wouldn't flirt with him. Married yes, but plenty of married women were glad to spend time with him.

She had an innocence about her, looked him straight in the eye, not like the nurses who gave him coy looks from underneath their mascara which Matron tried to ban. This woman treated him as if he was an irrelevance, a rather silly boy, as matron did.

Bit of a challenge. 'Would you like to have dinner with me? It must be miserable sitting in one of those poky little rooms every night. Bit of a woman of mystery aren't you? How about Friday? Could go to Swansea.'

'No thank you.'

He put on his little boy face which nobody ever resisted. He tilted his head forward a little, so that his soft brown hair fell over his forehead in an appealing kind of way.

'You intrigue me. I don't give up easily.'

'Excuse me, I've got to get the afternoon tea trays ready.' She looked down towards the ward.

'Matron's coming.'

He jumped up. Matron did not approve of doctors in the kitchen and she was thoroughly immune to his charm, as was Arianwen.

As she walked down the ward, Danny came shuffling up to her, a half smile on his undefined face. It was the face of a child, smooth, untouched by life, pale and grey from institutional life, an unfocussed look to him as if life had never offered anything worth his concentration. Danny had been in the home for a long time. He didn't know how long. Nobody on the staff knew and never showed any interest. He was one of the quiet ones. Not a nuisance in any way. Easy to overlook. It was difficult to say what was wrong with him. He had family somewhere, but they never visited. He limped a little and one of his legs dragged. He spoke quietly, mainly in monosyllables, as if he knew that he had nothing to say to the world, and nobody would listen to him. He rolled his eyes at the end of an utterance as a kind of visual punctuation. He was treated as a friendly old family dog, or servant, useful for sending here and there. He liked to help with the serving of food. Slow, but mainly efficient, he slopped the tea occasionally as he hobbled up and down, smiling at everybody, showing his few yellow teeth. Best of all he enjoyed clearing up and collecting the plates and bringing them to the end of the ward to the table which was used for serving up. He would have loved to wash up but he wasn't allowed inside the kitchen.

Arianwen was teaching him to read. She'd found him reading a book upside down and pretending to follow the words with his finger, his lips mouthing unspoken words. She'd taken the book from him and turned it the right way round.

'Shall I teach you to read, Danny? After supper every night for twenty minutes, after I've cleared up.'

He smiled his untidy mouth at her.

'Yes, Miss.'

'Did nobody ever teach you to read, Danny? Didn't you go to school? When you were at home with your family?'

'I never was at home. There was a big house with a lot of us, and then there was another big house with a lot of us. And then there was here. I like this house best.' He rolled his eyes and smiled at her, proud of his unaccustomed volubility.

'I'll start tonight. After tea.'

What else was there to do in the evenings? Try to read a book or a magazine, sit on her bed to stare at the walls and tame her thoughts, sit in the shabby sitting room which the volunteers shared with the nurses who regarded them as a nuisance, and made sure they didn't get the comfortable seats and they had to sit by the door on the hard chairs as if in a doctor's waiting room. The only other volunteer was Sidney who was training to be a doctor, and was terrified of the nurses, and sat on one of the hard chairs sipping tea and reading his medical text books and never spoke to her, which made her rather like him.

When she asked Matron if it was all right to teach Danny to read, she expected her to say no. Bewildered by so many rules, most of which seemed pointless, she thought there would be objections, although she couldn't see why.

'If you want to give up your spare time it's up to you. I don't think you'll have much luck. I think he's a bit simple.'

'He's not simple; low intelligence, perhaps, but with my help he might learn to read a little. That'll enrich his life. Don't think he's ever been taught. Nobody can learn without being taught. Not even the brightest child.'

'I suppose you know, you're the teacher, even though you're very young and idealistic. You'll learn in time that it's best not to take too much interest in the patients. That's not what you're here for. I'm the expert here. I don't suppose it'll do any harm. As long as it doesn't interfere with your proper duties. You volunteered as a ward orderly. If you think it's beneath your dignity then I suggest you look elsewhere. I don't know what you're looking for, or running away from, but you won't find it here.'

And that for Matron was the end of it. She never asked how Danny was getting on. The young woman was showing off because she was a teacher . Let her make a fool of herself.

Danny loved to hold a book in his hand. He loved to turn the pages as he saw some of the other men do. It was hard work. Harder than teaching any of the sniffly-nosed babies back in the village, and this was in English. All those phonics in English to confuse the faltering brain.

She taught him the old fashioned way: recognising letters, seeing, gradually, that letters set out in a certain way had meaning. By the end of the month he had made some progress.

'I'll be back during the Christmas holidays to help you again Danny. Keep practising.'

Like a child he had no concept of time. Christmas would happen in due course as it always had, as the daylight woke him in the morning before the nurses came to nag him. Institutional life was a grey fog of routine, occasionally dispersed by Christmas or Easter when the wards seemed more colourful and there was a quicker beat to the home's rhythms. The kind lady would come back and her sweet round face would encourage him and he would please her, even if it was hard work. Nobody else smiled at him and encouraged him as she did.

After she had gone, he held his reading book to him and stared at the words every night, mouthing those he remembered and followed them with his fingers and waited. The nurses laughed at him, but he put his book away in his cupboard every night and took it out first thing every morning even before he had his cup of tea.

At half term she told her mother that she would be away for Christmas.

'You can't do that. It'll be quiet, just the three of us, and Auntie Ella. I know it's difficult, Christmas is a time for remembering. We came to you last Christmas and when Ianto brought us down on Christmas Eve there was a bit of snow on Carn Fawr. It looked pretty, and you had that Christmas tree in the window with the lights and it looked so lovely as we came up the track, and Ianto started singing *Silent Night*.' Then she'd turned away, tears on her face, ashamed of herself.

'I'll come back for New Year. On New Year's Day, and can I bring a guest?'

'That'll be nice. Is it somebody who works there? Is she a new friend of yours? I'm glad you're making friends. There's not much to do in that village. I wish you'd come back to live here. There's a lot more life here. You could live here till...well, as long as you like.'

'It's one of the patients. He's got no family. Or none who show any interest in him.'

Her mother looked shocked. 'Is he one of those cripples? It won't be easy for him here. And is he all right in the head?'

'He can walk slowly, we can help him up the steps, and the mill house is all flat. He'll be no trouble. And he's not dangerous in any way.'

Her father came in, bringing the smell of winter with him.

He looked at the two women, alike in so many ways: small and determined little chins sticking out for battle.

'Nothing wrong is there?'

'Arianwen wants to bring one of the patients from that place home for New Year and she's going to be there over Christmas.'

'She's a grown woman and she's got to do what she thinks best. We can go to your sister's for Christmas as she asked. Save you a lot of bother. This patient chap, he's very welcome here. Somebody to talk to. Hope he likes radios.'

For once her mother had no reply for her husband. Her little face puckered as if she had something to say, but she turned to the sink and began to wash the dishes in silence.

***

A term passed. She'd always loved the second half of the Christmas term: the children over excited, the choir preparing for the Christmas concert, the children practising for their concert for proud parents, and walks round the village before dusk, houses lit and decorated, holly wreaths on some doors, the sense of expectation in chapel services. Now it was emptiness. The first hysteria of grief had gone, now there was emptiness, numbness, ever present guilt.

The school day seemed long, yet too soon she'd be walking back to the manse, too tired for one of her walks, walking quickly past the shop before she was accosted, and, in the manse, Mrs. Richards waiting with the teapot and kind words, her face anxious, wanting her to be herself again and how could she tell her she couldn't find the girl she was, gone somewhere into darkness or the grey infinite fog of her days.

Reverend Richards asked her to pray and once or twice she felt that something answered her, a quickening of the heartbeat, a new coolness about her as if her body had moved beyond her, taking her away, or was it herself answering from the distance of her dead spirit?

She learned to avoid them, the kind couple who treated her like a daughter who had been found for them. After her supper which was always early, she went to her room, saying she was tired or had lessons to prepare, and they said nothing, though yearning for the lost evenings when they'd sat round the table and drunk tea and talked about the village and the world. And in her room she lay on the bed looking at nothing and fell asleep in her clothes, and woke in the early hours, frightened, always that image in her mind, stark as etching behind her eyelids, gasping for breath, and lay awake a long time and then woke exhausted when Mrs. Richards brought her tea at seven thirty.

How could she go on living in this way, partly in the world and partly beyond it, this fraction of a life, a young woman still, every breath a kind of defeat?

One day, Hugh Jones asked her to stay after school for a brief chat. There was a time when they talked all the time, sitting together for school dinners, a cup of tea together in the afternoons when the last child was gone. Now she was solitary, her own prisoner, trudging out of school as soon as the children had gone. She no longer stayed to look proudly at the classroom, the colourful posters, always a jug of flowers on her desk, latest reading books on the shelf, and something interesting on the nature table: the skull of a bird, a nest, a fallen egg, The classroom had not been changed since that last terrible day: posters peeling, and some dusty faded items on the nature table.

It was November, the bleakest of months, and there was a hint of snow on Carn Fawr, and the wind had turned east, and the stove was blowing back smoke. Her classroom looked as forlorn as she did.

'You look so tired. How was half term? What did you do?'

'Went home. I didn't do much. What about you?'

'Tried to keep the children quiet. I wrote a poem.'

He looked pleased with himself. She had read one of his poems once, not fully understanding the complexity of form but something in it, a cry for humanity, made her heart stop briefly, as if she'd been taken into another world, a world where everything was sharp, a clarity which she'd never seen before, and, somehow, the kind, pragmatic man had become somebody else, somebody who awed her a little, a man who moulded words, till they spoke to her like prayer.

'What was it about?'

'Never ask a poet what he's writing about. It's terrifying, because when you try and explain it sounds quite pointless, trite and shallow, and you go back to it and yes it was trite and shallow, but this one, when I've drafted it some more, I might send it to the National Eisteddfod.'

'Another try?'

The previous year he'd come third, not the glory of the crown, but his name on the list somewhere. Not bad for a teacher from Penfro he'd thought. His wife had laughed.

'No money to be made from it. Why don't you write a novel somebody might want to read. Something with a story, not the whining self-absorption of poetry.'

'I would like to see you in the Chair.' Arianwen looked at his kind intelligent face, another one of the people who'd tried hard to help her over the last few months, but she had put herself beyond help, her world as distant from theirs as a far planet.

There was a time when she had gone to the Eisteddfod, as a student, and the summer before she started teaching, and always rather loved the overblown celebration of nationhood with the stalls and the mud, and the poor acoustics in the main tent, and the silliness of the Druids tripping along in the absurd robes. And she became later in life a member of the Druidic order, but that was when she was herself again, and that comes later, much later, when she had learned to laugh again, and there was somebody to laugh at her, a little portly thing in green robes rather too long for her.

'Sal would laugh at me. No money in it. Too many poets in Wales chasing too few crowns and chairs. But we are not to talk about me.'

And the beautiful brown eyes, soulful, so essentially Welsh, looked into hers, intense and fond and full of sympathy.

'I'm worried about you. You look so tired.'

'Is there something wrong with my work?'

'No, but the spirit's gone.'

'I do everything I've always done, the children are learning. Everybody who came in last year can read. They'll be ready for your class when the time comes, except for Carus and you and I know that she needs special education. I wonder whether there will ever be time when children like her will go to special schools where there are properly trained teachers to help them. We have a little bit of singing now and again.'

'I think you came back too early. You should have had more time off.'

'I think there was a limit to the amount of compassion the governors could show me.'

He smiled. 'On the whole they do what I tell them to do,' and he smiled the smile of a determined man. 'And I'm sorry, it's none of my business what you do in your school holidays, but this volunteering work you do, it must be exhausting. Why do you do it?'

'Because I think that if I don't do it, keep busy all the time, I'll be paralysed by sorrow and guilt and I'll never move again, or be whole again.'

'Why don't you do something easier, less painful? I can guess what some of the patients are like, it's not easy.'

'Listen, whatever I see again will never be as bad as what I've already seen.'

And the tears came and she was crying and he was horrified and ashamed.

He stood up, touched her on the shoulder.

'I'm sorry, Arianwen, how can I possibly understand what you've been through? I feel a great sympathy for you, but I know that's no help. There's nothing like the helplessness in the face of tragedy.'

'I've not told anybody before. I'm not sure whether he was dead when I found him.'

'I think he was, they ascertained at the inquest didn't they?'

'I think his eyes were open and they were accusing me. I caused his death. We were too far apart, too different. I destroyed him and I have to live with that for the rest of my life.'

'I'm sorry.'

'No, it's the first time I've told anybody that. I've never told my parents, it would upset them too much, and my friends they're frightened of me now, as if I'm not the person I was. I'm not I know, but at the core it's still me, and that's what I have to strive for, to be that person again. You're a good friend to me, you've not circled around, frightened of me. And I'm grateful, I know nobody can help me, only time and myself. It's bad enough losing someone through illness or accident, but this is different. I'm guilty and I sometimes hate him. Anger is destructive. I've always been a rational kind of woman, nice sensible Arianwen, and now I'm just a manic concoction of feelings and they've got to be unscrambled, and all the time there's the grief like some animal scrabbling away at me.'

'Have you spoken to your doctor?'

'He offers me tablets to make me smile, to make me feel dead and numb. I've got sleeping tablets but I never take them. What's the point of artificial sleep? I'm only deceiving myself and my body.'

She stood up. 'I'm going now and thank you. I'll try to look for that lost spirit.'

He watched her, as tiny as a child, an unhappy child, as she walked through the playground, and as she always did looked up and down although there was little traffic that time of day, only a tractor or a truck, and it being winter there were no children playing on the little bit of grass where they sometimes played amongst the sheep and their droppings.

The next morning, he heard loud singing from her classroom, not some dutiful little song, but something riotous, rather silly.

Christmas at the home was slightly hysterical, a bit of a pantomime in which Matron smiled, a grim, unpractised kind of smile as a concession on Christmas morning.

Mari came in for an hour to give the kitchen a quick sweep, and a cup of tea and to pick up the gossip.

'What are you doing here on Christmas Day? You should be at home with your husband.'

Every now and again she had a try, seeking out the core of Arianwen's mystery. Her questions had become rhetorical, there was no chance of answers, and she no longer waited, her sharp little eyes, which seemed to be permanently squinting against cigarette smoke, scrutinising Arianwen's face for truth.

'You'd better put that cigarette out. Matron's about.'

Mari swore and opened the window and threw the butt out at the winter-worn lawn. Then she waved at the cigarette smoke.

'I've got a load of his bloody family coming. Did the veg yesterday. Turkey's in. Everything's ready. Home for a glass of sherry now, and something stronger later. Made the puddings in

November. My sister-in-law made the cake. Hope she put a good slug of brandy in it or it'll be dry as sand. Cup of tea?'

'No thank you, Mari.'

'You sure? Tea keeps me going. They'll miss you, your family. You looking for a place in heaven? Done something really bad? Or you got religion bad? We had one of those last year, talked about God all day to the patients, one told him where to stick his god. God hadn't given him back his two legs what he lost in the war. Never did anything useful, just got in the way. I asked him what he'd done as well. Blushed. Never answered. Matron told him to leave in the end. Sorry, not much time for all this God stuff myself. That's what's wrong with Wales, too much God. Sorry, didn't mean to offend you. Right, I'm off. Hope the turkey's not too tough when you get it. That cook hasn't got a bloody clue.'

As she opened the door she turned back, 'I hear you're taking Danny home. He's beside himself with excitement, hope you don't regret it. Merry Christmas.'

Danny had been boasting in his garbled voice ever since she'd told him when she first arrived after discussing it with Matron who said: 'It might have been better if you'd made it just for Christmas Day. A few of them get taken by families for Christmas, if they're manageable, and if they remember they exist. Danny hasn't been anywhere since I've been here, and I've been here for getting on twenty years, except for the trip we organise in the summer to Barry or Porthcawl,' and she half smiled. 'He does enjoy that, especially paddling in the sea and sitting on the front eating an ice cream and getting it all over his face. Such a sad life he's led,' and then she was stern again, 'but he's not used to being in a family home. He's completely institutionalised, he's not used to organising himself. You'll have to be organising him all day.'

'I'm used to that, I'm a teacher.'

'He's not a five year old. Tell him exactly what to do. He'll be fine then. He'll be all right for getting to the toilet and washing, no problem there. Make sure he shaves every day. He manages stairs but takes all day.'

'My parents' house is all on one level, apart from one set of steps.'

'Bungalow?'

'No.'

'You're living in your parents' house? I take it you're a widow.

I'm not one to ask personal questions. There's far too much nosiness in this place as it is.'

And then, because Matron was not particularly kind and would not utter false sentiment and hollow sympathies, she told her.

'Please don't tell anybody else. I came here because it's far enough away from home.'

'Wales is a small country, somebody will find out soon. You can trust me, I'm not a gossip.' Arianwen knew that she would never like Matron, there was a coldness at her very core, she suspected, but she knew that she could trust her.

***

Danny sat in the front of the Mini looking proud and rather superior. Helen, the sister in charge of the ward, had helped him into the car, and then turned to Arianwen.

'I know he's a sweetie, but he'll tire you out and you look tired enough already to me. I don't know why you're doing this, but best of luck.'

Danny watched the unrolling film of scenery with a lopsided smile. He waved to a policeman standing by a telephone kiosk. As they climbed the hill to the village he looked confused.

'No houses, miss.'

'This is the countryside, Danny.'

'Want to pee, Miss.' She'd dreaded this. At the home he hobbled to the toilet and she'd hoped that they'd get home before he wanted to go, but he liked to drink about three cups of sickly sweet tea in the mornings before his breakfast.

She stopped the car.

'You'll have to go in that field there. There's a gap between the gate and the wall.' She helped him out of the car, and helped him to the gate. Then he was struck by shyness, and hobbled out of sight. He was a long time, and she became anxious, but when he appeared, the bottom of his trousers covered in mud, he looked happier.

'There's a bull, Miss, in the field. I was frightened it would come over, and I was scared to move and then I was brave. '

'I don't think a farmer would leave a bull in the field, unless it was tethered.'

'Look,' and he pointed to a docile looking cow grazing in tranquillity.

'That's a cow, Danny, quite harmless.'

They drove through the village, quite deserted, not a car or tractor. She felt quite sick with nerves. Three o'clock, or thereabouts, she'd told her mother. A good time, her mother was always at her best fussing round with teapot and cakes, laid on the table by the window with its view of the stream, and always where you could hear, like breathing, its muted sounds.

As they drove into the valley, through the trees, bare and waiting for rebirth, Danny looked about him, a child full of wonder. Often she'd wondered about that lost childhood, so different from her own, always in the light of love, always one of the blessed, one of the chosen.

'Did you go to school when you were a boy?'

'I don't remember.' That was always his answer. He was forty years old, she'd been told. Such a wasted life. How could she even contemplate the darkness of those forty years? Despite her teaching during the summer he did not seem to have remembered much and nobody else had the time or inclination to help him.

'Tomorrow we'll go and look at the river where I used to walk when I was a little girl, and then we'll do some reading, and we'll go for rides in the car.'

'That will be nice, Miss. And I will learn to read.'

They turned the big bend, where the road widened and then turned into the narrow lane to the mill. The trees looked as if they were standing back for their passing. From here, through the leafless trees, she could see the mill, a bulk in the receding late December light, a strange building, rectangular, like a slab of every day cake. So many windows, all grasping at the light now, and the redundant wheel on its side. Such a long time since she'd even noticed its beauty and its strangeness. Such a strange place to spend a childhood, yet somehow appropriate. Its dark confines had prepared her for her own darkness, and she was trained in solitude. It had been in the family for three generations. Had made them prosperous. The mills of Wales were dying, no place for so many of them now. And when she was gone, what would happen to it then? She felt a regret, a care for the fine old building as if it was an elderly relative she had once loved and now rather neglected.

'There's a man there.' Danny pointed. At his side she felt his tension. Danny was unused to strangers. Dad was standing where he always did to greet everyone, on the little bridge, one hand on the railing the other cupping a cigarette. She guessed that he'd been there for some time, an old coat over his shoulders. Watching and waiting. There was a patience to her father, unlike her mother and herself. If time was slow, let it be, nothing you could do about it.

He saw them and waved, a little round man, and she was full of love for him. Her father was all endurance, a happy man who liked his life as it presented itself to him day by day. He never challenged it, tried to wrestle with its ferocity, unlike her mother, always a bit cross with everyone and the world.

'That's my father.'

Danny slid down in his seat, his fists clutching the sides. Even in the cold little car she could smell his sweat, even though one of the nurses had given him a bath in the morning.

'This is where we stop. You'll have to walk the last part. Plenty of time.' Her father crossed the bridge and came over to the car. As she went round to the passenger door to help him out, her father was already opening the door. Danny shrank further down in his seat.

'Welcome to the cwm, Danny. You're not seeing it at its best today. You should see it when the trees are covered in leaves and when the sun is shining: the most beautiful place in the world. You'll like it here, Danny. Tea and cake ready, and the best blackcurrant jam in the world for the scones.' Something in his soft voice, his calm, and his smile reassured Danny and he allowed the much older man, a little shorter than himself, to help him from the car.

He led him over the bridge.

'Don't worry about the bags. I'll bring them later.'

'I'll bring mine.'

And she followed their slow progress over the bridge and along the side of the stream.

'Do you like wirelesses, Dan? I'll take you to the shed after a cup of tea. I'm repairing one for somebody at the moment. You can watch me. Get away from those women talking.' It occurred to Arianwen that men like Danny had not been taught any skills, let alone reading, just allowed to moulder away their days. Surely something could have been made of him? She would mention it to Matron when she took Danny back. Matron probably wouldn't listen, but perhaps something would penetrate her stubborn carapace. After all, she'd given in on the reading and the visit. She did painting with children, perhaps she could do painting with some of the patients? In that glass lean-to with the unwatered plants: a place of dust and hopelessness.

Her mother stood at the top of the steps, a teacloth in her hand, her best apron on over her second best afternoon dress. Concessions had been made, but not too many. After all, this was not an ordinary guest, not somebody she had to impress, but kindness was to be dispensed like alms. She came down the steps, cloth discarded on the rail: a plump little duchess greeting her weekend party.

'Mam, this is Danny.'

He stood looking shy. 'Hello, Missus.' And as he had been told, offered his hand for shaking.

Her mother took the hand offered and shook it.

'There's nice manners. Let's have a nice cup of tea. Perhaps you could show Danny his room and where the bathroom is, while I put the kettle on. It's all laid up.'

Danny looked frightened by his solitary little room. It occurred to her that he'd probably never slept in a room on his own before. The jug had a little bunch of dried flowers in it, matching the pale rose of the glaze.

It was a simple little room, a small bed, and a cupboard with one of the old jug and ewers on it, redundant now, since one of the bedrooms was converted into the pink bathroom Mam showed proudly to guests whether they needed to use it or not. There was a simple, brightly coloured traditional carthen on the bed, and a home-made rug on the wooden floor. It was Mam's way of making you feel welcome, tea and cakes and a nicely prepared room, not too many words, but in her practical way, eloquent as any.

The tea was heroic, the fire huge. Mam was enjoying herself. Danny looked at the table. Arianwen realised she was hungry.

'Bread and butter first, then cake.' Childhood came back to her.

They cut everything up for Danny. He had few teeth, and those were yellowed and brittle looking. He tried everything. It took a long time, and he struggled with the pretty cups and saucers, but she was quite proud of him. At the end he burped, and looked ashamed when she gave him one of her schoolteacher looks.

'Had enough, boy? Let's leave the women to it, and I'll show you the shed.' He took the old oil lamp from the window where he always kept it and lit it. Strangely for a man who loved the mystery of mechanisms, he scorned the torches Mam kept in the kitchen for emergencies. The smell of oil was acrid in the cosy room with its redolence of burning logs.

'Want the bathroom, boy?' and took Danny out, quite proudly, as if he were his son.

'Don't you stay out there too long, get that boy cold. Give him one of your coats. That old jacket is not warm enough. We'll have to look out some of Uncle Edward's stuff. You be back long before supper, and you'll need to bring in more logs for me. Do you like eggs, Danny?'

'Yes, miss.'

The two women cleared up in silence. As Arianwen wiped the sink, her mother, who had been bending down to put some crockery away, straightened up and looked at her. Not a glance, but a long appraising look, as if they were strangers.

'You look a bit better. Not so tired, and your eyes look as if they're seeing the world again. Still too thin, though. You ate a good tea. Those little sponge cakes are nice aren't they? Best butter in them. From Panterwyn. Best butter for miles. Do you remember going to the farm when you were little? Once we went to the dairy and saw old Mrs Davis turning the churn, and do you remember the loud thump of the butter as it was turning, and you cried a bit because you didn't know what was in there, and then when it came out she let you pat it into shape and put your initials on it, and we brought it home and you wouldn't let us eat it, till I made those scones you liked?'

'I thought the Tylwyth Teg had got into that churn and they were beavering away there turning the milk into butter.' She laughed at her childish self.

'Welcome back to the world, girl.'

It was a strange, hubristic thing to say. Her mother was quite wrong. She felt no better. Nine months had passed, gestation time, and now there would never be babies for her, but she did feel a little closer to her mother than she'd done for a long time and life moved on, muffled, distant, like somnambulist footsteps.

Then her mother did something she hadn't done for a long time, which she had not even done that dreadful morning when Ianto had brought her and Dad and hurled them along the lanes through a misty morning with the sun just breaking behind them in the east, and the whine of the brakes in the yard and the clucking hens, and she'd been sitting there in Tom's chair, by the range which was pulling properly for once as a kind of tribute, surrounded by kind, broad faced women, holding on to the dog's neck. Her mother had stared at her, but didn't touch her, as if the enormity of what had happened was beyond all feeling, beyond all possible expression. And Arianwen had been relieved. She never wanted to be touched again. There had been too many kind, inarticulate lips touching her face, dry and moist, an intrusion, and she had wanted to move away, but that long-embedded courtesy did not allow. Even in that extreme moment of her life the rules of civilised life prevailed. Now, at last she moved towards her daughter, took her by the shoulders, and kissed her, a quick cool kiss on her cheek.

'O, cariad fach'. And then she picked up a cloth and scrubbed at the kitchen table.

Later, after her father had brought Danny back from the shed, their faces shining with cold and the smell of frost on their clothes and the two men tried to watch the little television in the corner, there was a knock at the door and a voice from the hallway.

'Anybody at home?' Ianto. Even now a little surge of the blood when she heard his voice. Those riotous trips to Cardigan and back, and the singing would come back to her. They were reminders of happiness. Her happiest times had been to the rhythms of songs, but now music was quite alien, only the sound of her duty to the children. There were sounds in her head, but all was disharmony, and her ears were quite closed to music.

At the home she'd stood at the back when they sang the carols on Christmas Eve and she hadn't allowed her throat to bring up the words, checking the muscles as if suppressing the acid burn of vomit. And at the school Christmas concert with the proud parents gleaming, she'd played the piano for the children, exhorting them to sing, but her voice stayed down there in whatever depth from which song sprang. The children hadn't noticed, so intent were they on the noise they made.

'In the kitchen.'

'Cold out there. Cosy in here.' He looked expectantly at the teapot.

'Cup of tea, Ianto?'

'Lovely.'

'Drop of something in it as it's Christmas?'

'Champion. Hear you've got a visitor,' dropping his voice as if about to utter something shameful, 'from the home.'

'Danny's in the sitting room, go through.'

In all the years that he had been coming to the house, ritual call in the hallway, efficient wiping of feet on the old mat with the 'CROESO' fading under the history of so many feet, meaningful looks at the teapot, she never remembered him in the sitting room. Unlike most homes in the area there was no parlour or best room, a setting for pre-funeral gloom, and pre-wedding sipping of sherry, rooms cold with desolation as if they were suffering some kind of long hurt. The family sitting room, large and cosy and colourful, actually was a room where people sat and talked and listened to music and warmed themselves by the fire, you could hear the dying sigh of the wheel's slow turn and hear the shirring of the long gone loom and the call of the workers, and feel the spores of the wool on your face. It was a room which embraced and welcomed, but Ianto was a kitchen kind of man.

Ianto looked uncomfortable standing in the door way, larger than anybody in the family, cap in hand, looking subservient, not her Ianto, her singing chauffeur, her faithful friend.

'This is Danny, Ianto. Danny, we have a visitor. Ianto is one of my best friends.'

Danny was now doing one of the simple jigsaws she'd brought from the school for him to do, along with some reading books in English. He was uncertain whether he'd ever spoken Welsh, even though the first home he'd been in was in rural Carmarthenshire. English was the language of officialdom, so English was Danny's language.

The puzzle was of farmyard animals in high colours, very clean and shiny black and white cows, very white sheep, bright red hens and grass so green, a green never seen even in rain soaked West Wales.

Danny was looking angry; he was easily frustrated. She saw that an essential piece of sheepdog was on the floor. Ianto picked up the large wooden piece and the dog, a strange mongrel creature, was complete. Danny smiled.

'I'm Ianto.' And, like Mam, he offered his hand to shake. Nobody had ever shaken hands with Danny before today, but he obviously enjoyed it, and he took Ianto's hand and shook it hard, many times.

Mam appeared in the doorway.

'Cup of tea for us all in the kitchen.'

Danny, who loved his food and had a sweet tooth hobbled to the door. Her father took his arm, but he shook it off.

'I brought my old wireless for you to have a look at. I still prefer it to the television. Although I like to see the rugby. Nice and warm by the fire with a beer in my hand. Not like the Arms Park though.'

The cup of tea was one of Mam's spreads, cakes and sandwiches and the whisky bottle stood on the table for exclusive male use. Her father poured a few drops into his tea and then passed it to Ianto.

'Thank you, nothing like it for keeping out the cold.' He poured himself a good tot, and then turned to Danny. 'Drop, Danny?' and before the women could stop him put a hefty drop in Danny's tea.

Mam looked disapproving, but Danny was gulping and grinning, enjoying the warmth of the alcohol and the warmth of humanity.

The men ate Christmas cake, mince pies, and pancakes with strawberry jam, and then her father stood up and looked out of the window at the late December gloom.

'Let's look at that old wireless then, Ianto. Danny, you come with us. Ianto, bring the big lamp,' and Arianwen watched through the little kitchen window as he led them along the path with the trees still like giant sentries over them, the stream a shining stillness by their side. She saw the light of the lamp and their black forms moving, and the mist coming down thick, and they were medieval pilgrims searching for sanctuary. She opened the window to let some air into the stuffy kitchen and she could hear them singing as they made their progress. It was a rugby song and rather rude, and she smiled to herself, and her mother coming back from closing the outer door which they had not closed, saw the smile, quick as it was.

'I don't think it's a good idea taking him to chapel tomorrow, Arianwen, he probably doesn't know how to behave in chapel.'

'He enjoys the singing when we have services in the main sitting room on Sundays.' It was a sign of her mother's changed view of her that arguments now came to nothing. She seldom challenged this terrifying woman her daughter had become.

The chapel stood in the most exposed part of the village, charmless as chapels are, utilitarian buildings for a harsh religion.

Beautiful architecture is for churches in pretty villages. Its cemetery lay around it, bleak in January, the Christmas flowers and wreaths fading, or blown away to the hills, outrageous bits of holly and red flowers scattered in hedges.

Inside, the living sang. Not a bad turn out, after the festivities of Christmas, and the carols with their notes of hope. Now it was time for the old hymns, some beautiful, some dirges to the way of life passing, a life where the chapel and the minister are losing their powers. We are at the turning point, this is still a predominantly Welsh speaking area, before the incomers, and their all-powerful language swept up a whole way of life and threw it to the winds. The sixties are approaching fast, galloping changes just over the hill.

Danny's limp, and the way he drags his left foot behind him like a chain, and the way his face moves, the jaw working at a non-existent piece of food, makes him a focus for attention. The bored young, on the cusp of rebellion, dragged along by their parents, stare and giggle, the more tactful look away, and the obviously pious look at him with conjured sympathy, while scrutinising Arianwen for looks of madness or grief. Always a bit of a rebel in a quiet kind of way, never was the same after going to live with some odd family in Cardigan. What were her parents thinking, letting her stay away from home so young? Always a family that put itself above itself, and her father only an ordinary working man who fiddles with wirelesses, useful kind of man, but nothing for putting on airs. Arianwen and her mother with Danny between them like a prisoner, walked along the right aisle to their usual pew, identical little chins up in the air, two proud little women.

During the first hymn, when the deacons stood up and faced the congregation, and the minister, a man whose florid face spoke of an acquaintance with alcohol despite signing the pledge a number of years back, glowered at them as if he was already working himself up for a sermon which would remind them of the extremity of their sins, Danny looked round. His experience of organised religion was limited: the lukewarm vicar who came round the wards occasionally, hymns sung on Sundays, a prayer by an embarrassed nurse who muttered the Lord's prayer as if it was a punishment. Danny smiled, and muttered something to himself. He looked up at the empty gallery, he sniffed, as if the chapel's smell of damp, and polo mints, and moth ball and Vick were the incense smells of

Rome. Hymns were sung, prayers uttered, and then the minister, looking important, and eyebrows undulating with emotion climbed the steps into the pulpit as if he was ascending to heaven carrying all the sinful burdens of his errant flock.

Mints were unwrapped with noisy care, bottoms shuffled, throats cleared, and the main entertainment began. The captive young glanced around them, boys blushed at girls' flirtatious looks and tossed hair, the pious looked expectant as if close concentration would ease their way to heaven. Danny had by now exhausted all the possibilities of engagement. He shuffled and coughed, all the actions of the congregation exaggerated in his distorted body. He yawned loudly, waking up a farmer dreaming of Sunday supper, cold cuts with pickles, and beetroot, and a bit of that nice cheese.

Then a little fart, quite restrained, but quite audible, even against the rising crescendos of the minister whose redness deepened as he described the Gothic splendours of Hell. Arianwen smiled, such a tiny whisper of a smile, quite rare, and froze it quickly, but not quite fast enough, not before it was seen by one of the deacons, an ascetic man of few pleasures who frowned upon any mirth as if it was the very sins of the devil.

Danny tapped a tuneless tune on the hymn book which he was holding against him. The youngsters giggled, and the minister seeing that all was lost brought his oration to an end. There was a relieved shuffling and looking at watches and pleased smiles, supper would be a bit early tonight, and the youngsters smiled smiles of promise at each other, a longer sojourn round the back of the chapel with cigarettes beckoned.

The two women repeated their proud walk out of the chapel.

'Arianwen, my dear, I am so glad to see you. I hear you're doing splendid work at that school. No privacy in West Wales, my dear, your headmaster is a friend of an old friend of mine.'

The minister's wife, unlike her husband, was a true Christian, a highly educated woman, perceived by the village as having dangerously liberal ideas, who made it clear to all who would listen to her that she thought the way society was changing was rather a good thing, and that unlike her husband's god, hers approved of modern times. She was a source of embarrassment to her husband, and gossip and conjecture for the village and surrounding areas.

Arianwen was fond of her, and smiled her gratitude.

195

'And you're doing voluntary work as well. Such a good idea,' then she came closer, the intense grey eyes with their exotic fleck of green, looked in to Arianwen's, a probing sharpness which made her draw back. 'How are you really? If you want to talk, proper talk, not all this village code stuff, call to see me. I'll shut Edwin away in his study. There'll be no cakes, I leave that to worthy ladies like your mother, but I can make a decent cup of coffee, and there's always a bottle of something.'

'I might do that. Before I go back to school next week. I'm taking Danny back tomorrow, perhaps the day after. Perhaps I shouldn't have brought him to chapel. Your husband will be angry with me.'

'Made the sermon a bit livelier than usual, and shorter.'

And then she was away talking to an elderly couple, asking about their sons and their cattle, not quite saying the right things.

Many years later, when she was able to look back at that time with the objectivity of distance, she realised that looking after Danny, bringing kindness into his institutionalised life was not just some vague altruistic gesture, but an unconscious grasping for purpose. It had probably done her more good than Danny, and was ultimately a selfish act. And she felt rather ashamed. When she wasn't there Danny's life reverted to what it had always been, nobody bothered with his reading and in the years when she went back, every time, she started again, as if he was one of her particularly slow infants. He died young, and nobody mourned him, and after the sad little funeral she never went back to the home again, and wondered if she had really done any good at all.

A few days later she drove back for the spring term. The holiday had been so busy that she had little time to think, which was what she wanted. A new numbness was replacing the worst intensity of her suffering. Each day was an attempt at escape, of limbs moving, her body functioning, her mind occupied by quotidian concerns, and she spent her time exiled from feeling, each day a little vacation of the mind as though she was not the inhabitant of her own existence. She was a woman floating through her days, flotsam drifting on the tide, a doppelganger living another woman's life.

It was strange living with the Richards again, even though her marriage had lasted such a short time. Would she, when an old woman, look back at her life with Tom as a long ago storm, and would it in time become part of other turbulences? Such a short time as a wife, and before that the long haul of childhood and adolescence and young womanhood. Now it was like being twenty-one again, just out of college, waiting for life to take her. Not so long ago, but she was not that young woman, such horror in such a short time. After a childhood blessed with calm, and an adolescence spent during the war, which even with the red glow of Swansea burning patterns on her retina, and so much breaking of sad news in the village, had seemed remote.

Now the long climb would start, traversing the steepest of cliffs: life in her adopted village, teaching music to young people, preparing them for the Urdd Eisteddfod, one day, perhaps, the choir again, and as the first clouds of the day appeared from behind the hills Elwyn's cheerful face appeared to her as if he was urging her to live again. Smiling. Always smiling.

He'd come to the funeral and sang, yes, but like a stranger, he had not shaken hands with her as some of the choir had, embarrassed, with eyes averted. Driving carefully along the narrow lanes she felt a little song in her throat, not much more than a cough, something from childhood. Yes, one day she would sing again, but it was so slow, this pulling herself through the days. Today when she'd woken up there was that familiar shadow, that weight that came with the morning's memory, but after that, briefly, a respite from the blackness as she remembered that she was going back to the village. A sense of treachery assailed her. Her parents were ageing, their eyes asking her to be herself again, the little girl who'd brought them so much happiness. Now she had nothing to offer them.

'Have you thought of trying for a job nearer home? You could live here and drive to work. Better than going back to that place with all its memories. The mill is part of you, and it's full of happy memories and it'll be yours when we've gone, and you never know what might happen in the future.' She looked away from her mother's anxious face and watched the wheel turning, slower now as the water levels were low this winter, as if the stream had slunk away in despair, and she felt part of its sluggishness in her own dragging limbs.

Her father would mumble something at this point and scuttle outside, and looking out of the window she would look down on his white head moving towards the sanctuary of his shed.

'I won't get married again, if that's what you're thinking. I like that school. I've got a job to do. I don't think I'm in the state of mind to start at a new school yet. In a few years' time, perhaps, or go to work abroad in one of the Forces schools in the Far East. Get away from everything.'

Her mother looked hurt.

'Not too far. Your father would break his heart.'

Words, just words, and she regretted what she'd said. Sometimes she felt that in her own pain she had become quite oblivious to the pain of others.

'Don't worry about that now. I'm going back to a village where I've been made welcome. I like the Richards. They're kind, and I'm only a few miles away. I'll be home for a weekend soon. I'll take you to Carmarthen shopping and we'll have tea at that posh hotel and you can put on your best hat.'

When she left, her mother kissed her, a cold and formal kiss, and her father shook her hands as if she was a departing dignitary.

As she drove in to the village the rain was business like, but there was lightness in the west which suggested that she might have a brief walk after a cup of tea with the Richards. Every day during the holidays she had walked in the woods, a scuttling little figure, thinner than she'd been all her life, head down against wind and rain, or rare sun, a manic need for movement, as if tragedy could be left behind in the motion of arms and the legs and the blood's charge along her veins.

She stopped the car at a high point above the village. Here was the best place for walking, little streams with gorse growing along their shallow banks, the sense of the sea's turbulence close by, the salt suggestion of breezes, larks' calls in spring, the buzzards mewing as they climbed the thermals, so open, so much space.

There was liberty here, so different from the woods with the trees bending over her as if watching, a strange intimacy about them, like inquisitive neighbours, comforting in summer with promise of shade, but in winter winds manic strangers undulating in balletic movements and sometimes in the night she would hear giants crash in the woods, and in the morning her father would go and saw the great trunks. And it seemed to her that every time she went back, coinciding with her parents' ageing, there was a denudation of trees, the woodland thinner, like a head losing its hair, more spaces for flowers to grow, tiny aconites and primroses in spring and later the sea like waves of bluebells, and the mill was something organic evolving in time.

***

It was difficult not to laugh at Arthur. He had that silly name, a grand one with its allegiance to Wales's saviour king, waiting in some dark cave to deliver Wales from great danger. The only danger Arianwen could see was creeping Anglicisation: a threat to language and tradition, and when she went to Haverfordwest or Cardigan there were more English voices to be heard on the streets. The war, however had taught her about tolerance and she rejected the bitterness of some of her contemporaries.

Arthur was not a heroic figure. Even at five years old he was portly and self-important. His parents were prosperous farmers who regarded themselves as a cut above the smallholders who farmed most of the surrounding hills. They lived in a large modern house with a beautifully kept garden and Arthur came to school in a neat blazer and well pressed trousers. Other boys tormented him; pomposity was not appreciated in rural circles.

Two boys stood in front of her: Arthur crying, in his usual messy way, snot running down his pasty face, a loud keening which suggested a certain degree of histrionics, and skinny Gwyn, dark eyes defiant, not, she realised, the least bit frightened of her. Something would have to be done about Gwyn. Already at six he was a born leader, almost too clever, and a malign influence on other boys in the class; he spent most breaks charging round the playground with a group of malleable acolytes. In his sharp eyes there was, already, a challenge to authority.

'Right, Arthur, tell me what happened.'

'They called me fatty and that I'm silly.' Arianwen couldn't help thinking that it was a pretty accurate description of the rotund little figure in front of her, with his silly impractical clothes which made him stand out, when the others, even the wealthier ones, came to school in hand me downs. His indulgent mother allowed him too many sweets and his father had immortal longings for his prosaic little boy.

The two standing in front of her were fine examples, she felt, of the arbitrary unfairness of life, with Gwyn, already at six, showing signs of the dashing young man he would become: scholar, poet and fine sportsman, with the sweetest singing voice she'd ever heard. Life was very unfair.

'He took my sweets and -' more howls, building up to a crescendo and another slither of snot.

'And then?'

'He kicked me.' Arthur wailed, loudly. She could imagine the sheep grazing on the green bleating in horror.

'Did you, Gwyn?'

'No, never. Arthur is a tittle tattle and he was trying to trip people up.' Gwyn was indignant at this accusation, but she knew full well what the boys were like in the playground.

'I'm not sure either of you is telling the truth, so you'll both stay in at dinner time and tidy the cupboard till I get some truth instead of lies.'

They stared at her with hatred. Her justice was rough, yes. Arthur complained about something or someone every day, and Gwyn was rebellious and cheeky. Let them stay with her in the classroom on this bright, dry day. One of the girls came in with more complaints. Sometimes children exhausted her, but she realised that they made her, if not happy, at least less unhappy.

And over the years, so many Arthurs wailing their complaints and the clever Gwyns, ever defiant: the Arthurs becoming clerks and civil servants or even bank managers, and the Gwyns, the blessed, rebels and poets and politicians and teachers and even preachers, so many through those years, those lonely years. And, so many went back to the family farm, manacled like Tom to the unforgiving harshness and demands of the land.

And she went back to the mill as the years passed, and the wheel clogged with weed, and moss slowed it almost to stillness, and her parents slowed down to its motion, movement slower, and her mother fussed to a slower rhythm and her father went to the shed and picked bits of wiring up and put them down forgetting their purpose, and stared at the trees. When they fell, a man from the village with a chainsaw came to finish them off into logs which he took away to sell. The fireplace in the living room was now replaced by an electric fire with bright red coals and flames which flickered too fast. Modern life, garish with bright colour, had caught up with the old mill, and there was the occasional modern piece of furniture in pale wood which looked out of place in the dark room which had always looked as if it was settled cosily in its own segment of time, and now was like some old creature clutching on to life as the young gambolled about it.

On the weekends when she didn't go home she had started to go to chapel with Mrs. Richards. Uncertain now about belief she saw chapel going as something innocuous, meaningless, another village activity, which did no real good, essentially harmless, a way of passing time.

The faces looked at her: friendly faces, concerned, and a little curious. They were fond of this young woman. They'd watched her as a new teacher at the school, watched her drive back and fore to the village in that noisy little car of hers, saw her at chapel on the Sundays when she didn't go home, looked at her colourful dresses and watched her quick movements about the village, appreciated the cakes she'd brought from home for whist drives and concerts, heard her singing, not a first class voice but passable, and then the glorious speculation when she courted with Tom, with that quiet boy Tom, and a marriage and the watching of the waistline as she carried on teaching and was a farmer's wife all at once, trying to keep that dreary old house clean. And they'd known that there was a deep sadness in Tom, since that brother died, and his mother withdrew her love for him, as it followed the lost boy into his grave. An unhappy family, the sad little boy, but that final act, no nobody had expected that, and then the young woman transformed in one night into a tragic figure, somebody beyond their experience, like a glorious actress on the stage lit by darkness and sorrow. And they had not known what to say to her, and they'd gone through the centuries old rituals of mourning, baked the cake, knocked the door, and sat in silence with her, as her mother sobbed, her father stood outside the door, his face unsuited to tragedy, sculpted to bleakness, and his fingers shaking as he smoked his endless cigarettes, and she sat there, as if she was dead herself.

It was a long time, it was a short time. They were uncertain. The rhythms of country life were slow then. They didn't see the years passing or note time touching their faces, only felt it in the stiffening of their bodies.

The chapel going became easier, just part of Sunday like Mrs. Richards' roast and listening to a concert on the radio, and, eventually, when Reverend Richards decided that television was not the devil's instrument and another route to sin, the two women watched old films on Sunday afternoons with a cup of tea and a slice of sponge.

One evening returning home from meeting an old friend from college, the most beautiful late March evening of a brave sun and soft breeze, driving with the window open, she drove slowly past the village hall where the road narrowed. The hall, tin roofed, sweated when the mildest sun came out, and now all the windows were open to let out the mugginess caused by the choir, packed into the small building, and she heard the end of a song, something light hearted, obviously new to the choir, as the voices sounded as if they were tasting something strange, but she could hear the effort, and at the end a great deal of laughing and groaning. As she drove towards the manse she heard her voice trying out those little slivers of song she'd heard. After she parked the car she wanted to run back and join them and struggle that song into harmony, but it was not the kind of thing she did, running wild-eyed and eager into the hall, a welcome spectacle and distraction. She would do it the right way; a phone call and a chat.

***

The new choirmaster, not quite as pompous as his predecessor, nodded at her. He didn't really know her, but he'd heard her story, and had seen the tiny little figure at the shop where he sometimes called for sweets for his grandchildren. And the shopkeeper was always pleased to repeat the story, as they watched her quick walk through the village.

He had thought of a little speech of welcome when he saw her come in, and had it stored neatly in his mind somewhere between the harangue for the tenors and the tricky bit of a new chorus they were rehearsing, then realised that she would not welcome such treatment.

They were working on an oratorio for Easter, and there was a concert in three weeks' time, fund raising for repairs to the roof of the chapel: hymns, traditional folk songs, and a few favourites from the shows. Not the best time to be re-joining, but let her sing in the concert if she wanted to.

Arianwen nodded to the people she knew. There were many new members, people who'd moved into the village. There were more cars now and many lived in the village and drove to Haverfordwest and Cardigan to work. She saw a couple of mothers from the school who looked at her surprised, as if they could only imagine her as a fixed presence in the classroom, who slept in the stationery cupboard with the chalk and the sticky paper.

The choir was younger now. Old Hector Jones of the once soaring tenor had, most tactfully, been persuaded to retire. His voice crackled like a carrion crow's, and his eyes were too dimmed to read the music, but he sang in chapel on Sunday mornings, grinding through the hymns like an unoiled engine, his spirit still as strong as when he won the cup at Cardigan Eisteddfod and the adjudicator said that he was one of the finest tenors he'd heard for years.

Then Elwyn was there, late as usual, carrying with him the metal whiff of cold from the hills, the smell of cigarettes from the pub, and the distinctive smell of aftershave, not yet too common in this part of the world. And she felt his presence in the sudden tremor of her voice and the quickening of her pulse. He had that rushed look of the man whose life demanded that he play too many parts. He lived with his mother, somebody had once told her, a dutiful son. She didn't know whether his mother was still alive. She knew so little, only that he could sing, and that with him he always brought excitement and he could make people smile, bringing a special infusion of joy.

One of the young mothers of a little boy in her class stood next to her.

'David is settling in very well, Mrs. Thomas. He's a delight to teach.'

The mother smiled.

'We were so worried how he'd settle in. He'd only had a term in the school in Aberystwyth. And then we had to move because of my husband's job. Not very good timing.'

'He's a very bright little boy and good natured. No need to worry about him.'

The proud mother answered, her voice fading as if she was far away.

He was standing there not smiling as if searching for sorrow in her eyes, the first time she'd seen him since the funeral when he had not shaken her hand. It had been her one clear memory of that dreadful day. Pious gestures were not for him. His was not a personality for tragedy. He was for smiling and comedy, a springtime kind of character. It was a face for happiness.

Her smile for him was timid, and then she turned again to the young mother, who was quite unaware that her son's teacher had heard so little of her speech, and nodded as if agreeing with everything said.

The mother smiled and then turned to her neighbour.

The choirmaster clapped his hands and the choir assembled. By the time the rehearsal had finished, she really felt that she'd not been away, that the interregnum of horror was something that had happened to another woman, a tragic heroine driven mad by sorrow on a remote stage. But as soon as she was outside and looked at the cold eye of the moon, quite indifferent to earthly sorrows she knew that it was going to be one of those nights when she wouldn't sleep, and if she did, her dreams would be filled with horrors. One of those nights when Mrs. Richards, who heard and knew everything, would look away when she went down to breakfast. It was one of those nights when she would have liked to walk all night.

When she first came back to the village she had taken to walking up to the hills and screaming like Lear at her unfeeling Old Testament god, startling sheep who stared at her with their old woman faces, and then coming back to the manse and going straight up to bed, where physical exhaustion, or a tablet, would give her some sleep.

One of the women who helped to make the tea walked with her, one of those rare women who were not frightened by silence.

When they stopped at the manse gates, she looked down at Arianwen.

'It was good to see you and to hear you sing.' And walked away.

In the kitchen the Richards were drinking their milky drinks and for once she was glad of their company. They talked of the marriage of a local farmer to a wealthy girl from Cardiff.

'She doesn't look like a farmer's wife, all stilettos and make up,' Mrs. Richards said. 'Can't see her helping with the milking, and feeding the chickens and making brawn when the pig's slaughtered and helping with the lambing.'

'I wasn't trained in any of that either, Mrs. Richards. You have to learn. Give the poor girl a chance.'

Reverend Richards frowned on his wife's gossip, and changed the subject, handing Arianwen the paper.

'I've just finished reading this, would you like to have a go at it, then perhaps we can have a chat about it.'

And he passed her an article from the Western Mail on the decline of religion in rural Wales. It looked very dry. However, she would read it, and try to discuss it intelligently with poor Rev. Richards who could not find his intellectual equal in the village apart from Hugh Jones, who made little secret of his agnosticism, although he kept to the letter of the law by holding school assemblies and teaching religious studies to his class.

Easter, with all its symbolism and Christian pain, was coming and she had warned her parents that she would not be home till Easter Monday because of the concert on Saturday night. Her mother was disappointed when she phoned, and she heard her mother's long sigh along the airwaves.

'I was hoping you'd be home for Easter Sunday. I've ordered a lovely piece of lamb from the butcher's, and the minister and his wife are coming to dinner. I thought you could make one of your lovely apple pies. Can't you come early on Sunday morning?'

'We're having a little party in the choirmaster's house after the concert, and I thought it would be good for me to go, and start mixing with people again. It's a long time since I went to a party. Sometimes I feel that I have no life apart from other people's children.'

Her mother hated to lose a battle, but was pacified by the thought that her daughter was going to a party, and all its myriad possibilities.

'Shall we have an outing somewhere on Monday? I'll come home for supper Sunday evening, I love cold lamb and pickles. What about Aberystwyth? Dad loves a trip to Aberystwyth, a walk on the prom, and then tea in a nice hotel.'

'That would be nice. I haven't been to Aberystwyth for years. A walk on the prom would be lovely, but you've got to remember we're getting on, and we can't charge along like you do.'

On the night of the concert, she put on a black dress, as requested by the choirmaster. She only had one black dress. It was the dress that had been bought for her for the funeral. Sorrow and frantic walks had slimmed her down and she no longer had the appetite for Mrs. Richards' lovely food. The dress had been a little tight then, when she was really just a girl, but now it fitted her perfectly, its classic lines showing well her curves and the newly slim hips, but she didn't want to look like a tragic widow any more, at least not for tonight, the music was what was important. There was a pair of earrings she'd bought in Paris, fine for Paris, but rather big and showy for Welsh villages. They'd never been worn since. She put them on, they suited her. Her hair was longer now, and there was a shine to it. Eyeshadow and her reddest lipstick and she smiled at her reflection, like a defiant teenager waiting for her mother's anger, and then her highest heels, black patent and very glamorous, bought on a long ago trip to Carmarthen.

Mrs. Richards was using the new phone in the hallway, her Saturday evening call to her sister in Cardiff who she never saw, with whom she conducted weekly phone calls which seemed to be a series of misunderstandings and confusions. The Reverend and Arianwen had often exchanged smiles listening to an exasperated Mrs. Richards.

'I didn't mean that, Gwen, listen. It was Tuesday not Wednesday, I told you. It's the day the baker comes. The butcher comes on Wednesday.' Her voice rose in exasperation and her round little face puckered with frustration.

She stopped mid-protest and looked at Arianwen and after a look of awe, or shock, smiled.

'Oh, you look lovely. Tom would have been so proud of you,' then blushed in embarrassment and turned back to the voluble squawking at the other end of the line.

***

The choir were gathering at the front of the chapel, the men looking embarrassed in their bow ties and dark suits, the women looking as if they were strangers to themselves and rather self-conscious about it. They smiled, and appraised, and looked superior as they listened to the men.

'We look as if we're going to a bloody funeral.'

'We didn't have to dress up like a load of pansies with old Edwards.'

'You look better without cow shit on your trousers.'

'Bur our singing's much better now, and I like getting dressed up and making a bit of an occasion of it, so stop moaning, you miserable old fools,' one of the women said. 'Arianwen, cariad fach, you look lovely,' and they all looked at her, men and women, as if they'd never seen her before, and a couple of the men traced the length of her body with their eyes, languid and slow, and she felt something she hadn't felt for a long time, something she'd felt in the early days with Tom, a sadness and yearning in her body, but something which Tom's embarrassed fumblings had somehow never assuaged, and throughout their short marriage it had always been there. And then, nothing, no yearning, just the empty darkness of her widowhood.

Arianwen was too astute to deceive herself that the night of the concert was her entry to the promised land of recovery. That took much longer. However, it was an evening which she remembered for a long time, ordinary, pleasant and she sang again, not with the old spirit and joy, but it served as a beginning. She was not herself again, the handy little cliché which occurred to those who watched her, to place and rationalise the small changes they saw in her: colour, a smile, a pleasure in the music which had always been such an important part of her. The eyes which had avoided contact for so long, dark and dead, as if some vital illumine was gone, looked up as if she was saying, 'I am here again, not fully, but a part of me is what you want me to be.'

And Elwyn watched her. He didn't smile. He saw something which had been lost to him, his life was not always what it appeared to be, the elaborate comedy sketch which he'd composed for the world, the smiling man, the funny man, efficient at work, a natural leader, hard on shirkers, generous with praise for the industrious, good to his mother, even though he saw her sometimes as an intolerable burden, as his life crept past him, he watching, a spectator of his own invented life.

The concert went well, fewer errors than with the old choir-master, and the new one smiled. He knew the benefits of praise.

'Not bad, folks. Some sopranos, just a little bit slow, and tenors, a little more oomph perhaps, but not bad, not bad. Rehearsals for the summer concert begin next week, and we may be singing in the cathedral later in the year, and I think we're ready to try the Cardigan Eisteddfod. Right, back to my house. My wife and her mother have prepared enough food for an army. And I'm sure everybody's thirsty. Dai Aberfrenni brought round a cask of home brew earlier and there's wine and sherry for the ladies.'

His house, a large villa which had once belonged to an auctioneer from Haverfordwest, was at the end of the village, and after taking the congratulations of the audience they walked along the dark pathway, some of the men singing hymns in low voices, the music still bubbling in their throats.

The large house was lit up at every window. Inside it was spacious and warm, and furnished in a modern way with light furniture, bright rugs, plants and bookshelves, and there was a harp in the corner of the sitting room. She remembered the Morgans, the harp always wakening memories of that enchanted interval in her life. There had been a time when she had thought of learning how to play it properly. Music, she knew, and the concert had reinforced that knowledge, was the way in which she could find a place in the world again.

Usually village gatherings offered cups of tea, and a bottle of sherry to be drunk in tiny glasses, but here as well as the promised sherry and huge cask of homebrew, there was a table laid out with spirits, and bottles of red wine, and a couple of white wine bottles in glass coolers. She remembered the strong red wine she'd drunk in Paris that week when all her life was there like a big apple waiting to be peeled, but worms had waited.

Yes, there were happy memories before her life changed forever. Soon she must go abroad again. The thought of teaching somewhere in the sun still appealed, and again, that constant cliché, start a new life. But how could she do that to her parents? She was burdened with that unique sense of responsibility of the only child.

The other table displayed a most impressive variety of food, *a good spread* in West Wales parlance, her mother would have approved. Hannah, the choirmaster's wife, was a tall woman, immaculately dressed and skilfully made up in the Elizabeth Taylor mode. Her mother would not approve of that. She still pursed her lips at eyeshadow, but lipstick of a pale shade was tolerable and she admitted to herself that Arianwen looked better, more alive somehow when she used it. Lipstick in chapel she was still uncertain about, although when Arianwen challenged her she could not quite find her way round the serpentine maze of her thinking. Times were changing, and the century's changes were rushing along, overtaking time itself.

A glass of red wine, not as good as her memory of that first Parisian wine, but what could compare? In her mind memories of Keats's *vintage of the warm south,* and on that Welsh evening she shivered as she thought of warm places, and as she sat amongst the women, listening as the conversation reverted to familiar topics: gossip, children, chapel matters, she felt that she was the inhabitant of two worlds: the kind and stolid village and another exotic world, which beckoned her with warm seduction.

The men, relaxed now, jackets and ties discarded, faces red with beer and whisky, stood in a circle round the choirmaster and Elwyn, glasses in their hands, swaying slightly as their sense of gravity diminished, some with their arms round each other's necks like rugby players. There was an exclusivity, an intimacy to the world of men which she could not understand. Tom had not been one of this kind, although a tuneful enough member of the choir.

Some of the women looked away, bored, even irritated by such male solidarity, not conscious of their resentment that their men, stolid, silent hardworking types, harmless enough most of the time, could with others assume a kind of glamour, of otherness which closed them out.

And now there'd be proper singing, something tribal and instinctive. Hymns first, then folk songs, and *Sospan Fach,* and then somebody daring, Elwyn probably, would introduce something more scatological. And the women prepared to be shocked, and rather enjoyed it.

When they stopped to replenish their glasses, he left the circle of men and came to her, serious now, readjusting his face for her tragic status, but Barbara Jones stopped him, a music teacher at the grammar school, plump but pretty, vociferous and liked by men, especially married men, and she led him away to a corner, and she could hear them laughing, the sound breaking through the discordant sound of male and female voices.

She turned to Joan Davies, whose son she had once taught.

'How's Sam?'

'Third year at Cardiff University. Going to be a vet, another four years, but he wants to work with large animals, so he's hoping to come back to Pembrokeshire or Cardiganshire. Dai's disappointed he's not going to take on the farm, but he's proud of him. He was too bright to be a farmer. He liked the animals, but was never too interested in the day to day grind. Dai reckons the good times are coming to an end for us small farmers. The young people want to move away. The world's changing fast. When the time comes we'll sell the farm, keep a bit of land and build a nice bungalow somewhere, and live a bit.'

Arianwen looked at the woman's lined peasant face and the large hands worn by hard work, and felt a sadness for her. So many conversations now were elegiac for a time which was creeping away from them, but life would be easier from now on. And life was changing. The years were galloping along, and even here in this remote corner of the country, young people were changing, more rebellious, even the little ones, and so many going to university, and then coming home full of contempt for parents and their way of life, strangely dressed, and the girls drinking pints with the men in the pubs and smoking and expressing their opinions in loud voices.

Part of her regretted the past, but she was a modern woman and saw that it was good for women to have more freedom than her generation, perhaps the last generation to listen to their mothers. She envied them their recklessness, their confidence, and they would be better wives and mothers in the end. Women were changing and she'd read books and articles coming from America. So much anger in so many women. She was a free woman, but what pleasure was there in that? Freedom so bitterly acquired. Already the reality of her marriage was a memory. She remembered the end, but the day to day life on the farm, the meals and the evenings, lonely evenings with him sleeping by the fireplace, the dog at his feet and she looking round the darkness of the kitchen, discontented, those she remembered as if she was looking at a lonely figure on a stage, set in darkness, one weakish spotlight on her. Had she, even then, felt regret? The emotions of the woman on the stage were unknown. Childhood she remembered quite clearly, as if she was already old, but her marriage was something discarded, a tedium made extraordinary by its end. The nightmares had stopped: that last walk to the barn, and the dog's fur stiffening under her hand.

She smiled at everybody in the room and accepted another glass of wine. No more than two glasses. After all she was a school-mistress, and dignity must be retained at all times, and the choir, loyal as they were, would not deny themselves a gossip about a teacher stumbling around with a glass in her hand.

Elwyn had gone back to his male cronies, and after a few jokes, it was time for more singing, and there was a greater beauty to their singing than in the formality of the chapel with its ghosts of deacons and angry priests terrified of those unyielding Victorian gods. Somebody called, 'Arianwen, cariad, play the piano. Let's do it properly now.'

And she did so gladly. More favourites: the songs of that delightful state of light inebriation where the world seems a good place, a quite disconnected mixture of hymns and folk songs and songs from the musicals, some of the cleaner rugby songs leading always to the great pinnacle of *Hen Wlad fy Nhadau*, and the women would wipe at their eyes with lace trimmed hankies. How she'd always loved a singsong as a child when family came on Boxing Day, and later at college after choir rehearsals.

At midnight a large group left, all the women, most of the men including Elwyn, still singing down the path, the women hushing them.

'You'll wake the village up, and there'll be angry looks in chapel tomorrow.' In the distance dogs barked and in answer a sheep called from its shelter by one of the dry stone walls.

Arianwen stayed to help the choirmaster and his wife clear up. Hugh Jones was there too, invited because he was a friend of the family, and in the kitchen the four of them gossiped as they washed up: Hannah washing, a cigarette in her mouth, and Arianwen and the two men drying.

They sat round the kitchen table; Hugh drew a picture of a daffodil in the steam on the window.

'Easter card for you, Arianwen.'

'I ought to be going Hannah, you must be exhausted. You worked so hard preparing all this lovely food.'

'No, Arianwen, stay and have a sober cup of tea, and we'll finish off leftovers. A midnight feast. How I envied those girls in those boarding school books living away from home, getting up to all sorts of adventures, and I just had to walk home from school where my mother waited for me, and told me to change out of my uniform even before I'd put my nose through the door, and then there was always home-made plum jam for tea because we had a plum tree in the garden and had too many plums. I would have done anything for strawberry jam from the shop like everybody else. I suppose if I was at boarding school I'd have hated it, and cried for Mam and plum jam every night.'

The choirmaster laughed. 'Well I went to boarding school. I hated it for about two years and then loved it. Mainly because of the music master who did everything to encourage me. Gave me ideas of musical greatness, but I'm only an amateur.'

'I went to the grammar school in Cardigan, but because of where we lived I had to board. I hated the first place, but loved the second one which was total chaos. I was so happy there. My first encounter with Bohemian types.'

They heard the sadness in her voice, and looked uncomfortable.

'What about you, Hugh?'

'Lived at home, went to the grammar school, then Aber, then teaching. The usual story: marriage and children.'

They drank tea and ate leftovers, and gossiped about the village and talked about the concert. The room was heavy with alcohol and condensation and the satisfactions of success. John, the choirmaster was effervescent with ambition, and plans for further concerts and his choir soaring to the heights.

Long after midnight, Hugh stood up.

'I'll walk you home, Arianwen.'

'No, you'll be going in the wrong direction, it's only a few yards.'

'No, I'll walk you home, I don't want my assistant teacher being mauled by a rampaging sheep or falling down a ditch.'

He looked tired, even though it was the weekend, as if tiredness was another limb which he carried around. Bruises under the pale brown eyes, an infinite sadness about him. She knew that after a day's teaching he went home to cook the dinner, as his wife now had a teaching job in Cardigan, and often stayed till late, driving her noisy car back when half the village was asleep. The youngest child was a bit of a problem, a morose boy who worked hard at school, but had no friends and could be seen wandering around the hills, a solitary figure muttering to himself. He reminded her a little of Bedwyr at his most difficult, but Bedwyr had an unconscious charm which Sion Jones lacked. It was not often now that she thought of that warm, eccentric family, but she remembered somebody telling her that Bedwyr was now well on his way up the academic ladder, doing exactly what he wanted which was what Bedwyr had always done. Of the others she knew nothing, but if there had been any major tragedies, she knew that the efficient West Wales communication mechanism would have let her know.

The Morgans had come to the funeral, her mother had told her, one of that huge mass of black clad people who'd stared uneasily at her, inarticulate, terrified, paralysed by the force of tragedy in their midst, when she was far beyond their sympathy and love.

A tidy man who liked order, she knew that after all the housework and cooking, Hugh would go up to his study and write. Occasionally he would read a poem to her, complex and disciplined, and she would try to convey her admiration, but she was not clever enough for the astute critical analysis he wanted. He had never won at the Eisteddfod, a great disappointment to him. Now he was writing a novel. She'd read the first chapter: perfect prose, unwittingly autobiographical, it was not the kind of book she would read at night. It was bleak, nihilistic, allowing no light in the darkness of the world. These days she preferred something more light-hearted, escapist nonsense.

Outside it was completely dark, one of those cloud ridden nights, not even that faint lightness from the direction of the sea. It was silent, nothing was alive, even the sheep which bleated all night were quiet, and there was, as always, the memory of the sea in the slight salt breeze. So different from the valley which always had the damp smell of something primeval, the trees closing in like inquisitive beasts. And always the whish and the whirr of the wheel, tired, creaking, an old thing waiting for death.

'Lovely evening, I do believe singing is good for the soul. How I envy you all.'

'So true. I remember one of the wiser tutors at college saying to me, 'Let the children sing' and those poor mites from poor homes needed to sing, not many reasons for singing in their lives.'

He stopped and turned to her. 'Sal's left me. No real explanation. I don't know whether there's somebody else, I rather doubt it. I don't think marriage suited her. She's one of these independent women. Not like you, I think you were made for marriage and children.'

Then silence till he spoke again and his voice was so low she hardly heard him. 'I'm sorry, that is so tactless, for somebody who calls himself a writer, it showed so little understanding of the human heart.'

'Don't apologise. It's time people stopped considering everything they say in my presence because they're frightened of hurting my feelings. My feelings have been hurt in the most terrible way possible, so nothing can hurt me ever again. I'm protected from further tragedy. I've got a knight's armour round me.'

'You're a woman of great courage.'

'Rubbish, I muddle along from day to day. That's what we all do. Why do human beings try to give themselves such fine motives? We live and we die, and all we can do is try to be as good as possible and as happy as life will let us be.'

'I think there will be a time when you'll be happy again, Arianwen.'

'We shall see. That's what my mother always used to say, when really she meant 'no'. Enough about me, what about you, what will you do?'

'Carry on exactly as I am, muddling, as you so inelegantly call it, but you're right. It's what we all do. If you're religious, as I believe you are, and I'm in a slough of indecision, then you believe in that mysterious divine order. It's difficult with the memory of war still vivid in our minds and the world tumbling along with wars somewhere all the time. Even evolution lacks order, survival of the fittest looks pretty arbitrary and quite ruthless.'

'You're far too deep for me. How is Sion taking it?'

'As you know, Sion does not communicate emotion in any recognisable way. He is away in dreams or nightmares. As far as I can see, he's happier. Two warring parents do not create a state of harmony. Since Sal left last week he has actually cleared up after supper, and asked how I feel. Lack of a mother may be the making of my son. That may sound trite, but she upset his equilibrium, overprotective one minute, indifferent the next. The village believes that she has gone to visit her mother who is recovering from flu. Unlikely, as she and her mother despised each other, but it will do for now. Inevitably, the truth will out and I can expect daily deliveries of cakes and stews as if I was bereaved. I may sound flippant, but I am in some pain, but somewhere in my writer's cold heart and my teacher's rationality there is the indication that it might be for the best.'

She couldn't see his face but could imagine the lines of pain on its paleness. Quite unable to think of anything to say she waited for him to speak again.

'If only I had met somebody like you. I see your courage, and the way you come to terms with the world and what it has done to you. I see a tranquil centre to you, something which Sal so sadly lacked. I loved her so much when I first met her at Aberystwyth, she was like the wild wind that sometimes blew us along the prom. She was so turbulent, so passionate. Marriage to a schoolteacher and second rate poet was not for her. She wanted drama in her life, to live her life always at the centre of the tempest. I like the quiet shores of life. Sorry, I sound pretentious. It's the writer in me. I have to stand aside and watch my life like a play and comment on it like some ghastly Greek chorus. At another time you and I could have been happy.'

He leaned forward. He was tall and rather frightening, but she let him kiss her cheek, and felt his cold dry lips on her cheek which was flushed and warm.

'Good night, Arianwen.'

She felt the sadness of the arbitrariness of life. How perfect a life she could have had with Hugh Jones: so compatible, harmonious, she his mouse-like muse. The schoolhouse would be transformed, a family home, a centre for music and culture, and in time she might make something of that strange troubled boy with his father's dark eyes, but anxious, whereas his father's eyes were full of a writer's wonder at the world . But those were silly dreams, and she was a pragmatic woman.

Inside the manse she crept upstairs like a delinquent child, pleased that the Richards were asleep and wouldn't smell alcohol on her breath. They were dear to her, like second parents, but they were finding it difficult to adjust to the galloping world of the sixties, bemused by so much change in their beloved village.

And the world moved on, and the millwheel turned, and Arianwen moved towards her fate.

CHAPTER 21

It was the end of another concert, another celebratory and self-congratulatory party at the choirmaster's house, and again four people cleared the kitchen and sat round the table with mugs of tea and tried to descend from the glories of the night.

Hugh Jones wasn't there. At the end of term he'd left for a walking holiday in the Alps with Sion. 'It sounds like something out of a pre-war novel, Somerset Maugham or somebody, but I'm rather looking forward to it, and believe it or not, so is Sion. I haven't been abroad for such a long time. I might manage some new poems and I shall work on the novel. I'm determined to finish it. It's been sitting in a drawer for far too long. What are you doing?'

'I shall stay here for a week or so. I'm going to take Mrs. Richards out a couple of times. She wants to go and have a look at the Cathedral. I think she's decided that it's sufficiently plain not to offend her Nonconformist sensibilities. Then home to my parents, and I shall take them out for days. Then I might go away on my own somewhere. I want to go abroad again someday. I did enjoy Paris. Such a long time ago.'

'You should be doing something more exciting than driving old people around. I think sometimes your sense of duty overwhelms you. Admirable, I suppose, but nothing wrong with a bit of selfishness occasionally.'

And, now, it was Elwyn who sat across the untidy table, dark eyes glinting in post-concert euphoria. He smiled at her.

'You look tired, Arianwen.'

'I am. The summer term is a long one, and the children get tired of being stuck inside on hot days, and the last week was exhausting, with the school concert, and then the outing to Tenby, and one naughty little boy wandered off and another ate too much ice cream and was sick in the coach. Such are the joys of a teacher's life.'

She was exhausted, and the years were passing, all the same, and she couldn't bear to think of the years since Tom's death, that feeling of paralysis, unable to move in any direction. Hers was a peculiar kind of inertia, and now she knew that the time for change was there, nudging at her, an impatient companion pushing her forward. Occasionally, she would send for forms for jobs abroad, somewhere warm, somewhere where she could do some real good, where nobody knew her history and nobody looked at her with pitying eyes, denying her the privilege of ordinariness. And even though she sometimes got as far as filling in the forms she never posted them.

'I'll be going, I'm dropping on my feet.'

'I'll walk you home.' Elwyn stood up.

She almost laughed. She remembered that last party when another man had walked her home. There were few escorts for widows approaching middle age.

Outside it was warm, and towards the sea there was still the last light of the setting sun, a faint shimmer of silver, and only the shyest of breezes.

'Nice to get some fresh air. Hot in that kitchen. They should have had the party outside.'

'And all the village complaining about the noise, and the songs you men sang, not the kind of thing to waft through people's windows in the early hours, and some are probably jealous they weren't asked, even though they're not in the choir. You know village life, nobody likes being left out.'

'You're right. And there's probably some old hag staring from behind the curtains right now. Let's give them something to look at.' And he took her by the waist, and humming the Blue Danube waltzed her along the lane, almost tripping over a sleeping sheep.

Surprised by laughter and a surge of joy she tried to be cross with him.

'I've got to live in this village. Mrs. Richards will be alerted to my notoriety, dancing through the village late at night. She never castigates, but her look of bewilderment is far more censorious, and if some of the gossips saw us, it'll be round the village and North Pembrokeshire by ten o'clock tomorrow morning. That's what villages are like.'

'I'm glad I live an anonymous life at the edge of town.'

'You, anonymous? Never. You're the rollicking boy of Pembrokeshire, all those concerts you and the boys sing. Everybody talks about you with a laugh in their voice. How do you do it? Is there never a time when you're serious?'

She looked up at him, a stocky kind of man, not much taller than herself, his face hidden as darkness deepened. He was a man who had disturbed her consciousness for many years, yet a stranger. In those long mourning years, everybody had become a stranger, onlookers in the progress of her life. Elwyn was an enigma, a man for the stage, a performer who played his roles convincingly: the clown, the amiable man in the pub and the valued member of the choir. It occurred to her that she only knew him as a man off duty.

Somebody had told her that he was a manager in an office in the market town on whose edges he lived. That was the other side of the man. This was the first time she'd considered other facets of his character, a man she always knew she found attractive, because he made her laugh, and poor Tom had never made her laugh.

'I'm serious most of the time, at work, looking after my mother; you see the light side of me. We need laughter to defeat the pain of living, and you little Arianwen should know that better than most. Your time for laughter will come again. Believe me. Life's tested you quite enough. I haven't the imagination to even try to feel what you've been through. I've loved and lost, but it was nothing, just a little butterfly flicker on the petal of a flower. You know the real meaning of suffering. My father died when I was very young, and I saw my mother's pain, and she changed, my carefree laughing mother. It was as if laughter and joy was drained out of her. She was one of those old fashioned women. Marriage and motherhood was everything to her, all she ever wanted. My father rather spoilt her. She was bereft without him, quite hopeless. I had to grow up pretty quick. She depends on me completely. Oh, such serious talk at three in the morning.'

He waved towards the upstairs window of the shop.

'Lady in the shop, if you're watching behind your net curtains, I'll sing you a lullaby,' and he threw his arms wide in operatic gesture and sang a traditional Welsh lullaby full of pathos.

Arianwen felt a diversity of emotions: laughter, and then a sadness about all that she had lost: the children never born and a life on the farm which she would have made a decent one, a comfortable home for all of them, and Tom would have had his dynasty, and he wouldn't be thirty years old lying in the graveyard just round the corner. Again she felt the bitterness, the anger, and then Elwyn got down on one knee to do his much loved imitation of Al Jolson, and the bitterness was replaced by schoolgirl giggles.

'Oh lady in the shop, cariad. What a night you've had watching the village schoolmistress dancing at three in the morning with the mad man from the choir. It'll be round the village tomorrow.'

'I don't think she would like to admit that she'd been hovering behind the net curtains. The fiction is that the gossip all comes to her, and that it's other people who spread it. The good lady is the very model of tact and diplomacy. Now I'm going home. I need my sleep for Sunday and I've had enough lunacy for one night. It's not conduct becoming of a woman who lives in the manse.'

As they walked the brief distance to the manse he hummed quietly to himself, so softly that she could hardly recognise the song. Then she realised that it was *Myfanwy*, a song she'd found rather sentimental and over praised, although hearing it sung by a good male voice choir it could set the emotions soaring. Now she felt the tears, whether sentimental or real she was uncertain, and when he took her hand as they stopped at the gate it seemed quite right that he should do so, and the light kiss on her cheek was preordained and she felt that those lips had touched her throughout her life.

Another Wednesday, another choir practice. He wasn't there. Over the last few days, stretched on a rack of impatience, she'd thought of him too much, feeling rather silly and schoolgirlish, behaving as she had when she'd had a very silly and completely misguided crush on a sixth former when she was in the fourth form. He'd hardly looked at her, but every encounter when he passed her in the corridor between lessons and when he'd brushed past her on the way to morning assembly had been full of invented meaning. How very silly she'd been. And how very silly she was being now: widowed woman, thinking of a man who had made her laugh and played the fool as he walked her, quite innocently, home.

Two days in the classroom with the children restless because of wind and rain had given her some respite from her reveries, and a fight in the playground, and somebody being spectacularly sick in the main door way, and the Head being summoned to Haver-fordwest for a pointless meeting, leaving her with the whole school to keep occupied, all had helped, but he was there when she woke up and in all the quiet unaccountable moments of the day his smiling face was there and she wanted to kiss his cheek with the evening stubble which gave him a devilish look.

The weather was still foul. All the drama of wind and rain that the Irish Sea could throw at them was quite relentless. The women came in with dripping umbrellas and old macs which steamed in the warm kitchen.

'Dreadful day, doesn't seem to have stopped for the last week,' somebody said, and everybody else joined in.

Arianwen, despite her exhaustion after her two dreadful days at school, felt the lightening around her heart which was a familiar Wednesday emotion, one which she had never tried to analyse, but was, she was certain, something to do with the transcending freedom of music.

Ann Jenkins, a mother of a child in her class, came up to her. As she listened to Ann's much repeated encomium of her son's myriad talents and special requirements as a 'sensitive child,' thinking of the robust little boy who sailed quite happily through his schooldays with little visible effort, and would, she was quite certain, continue to do so until he could escape his mother's obsessive love, she was watching the door. Each time the door opened, bringing sounds of the storm, and somebody came in laughing or complaining, who was not him, she was disappointed. Angry with herself, she tried to shake it off like the raindrops in her hair.

As the choir gathered into its familiar shape, and the choirmaster began with his ritual cough and a wave of his baton, she turned to a fellow soprano.

'Where's Elwyn tonight? I thought it was quiet and everybody well behaved.'

'I heard him tell somebody last week that he was taking his mother to Torquay for the week. She's had very bad flu, and he hopes it'll help her recovery. I hope the weather's better than here, or it won't do much good. The old girl's a bit of a trial, I hear, although you wouldn't think so with him always being so cheerful all the time would you? You're right, it's quiet without him, not the same type of hwyl somehow, and he's a lovely tenor. Pity he's never married. Watch out, here comes the second cough and another wave of the baton.'

She sang with her usual fervour. In singing there was a kind of forgetting, not escape, but the music, and her own part in it, mediocre as it was, took her away from sorrow, the frustrations of the day, and her disappointment that he wasn't there.

As a widow, and by the standards of society, and in particular that close knit obsessively observational community, she had certain rules to follow: widows did not think too much about their feelings, they got on with their lives as efficiently as possible. As a widow she should not think too much about a man who patently regarded her as an acquaintance, no more, but he had been there at the borders of her consciousness ever since she moved to the village.

When she thought of Tom, and she realised as the years passed that she did so less frequently, she saw him as an episode in her life, something which came quickly and passed quickly. The trip to Paris, working at the home, they, too, were episodes, and that glorious life at the Morgans, all episodes, strangely jumbled, an untidy narrative. Such chaos, a sclerotic stumbling from one place to another.

She walked slowly back to the manse. The rain had eased, and she breathed the freshness of damp grass, and the softness of the breeze. Approaching middle age, living still with the old couple, a bit like living with her parents. It was time to think again of change, her life was static, it was now time she looked fate straight in the eyes. Nobody could lead her life for her, and within her strict sense of duty, she would live it.

**

However, in the weeks to come her resolutions would change.

Coming out of the bank one morning, her mind was full of the interview with the manager who had advised her how to reinvest the money from the farm and its land, which had been accruing interest over the years.

'A tidy sum. It's done well over the years. Have you thought what you might do with it? I see you're still paying rent. What about buying your own little house? Some nice little places here in town.'

'I'll think about it. I know it's ridiculous my paying rent when I could have my own home. I suppose I like company. I don't know whether I'm ready to live on my own yet.'

His broad well-fed face fell into the jowls of sympathy. He knew her history. Very sad. Pleasant looking little woman too, sat there in a nice little red dress, good shoes, and gloves on those little hands, something very appealing about a woman wearing gloves. He could imagine her taking off those gloves and then coming over to touch him with soft little white hands. But he was a respectable bank manager, and on the council, and such thoughts were not quite right, and him a chapel deacon as well.

They'd shaken hands at the end of the interview, and he went back to attend to his letters, and to think what he'd have for his dinner at the café across the road.

'Arianwen.' She looked up. She'd been thinking of a bungalow, surrounded by the heather and gorse, purple and yellow clashing colours, but so beautiful in nature, on a hill overlooking the village, very modern, no chance for gloomy corners, and a big window where she could look up from a book and look towards the hills and be enchanted, lifting her eyes to the hills for aid which might come. She was never certain. She'd studied Wordsworth at school and had been rather taken by his almost religious adoration of nature.

'Elwyn.' She touched her face, hoping that no blushes showed. She was too old for blushing.

They stared at each other. He looked well, his face browner than usual, healthier looking.

'How's your mother? I heard you took her to Torquay to recover from 'flu.'

'Much rejuvenated, I'm pleased to say. She got pally with some other ladies of a similar age and they sat in the lounge together playing cards and enjoying malicious observations of the other inmates. So I was lucky, I didn't have to take her for 'spins' along the coast and spend hours in musty old teashops drinking weak tea and eating dried up old cakes. So I was totally free. I drove to remote places, walked and sang as I walked, caught up with some reading, and went to concerts, and went to the pubs and joined in the bonhomie.'

'Do you like doing things on your own?'

'I think I do, not that I've got much choice. I'm thinking of a foreign holiday sometime. It's a dream really, mother would have a fit.'

'It's easier for men. Didn't you go abroad in the war? You were just old enough weren't you?'

'Just about. I never got farther than Brawdy. Because I'd trained as an accountant, I was desk bound. Lucky really, I suppose.'

The rain which had been threatening all morning, suddenly

announced itself in a tremendous downpour as if the clouds had suddenly decided they wanted some drama. The rain was sliding down the back of her neck, and her hair, carefully combed before going to see the bank manager, was already slicked to her face, and the water was running into her eyes.

'Sorry, I'm going to have to run to my car.'

He stood in front of her smiling as the rain spattered his face, as if Welsh weather patterns were incapable of affecting him in any way, a happy man in a dreary street standing in the rain. She remembered a long time ago seeing that film with Gene Kelly singing and dancing and cavorting round a lamp post, laughing against a downpour. It seemed possible Elwyn would do something similar. Damp and cold, she remembered the night he'd waltzed her outside the village shop, watched by the indifferent stars and sleeping sheep startled into bleating, and his hand tight on her waist almost to the point of bruising her.

'You'll be drowned before you get to the car. Over there,' he pointed to the café across the street. 'Tea and cakes, best antidote to rain I know. Welsh cakes, lots of butter,' and he took her by the hand as if she was a child who needed guiding across the road.

It was the café much modernised, where, that lifetime away, she had first come with Tom, but that was another woman in another time. Memory could not be allowed to spoil this. She was young again.

Laughing, she allowed herself to be pulled along, and before they went through the door with its tinkling Swiss cowbell they stood outside shaking themselves like dogs, and laughing, laughing at each other, and laughing with each other.

The café was steamy and full. There was one little table near the counter where the large spitting urn added to the tropical humidity. The hissing muted the sounds of speech, and the waitresses in their dark dresses and white aprons, their movements quick and impatient, intensified Arianwen's feeling that she'd walked into another world, and the county town with its damp earthiness, and air of important business was quite remote.

They sat at the small table, knees almost touching, Suddenly, she felt rather shy as if she was being entertained by a complete stranger. It was the first time she'd been alone with him. The waltz on the green was of another dimension, out of time, another woman, something confected from the magic of singing and the wine and the euphoria of success.

He slid the hand-written menu over to her; written in English and Welsh, an innovation.

'I see that the spelling's as bad in English as it is in Welsh, imagine being illiterate in two languages. Takes a bit of doing not to be able to spell in Welsh.'

The proprietress, recognisable by her old-fashioned flowery dress, and her age, was standing over them, notebook in hand. It was obvious she's heard every word they said.

'Can I take your order now?' She was a big woman with a tiny squeaky voice. Arianwen glanced over at his face, and saw the threatening laugh spreading across his lips and in the crinkle of his eyes and looked away towards the steamed up window and felt the laughter, a burp-like eruption inside her, something alien come home after a long journey away, a prodigal returned.

'Tea and Welsh cakes for me,' and he looked over at Arianwen who knew her face was now quite pink with the effort of control.

'I'll have the same.'

'Proper butter,' he said. 'None of this margarine nonsense.'

The proprietress looked down at him over her huge bosom and impressive chins.

'We always serve butter, sir.'

And with great dignity she walked back to the counter.

'Definitely stately as a galleon, pity she's got no foghorn.'

And then she laughed properly, and it was like a rebirth, an emergence into a new world of possibility and hope and light and the music again a part of her, organic, growing out of the heart.

'What luck bumping into you. Not teaching?'

'School holidays.'

'Of course. If you've no children you forget these things.'

There was a sudden silence between them and the laughter was gone. Perhaps she only imagined the sadness in his dark eyes and then he smiled.

'I don't think I would have been a good father. I've not even been a husband yet.'

And then he looked across at her with that honesty and directness which so few people showed when they met her.

'You should have had children. I'm sure you would have made a lovely mother. After all, you had enough practice looking after other people's children all these years.'

'Motherhood is different, and teaching is not just looking after other people's children, it's about educating them, helping them to live their lives.'

'When they're that young what can you teach them, apart from reading and writing and sums?'

'Reading and writing and sums are actually quite important. I suppose you're one of these people who think that proper teaching is what takes place at secondary schools, that primary schools, especially for the younger ones, are just a baby-sitting service. I dare you to say that to Mr. Jones. He'd demolish you in no time. He's a great believer in early years learning. Remember, we learn language in our early years. Never underestimate the brain of a four year old. And,' she added wearily now, 'I was hardly married long enough to have children.'

'I'm sorry. I've upset you.'

'No, at least you talk to me as if I'm a real person, not some delicate object which has to be treated with special care.'

'I'm sorry. I don't always think before I speak. Over the years it's got me into quite a lot of trouble.'

One of the young waitresses brought their tea and cake over. A skinny little thing, just like Doris used to be, nervous, almost spilling the tea.

'Poor child. I'm sure that proprietress is a bully. Look, definitely proper butter, yellow as a daffodil,' and then he squeaked, sounding just like the proprietress, 'shall ay be mother?'

They sipped the tea in silence. When she'd got in the car that morning she'd never thought it would turn out like this, happiness with raindrops and Welsh cakes. Sat at a cramped table, in this café, hardly a romantic meal, but suffused with a promise which transformed its quotidian setting.

And she was to remember this for years.

PART 3

CHAPTER 22

The middle years pass quickly. From the height of her forty years she looked back at childhood and young womanhood as if across a river, a turbulent river, not the sluggish stream of the mill, with its dark shadows and the trees looking down on it almost with a kind of affection, and the little bridge across it which always creaked right in the middle and if Dad was in the garden Dad heard and turned round and waved to her.

Now across the turbulent river of her life she saw a child walking home from school. First holding her mother's hand, then later on, on her own, more slowly, dreaming and singing to herself a poignant old folk song or some American song she'd heard on the radio. And then, later, in her school uniform getting into Ianto's taxi, at first eager, and then later, more slowly, as if she didn't want to leave the Morgans behind, and then a young woman with a young man at her side, diffident, his mind turned in on his past and the long burden of his family chained to the farm's tyrannies. And then she was alone again, and her movements slow as if old age had arrived early, stiffening her limbs, and later, much later, there she was again with another man at her side and even across the river she could hear laughter and singing, both singing, an alto and a tenor, blending, harmonising.

If you visit the mill now it is much changed, there are more spaces, the trees have been chopped, swathes of lawn, everything modernised in good taste, a charming place to stay, especially if you want to leave the city behind and breathe the air of the valley with its ancient magic, and on cool nights you can hear the owls calling away down the valley.

However, if you know the history of the mill, you can see the bustle of the nineteenth century when mills abounded in these valleys, quiet places where the world seldom intruded, and they spoke in rapid Welsh and a visit to Newcastle Emlyn was a day's venture.

Arianwen's mother died, not in the mill, away, staying with a cousin. Her father died near the stream one freezing day. He had been lying in the cold for a whole day till the postman found him.

Tragic they all said, Arianwen hoped it was quick, and knew that for him it was the right place to die, not in the big bed in her parents' bedroom, where she had been born, like other earlier generations. Outside, in the cold air, close to his beloved stream.

A day in late April. Every room was empty. The company she'd hired had done well. Everything was bare. She walked through the bareness, her mind clear. Nothing was left of any of them, of her parents, of those who had lived there before them. For Arianwen there were no ghosts, no voices calling from the past. The wheel was almost still now as if it knew that it no longer had any function, a loyal worker pensioned off, quite redundant. The women she'd hired to clean had done well. The empty rooms shone with industry. Outside, spring was quite ostentatious, primroses on the riverbank, and wild garlic, her mother's daffodils still in flower in this dark valley, and blackbirds fighting, everything furious with new life. After rain everything looked clean, even the sky.

No dark places for shadows now, so much more light now it was empty. In the kitchen one of the taps was dripping and the old sink had a blue streak. Strange that Dad hadn't repaired the tap. He loved that kind of job, rolling his sleeves up, his face stiffening in concentration, humming something tuneless. Mam would be nagging, bending to take something out of the oven, tutting if a cake hadn't risen or a joint wasn't quite ready. She turned the tap but it still kept dripping. It was the new owners' problem now. Nice enough people, English of course. Only the English had the money or the vision. Not very good at big changes, the people of the valley. So many incomers now. Some people got angry about it, but somehow she couldn't. Better than the old place falling into ruins like so many of the old mills, jagged stones by secret streams. No point in being sentimental or looking to the past.

'Have you had enough time now, I'm starving. There's a nice pub in Cenarth does lovely food. Nice drop of beer as well, as you're driving.' He'd stayed in the garden while she walked round, his idea not hers, but she appreciated it. Now he climbed up the steps to meet her.

'Yes, I've said my goodbyes.'

'No tears, you're very brave.'

'My parents aren't here now, so it means nothing really, it's just an old carcass.'

'So much history here. When you were brought up in a little terraced house this kind of place is so romantic. I just feel sad that I never saw it when it was your home, with your parents here.'

'Mother could be quite fearsome. Tom was terrified of her.'

Now she could talk about Tom as if he was somebody she'd known at school, some passing acquaintance, and Elwyn's eyes no longer dimmed when she said his name.

'She wouldn't have terrified me. I'm good with women, and I looked after my own mother, who wasn't easy for all those years.' It was a long time now since his mother had died, and she could never quite see how much he mourned her, if at all. She knew him so well now, but there was still a little world of mystery behind the laughing eyes, but she had all her life to explore that world.

'You'd have liked my father. He was a lovely man.'

And then he took her hand, and she locked the door with the ridiculous big key, cold and heavy in her hand, and it stuck as it always had. Her father had never managed to fix it, despite hours of gentle cursing, and fiddling with oil cans and screwdrivers.

Then down the steps. Already there was bright green moss growing on them, as if the garden was watching them, waiting for them to go so that it could take over the house and win back what was taken from it all those long years ago.

She'd been planning her announcement for a long time. It was like telling her parents about Tom all over again, but now she was twenty years older, and settled in widowhood everybody had thought, till they realised that the friendship with Elwyn was important.

He'd asked her over a cup of tea in the café, the one in Haverfordwest he'd taken her to on that rainy day.

'It's sentimental, I know, but I'm a silly Welshman, not that I'm mean, mind, perhaps it should have been at a hotel somewhere over champagne, not tea and Welsh cakes, but somehow they've become a symbol of you, sunny with butter and cosy.'

'That's not very glamorous, and I've got my new frock on and just had my hair done.'

'And lovely you look, cariad, a bright little primrose of a woman,' and he started singing. The proprietress looked over at him disapprovingly, the respectable shopping ladies in floral frocks looked at him, most smiled, there was after all something rather charming about this stocky little dark man with his amiable face and thick brows. One of the teenage waitresses giggled and forgot to look bored.

'Right, I'm doing this properly,' and he did, down on one knee, wide and silly arm gesture: a pallid Al Jolson.

'Will you marry me?'

'Of course, you silly man, and get up off that floor and stop making an exhibition of us both. I've got to say yes so that we can get out of this place with some dignity.'

A pupil's mother was sitting near the window, her mouth wide. She could see the sentences forming in the woman's sharp eyes.

'Right there in front of everybody, and that man who sings in those concerts down on his knee singing, and kissing her hand.'

Then he sat back into his chair, looking like a prim heroine in Austen and dabbed at his lips with a napkin, and poured more tea.

'Bit stewed, shall I ask for some more water? You've gone very red,' then looking anxious. 'You did say yes, didn't you?' The proprietress was looking rather cross. Such fools in her café, middle aged people behaving like that. The young waitresses giggled by the urn and whispered and stared at the little dark woman and the mad man escort. Tea sippers and cake nibblers looked away. Entertainment was over, they looked at the long boredom of another Saturday afternoon.

Outside she looked at passing afternoon shoppers. They looked different, as if a special light was shining, and each person was like a sharp black outlined drawing. Sounds loudened and the taste in her mouth was not that of stewed tea or the slipperiness and salt of butter, but something unknown, quite magical, *ambrosial* was the word, and there was music in the passing voices and the sound of passing traffic, and she looked to the sky, not even a smug cloud sailing in from Ireland.

It was Monday morning and it was raining, and she couldn't leave it till Friday or Mrs. Whatever-her-name-was would have it round the village by midday; the playground communication system was very potent, even in those days before mobile phones.

Reverend Richards, very old now and finally retired, was reading the paper, eyes close to the print, and Mrs Richards tiny as ever, and a little bent, and slower in her movements, was standing at the stove stirring the porridge.

'I'll just have toast today, I'm not very hungry.'

'Are you not well?' She turned round, this woman who had tried so hard to replace her mother and had almost succeeded, all anxiety, the spoon in her hand dripping milk on her immaculate floor.

'No, I'm fine, very fine, actually. Elwyn and I are getting married.'

Mrs. Richards dropped the spoon on the floor, ignored it, there was the slight whiff of burning from the porridge.

'O cariad, o cariad.'

Rev. Richards stood up and took the saucepan off the hob and put it on top of a pile of newspapers on the table.

'For heaven's sake, woman, stop saying "o cariad" and congratulate her. Wonderful news my dear,' and he shook her hand, and, rather shyly, kissed her on her cheek.

Mrs Richards sat down, and started crying.

'I think she's pleased,' her husband said.

'You'll come out of retirement to marry us, won't you?'

'Of course, of course.'

'Your suit will have to be let out. You've put on weight since you've retired. And I'm going to have a new hat. Something brazen,' and she looked round at them defiantly.

'And bring him to tea on Friday,' she stood up as if ready to start baking, and in her excitement knocked over the porridge pan. 'We won't be in the manse much longer, so make it soon.'

'Toast for everybody today, I think.' Arianwen smiled at her as if she was one of her new infants, then sponged off the table, and got the mop out to clean the kitchen floor. It seemed a very prosaic way of celebrating her news. Rev. Richards was reading the paper again and smiling as though the world was full of good news, and Mrs. Richards was excitedly hacking away at a loaf of bread, huge uneven slices far too big for the ancient toaster.

'I'll do it.' And she took the knife away from the little woman's shaking hand before she carved a finger off.

It was still raining outside, and she took her umbrella from the stand, and put on her everyday mac. She shivered as she felt its cold on her arms. She looked outside at the filmy landscape, the hills quite lost in deep cloud. Happiness was unwieldy, errant like flying clouds and the blowing rain. Again she was soaring, and she felt at one again with the little girl wandering down the lane holding her mother's hand, asking questions which her mother never answered. Her mother's face was in a passing cloud, kindlier than in real life. She put away the chimera of her happiness and, a stolid little woman, stood outside putting up her umbrella.

***

It rained all day, the guests scurried in under their umbrellas, and the nastiest wind since November, spiteful and unrelenting, blew in from the Irish Sea, rattling the windows of the old chapel.

The guests moaned, as do most, who despite all experience of reality, expect wedding days to have a special dispensation of sun, even in undependable West Wales.

'Couldn't she have waited till summer?' one farmer, straitlaced in his black suit, uncomfortable in new shirt and tie, complained to his wife who was contemplating the unfamiliar but reassuring image she saw in the mirror.

'Yes, a bit of sun would have been nice. If anybody deserves a bit of sun, it's her. I've never seen her look so happy as she's been these last few months. That suit's a bit tight, I told you to cut out the cakes, but you wouldn't listen. I'm glad I did,' and she looked again at the reassuring image in the mirror.

'There'll be no beer I suppose.'

'Of course not, there'll be tea and cakes and sandwiches. You know what the old Reverend is like. Never touched a drop in his life. He and the missus are paying for the reception. That's their gift to Arianwen. She's been like a daughter to them.'

She wore a red suit, like a little poppy, and no hat, shocking elderly matrons whose hats were safely embedded in their perms, as was their lipstick to their puckered lips. and the powder, orange to the jaw, exaggerating the grey battlefield of their necks.

Arianwen's hair shone a suspicious black, and was rather curlier than usual, and silky, and he longed even there in the chapel to run his hand along it, and the white smoothness of her face, and kiss the brown eyes bright with love. They dispensed with formality and held hands right from the beginning of the ceremony, as if they'd spent too much time waiting for each other. The choir sang, something complicated and rather too clever, and the farmers' stomachs rumbled, missing midday dinner, and the little girls from the infant class who were to stand in line outside the chapel holding

231

posies wriggled their little bottoms on unfamiliar wooden seats.

Arianwen's youth choir sang something Welsh and simple, one of the old airs, and the hatted ladies snuffled, and their men looked at the ceiling which needed painting and bit their lips stoically, and thought of their own wedding days and looked at what their wives had become. Something to be said for starting again when you were older. Those two standing in the front holding hands defied age and the wearying business of life. Something heroic about them.

Afterwards, in the little hall adjoining the chapel, it looked as if the whole village was there. And the complaining men were happy because Elwyn had insisted on beer, and Mrs. Richards had said to the old minister, 'Times have changed, no harm in a drink. Beer for the men and sherry for the women.' And he'd rolled his eyes to the ceiling and consulted with the god who as he got older was becoming vaguer and, frequently, a less insistent presence, and said *yes*. What did it matter? The world had changed so much, and the dogmas of youth seemed so far away.

And it was noted by the hatted Valkyries that Mrs. Richards had more than one sherry and was red-faced, and smiled as if she was Arianwen's proud mother, and it really was a very nice outfit she was wearing, if rather bright and modern. She'd made Rev. Richards take her to Swansea, Carmarthen not offering such sartorial choices.

And before they left, Arianwen and Elwyn sang *Myfanwy* and then everybody joined in. The farmers thought about the milking and the tyranny of their lives and began to shuffle, and their wives, two generous sherries downed, who were now beginning to enjoy themselves, looked reluctant, but they were farmers' wives and knew their duty. Something simple for supper tonight, bread and cheese, and an early night or a doze in front of the television, before chapel tomorrow, and the roast at midday and the whole pattern starting again.

***

And we come, after many years, too happy to be chronicled, to an afternoon in April when they ran out of milk, and Elwyn waited for his Arianwen to come back from the shop. And, somewhere above those gorsed moors their singing might still be heard on quiet nights.

The End

About the Author
Angela Johnson

Angela Johnson was born in West Wales, and is a Welsh speaker. Her work is often inspired by the Welsh countryside, and the characters she knew in childhood, and the tales they told.

She was an English teacher and taught in a number of schools in the South East of England She then studied Creative Writing at the University of Kent. Her novel Harriet and her Women was shortlisted for the Impress Prize for Fiction, and she has won the Poetry Prize at the Folkestone Arts Festival.

She lives in Kent, enjoys travelling to look at birds and plants in exotic places, and is a passionate environmentalist, and, latterly, is spending too much time fulminating about politics.